Dessert at The Beach House Hotel

Judith Keim

BOOKS BY JUDITH KEIM

THE HARTWELL WOMEN SERIES:
The Talking Tree – 1
Sweet Talk – 2
Straight Talk – 3
Baby Talk – 4
The Hartwell Women – Boxed Set

THE BEACH HOUSE HOTEL SERIES:
Breakfast at The Beach House Hotel – 1
Lunch at The Beach House Hotel – 2
Dinner at The Beach House Hotel – 3
Christmas at The Beach House Hotel – 4
Margaritas at The Beach House Hotel – 5
Dessert at The Beach House Hotel – 6

THE FAT FRIDAYS GROUP:
Fat Fridays – 1
Sassy Saturdays – 2
Secret Sundays – 3

THE SALTY KEY INN SERIES:
Finding Me – 1
Finding My Way – 2
Finding Love – 3
Finding Family – 4

THE CHANDLER HILL INN SERIES:
Going Home – 1
Coming Home – 2
Home at Last – 3
The Chandler Hill Inn Series – Boxed Set

SEASHELL COTTAGE BOOKS:

A Christmas Star

Change of Heart

A Summer of Surprises

A Road Trip to Remember

The Beach Babes

THE DESERT SAGE INN SERIES:

The Desert Flowers – Rose – 1

The Desert Flowers – Lily – 2

The Desert Flowers – Willow – 3

The Desert Flowers – Mistletoe & Holly – 4 (2022)

SOUL SISTERS AT CEDAR MOUNTAIN LODGE:

Christmas Sisters – Anthology

Christmas Kisses

Christmas Castles

Christmas Stories – Soul Sisters Anthology

Christmas Joy – (2022)

THE SANDERLING COVE INN SERIES:

Waves of Hope – (2022)

Sandy Wishes – (2023)

Salty Kisses – (2023)

OTHER BOOKS:

The ABC's of Living With a Dachshund

Once Upon a Friendship – Anthology

Winning BIG – a little love story for all ages

Holiday Hopes

The Winning Tickets – (2023)

For more information: **www.judithkeim.com**

PRAISE FOR JUDITH KEIM'S NOVELS

THE BEACH HOUSE HOTEL SERIES

"Love the characters in this series. This series was my first introduction to Judith Keim. She is now one of my favorites. Looking forward to reading more of her books."

BREAKFAST AT THE BEACH HOUSE HOTEL is an easy, delightful read that offers romance, family relationships, and strong women learning to be stronger. Real life situations filter through the pages. Enjoy!"

LUNCH AT THE BEACH HOUSE HOTEL – "This series is such a joy to read. You feel you are actually living with them. Can't wait to read the latest one."

DINNER AT THE BEACH HOUSE HOTEL – "A Terrific Read! As usual, Judith Keim did it again. Enjoyed immensely. Continue writing such pleasantly reading books for all of us readers."

CHRISTMAS AT THE BEACH HOUSE HOTEL – "Not Just Another Christmas Novel. This is book number four in the series and my introduction to Judith Keim's writing. I wasn't disappointed. The characters are dimensional and engaging. The plot is well crafted and advances at a pleasing pace. The Florida location is interesting and warming. It was a delight to read a romance novel with mature female protagonists. Ann and Rhoda have life experiences that enrich the story. It's a clever book about friends and extended family. Buy copies for your book group pals and enjoy this seasonal read."

MARGARITAS AT THE BEACH HOUSE HOTEL – "What a wonderful series. I absolutely loved this book and can't wait for the next book to come out. There was even suspense in it. Thanks Judith for the great stories."

"Overall, Margaritas at the Beach House Hotel is

another wonderful addition to the series. Judith Keim takes the reader on a journey told through the voices of these amazing characters we have all come to love through the years! I truly cannot stress enough how good this book is, and I hope you enjoy it as much as I have!"

THE HARTWELL WOMEN SERIES – Books 1 – 4

"This was an EXCELLENT series. When I discovered Judith Keim, I read all of her books back to back. I thoroughly enjoyed the women Keim has written about. They are believable and you want to just jump into their lives and be their friends! I can't wait for any upcoming books!"

"I fell into Judith Keim's Hartwell Women series and have read & enjoyed all of her books in every series. Each centers around a strong & interesting woman character and their family interaction. Good reads that leave you wanting more."

THE FAT FRIDAYS GROUP – Books 1 – 3

"Excellent story line for each character, and an insightful representation of situations which deal with some of the contemporary issues women are faced with today."

"I love this author's books. Her characters and their lives are realistic. The power of women's friendships is a common and beautiful theme that is threaded throughout this story."

THE SALTY KEY INN SERIES – Books 1 – 4

<u>FINDING ME</u> – *"I thoroughly enjoyed the first book in this series and cannot wait for the others! The characters are endearing with the same struggles we all encounter. The setting makes me feel like I am a guest at The Salty Key Inn...relaxed, happy & light-hearted! The men are yummy*

and the women strong. You can't get better than that! Happy Reading!"

FINDING MY WAY- "Loved the family dynamics as well as uncertain emotions of dating and falling in love. Appreciated the morals and strength of parenting throughout. Just couldn't put this book down."

FINDING LOVE – "I waited for this book because the first two was such good reads. This one didn't disappoint.... Judith Keim always puts substance into her books. This book was no different, I learned about PTSD, accepting oneself, there is always going to be problems but stick it out and make it work. Just the way life is. In some ways a lot like my life. Judith is right, it needs another book and I will definitely be reading it. Hope you choose to read this series, you will get so much out of it."

FINDING FAMILY – "Completing this series is like eating the last chip. Love Judith's writing, and her female characters are always smart, strong, vulnerable to life and love experiences."

"This was a refreshing book. Bringing the heart and soul of the family to us."

CHANDLER HILL INN SERIES – Books 1 – 3

GOING HOME – "I absolutely could not put this book down. Started at night and read late into the middle of the night. As a child of the '60s, the Vietnam war was front and center so this resonated with me. All the characters in the book were so well developed that the reader felt like they were friends of the family."

"I was completely immersed in this book, with the beautiful descriptive writing, and the authors' way of bringing her characters to life. I felt like I was right inside her story."

COMING HOME – "Coming Home is a winner. The

characters are well-developed, nuanced and likable. Enjoyed the vineyard setting, learning about wine growing and seeing the challenges Cami faces in running and growing a business. I look forward to the next book in this series!"

"Coming Home was such a wonderful story. The author has such a gift for getting the reader right to the heart of things."

HOME AT LAST – "In this wonderful conclusion, to a heartfelt and emotional trilogy set in Oregon's stunning wine country, Judith Keim has tied up the Chandler Hill series with the perfect bow."

"Overall, this is truly a wonderful addition to the Chandler Hill Inn series. Judith Keim definitely knows how to perfectly weave together a beautiful and heartfelt story."

"The storyline has some beautiful scenes along with family drama. Judith Keim has created characters with interactions that are believable and some of the subjects the story deals with are poignant."

SEASHELL COTTAGE BOOKS

A CHRISTMAS STAR – "Love, laughter, sadness, great food, and hope for the future, all in one book. It doesn't get any better than this stunning read."

"A Christmas Star is a heartwarming Christmas story featuring endearing characters. So many Christmas books are set in snowbound places...it was a nice change to read a Christmas story that takes place on a warm sandy beach!" Susan Peterson

CHANGE OF HEART – "CHANGE OF HEART is the summer read we've all been waiting for. Judith Keim is a master at creating fascinating characters that are simply irresistible. Her stories leave you with a big smile on your face and a heart bursting with love."

~Kellie Coates Gilbert, author of the popular Sun Valley Series

A SUMMER OF SURPRISES – *"The story is filled with a roller coaster of emotions and self-discovery. Finding love again and rebuilding family relationships."*

"Ms. Keim uses this book as an amazing platform to show that with hard emotional work, belief in yourself and love, the scars of abuse can be conquered. It in no way preaches, it's a lovely story with a happy ending."

"The character development was excellent. I felt I knew these people my whole life. The story development was very well thought out I was drawn [in] from the beginning."

A ROAD TRIP TO REMEMBER – *"I LOVED this book! Love the character development, the fun, the challenges and the ending. My favorite books are about strong, competent women finding their own path to success and happiness and this is a winner. It's one of those books you just can't put down."*

"The characters are so real that they jump off the page. Such a fun, HAPPY book at the perfect time. It will lift your spirits and even remind you of your own grandmother. Spirited and hopeful Aggie gets a second chance at love and she takes the steering wheel and drives straight for it."

DESERT SAGE INN BOOKS

THE DESERT FLOWERS – ROSE – *"The Desert Flowers - Rose, is the first book in the new series by Judith Keim. I always look forward to new books by Judith Keim, and this one is definitely a wonderful way to begin The Desert Sage Inn Series!"*

"In this first of a series, we see each woman come into her own and view new beginnings even as they must take this tearful journey as they slowly lose a dear friend. This is

a very well written book with well-developed and likable main characters. It was interesting and enlightening as the first portion of this saga unfolded. I very much enjoyed this book and I do recommend it"

"Judith Keim is one of those authors that you can always depend on to give you a great story with fantastic characters. I'm excited to know that she is writing a new series and after reading book 1 in the series, I can't wait to read the rest of the books."!

THE DESERT FLOWERS – LILY – "The second book in the Desert Flowers series is just as wonderful as the first. Judith Keim is a brilliant storyteller. Her characters are truly lovely and people that you want to be friends with as soon as you start reading. Judith Keim is not afraid to weave real life conflict and loss into her stories. I loved reading Lily's story and can't wait for Willow's!

"The Desert Flowers Lily is the second book in The Desert Sage Inn Series by author Judith Keim. When I read the first book in the series, The Desert Flowers-Rose, I knew this series would exceed all of my expectations and then some. Judith Keim is an amazing author, and this series is a testament to her writing skills and her ability to completely draw a reader into the world of her characters."

Dessert at The Beach House Hotel

The Beach House Hotel Series – Book 6

Judith Keim

Wild Quail Publishing

Dessert at The Beach House Hotel is a work of fiction. Names, characters, places, public or private institutions, corporations, towns, and incidents are the product of the author's imagination or are used fictitiously. Any resemblance to actual events, locales, or persons, living or dead, is coincidental.

No part of *Dessert at The Beach House Hotel* may be reproduced or transmitted in any form or by any electronic or mechanical means, including information storage and retrieval systems, without permission in writing from the author, except by a reviewer who may quote brief passages in a review. This book may not be resold or uploaded for distribution to others. For permissions contact the author directly via electronic mail:

wildquail.pub@gmail.com

keim.judy@gmail.com

Published in the United States by:

Wild Quail Publishing

PO Box 171332

Boise, ID 83717-1332

Dedication

For my readers who kept begging for more stories about Ann and Rhonda

CHAPTER ONE

On this late August day, I walked with my business partner, Rhonda Grayson, along the sand in front of The Beach House Hotel, the upscale boutique inn we'd created out of her seaside estate on the Gulf Coast of Florida. Looking at it from this angle, it resembled a pink diamond, bright and beautiful, sparkling at the edge of the beach.

It was rare for the two of us to have time like this; being out in the salty air was a pleasant way to talk business and help the creative juices to flow. Bernhard "Bernie" Bruner managed the hotel, but Rhonda and I were the unique forces behind the operation.

As friends and partners, we were as different as two people could be. Rhonda was a free spirit who said whatever was on her mind while I, a product of my strict grandmother's upbringing in Boston, still cringed at some of her words as I took care of the many small details of the business. But from the beginning, we complemented each other's skills and had grown to love one another like sisters who accepted the best and worst about the other.

Rhonda's cell phone rang. She checked caller ID. "Vice President Swanson," She stopped walking and straightened. "Good morning, Madame Vice President," she said and grew quiet. "Uh, huh. I see. Sure, I'll talk to Annie about it and get back to you. But I'm going to say yes right now."

I waited while Rhonda ended the call and turned to me. "It's another favor," she said and shared the details.

"What do *you* think we should do, Annie?" Rhonda asked me. "Having the vice president of the United States appeal to us to do something for her isn't anything we can turn down. "I know," I said. "But the last time we did Amelia Swanson a favor, we almost got killed." Memories of the shooting still haunted me.

Rhonda grinned. "You know what she said about us? She called us sweet as pie, like one of Jean-Luc's desserts. How do you like that?"

"A southern expression that serves her well." I stopped walking and studied Rhonda. As usual, she wore a colorful caftan, had her dyed blond hair tied in a bunch at the base of her neck, and wore all the sparkly diamonds a walk on the beach would allow. "I'm not sure this is a wise idea."

"Look," said Rhonda. "According to Amelia, the girl needs a safe place to stay, somewhere away from any news people until her baby is born and she turns her over to the parents she's chosen to raise her."

I sighed with indecision. I'd heard the argument before.

Rhonda pressed on. "Amelia told me the young girl doesn't want anyone in D. C. to know anything about this unfortunate business."

"I think we should help her," I finally admitted, "but I want Amelia to understand we run a hotel, not a haven for women who need help. I'm happy to serve on the board of her non-profit, but owning and running a hotel is a constant struggle to survive against competition and the forces of nature without adding this kind of situation to the mix."

Rhonda flung an arm across my shoulder. "I knew you'd go for it! I already told Amelia we'd do it."

"Yes, I know," I said, "but to be fair we need to warn her that the girl will stay in a regular room, not at the guesthouse. Fall weddings are about to start up, and the guesthouse is booked from now through fall."

"But we can protect this young woman from any curious press just like we did for Amelia's sister, Lindsay. I'll call her when we get back to the hotel. She said she'd send us more information soon."

Rhonda knew me well. I'd never turn away a call for help. But it was ironic we'd be assisting a girl who didn't want to raise her baby, while my daughter, Liz, was trying for one. Liz had been doing so for only a few months, and she tended to be an over-achiever, but still ...

"I love you, Ann Sanders," Rhonda said, grinning at me. "It'll all work out. And if the girl is as smart as Amelia says, maybe we can find a job for her at the hotel after she has the baby."

I held up my hand. "Whoa! One step at a time. When will this person arrive?"

"Sometime tomorrow. She can't fly at her stage of pregnancy, so a friend is driving her here."

"Tomorrow? Thanks for the heads-up." I rolled my eyes but couldn't help laughing. "You're something else."

"Yeah, I know. Sweet as pie or whatever dessert you want," said Rhonda, elbowing me playfully. "Wonder if Consuela or Jean-Luc have pie on the menu. It's sounding really yummy."

I looped my arm through Rhonda's. "We'd better head back and let Bernie know about this latest development."

"With a stop in the kitchen," Rhonda said. "If Consuela hasn't made any pie, one of our famous cinnamon rolls will do. Or any dessert at The Beach House Hotel. I love them all."

"Me, too," I said. Our cinnamon rolls were one of the reasons that interest grew so rapidly in the hotel back when we first opened over five years ago. They continued to serve us well now.

As we walked back to the hotel, I turned to Rhonda. "Doing this favor for Amelia won't be a piece of cake."

Rhonda looked at me, and then let out a raucous laugh. "Good one, Annie!"

I grinned. Still, I knew getting involved in things like this didn't always work out the way we thought they would. We'd already proved that. But my heart had already gone out to this young woman who needed a safe place to stay.

Inside the hotel, I followed Rhonda into the kitchen. I greeted Consuela, who handled the breakfast rush, with a hug and then grabbed a cup of coffee to go with the cinnamon roll she handed me on a plate. There was something about the smell of butter and cinnamon that made me think it was going to be a good day.

In our office, I studied the financial report from yesterday while Rhonda checked bookings for the holidays ahead. We were already working on ads for that time even though Labor Day hadn't yet arrived.

My phone rang. *Liz.*

I held my breath and picked it up. "Hello, sweetie, how are you?"

"Okay," Liz said, sounding down. She desperately wanted to start a family. She was healthy, and so was her husband, Chad. I figured it would happen soon. Just not soon enough for her.

"You sound a little down. Why don't we have some fun to brighten your day? Let's meet for lunch. You can show me some of the new jewelry you've designed. You know I always love to spend time with my sweet daughter."

"Maybe tomorrow," Liz said. "That would be lovely. Thanks, Mom. Love you."

She ended the call, and I let out a sigh.

"No news?" Rhonda asked.

"Not yet," I replied, feeling a twinge of envy. Rhonda's daughter, Angela, had just had her second baby, and Rhonda was delighted with the idea of being a "hot granny," as she called herself.

"We'll be careful about mentioning the new project to Liz," Rhonda said.

"Thanks." I wondered what other news would come our way. So far today it hadn't been that great.

I settled back into my routine of going over sales figures while Rhonda went to check on staffing with Bernie. In the slower months, we gave some of our staff time off. Soon, though, things would be picking up.

Later, I was still engrossed in updating spreadsheets when Rhonda burst into the office.

"Annie! You're not going to believe this. You know the hotel on the beach in Sandy Isle, just up the beach from us? Guess who the new owners are?

My heart sank. Rhonda got a certain look on her face when she talked about a certain person that we both detested.

"Oh no! Are you thinking about ...?"

"Brock fucking Goodwin? You bet. The bastard is in cahoots with Aubrey Lowell from the Sapphire Resort Collection. I don't know how he managed it, but he's a part-owner with Aubrey and a few young hoteliers who scraped up the money to buy it."

The morning that had been upsetting now threatened to make me sick. "I didn't even know the hotel was for sale."

Rhonda faced me, hands on her hips. "It hasn't been doing well for a couple of years, but I didn't think the owners would sell. They've owned it for only a few years."

"Enough to get discouraged," I said. "It was just a

standard hotel. What are they going to do with it?"

"Bernie told me they're upgrading it. They've already started. Aubrey told him they're going to do everything at their hotel that we wouldn't allow them to do here." Rhonda sank onto her desk chair and faced me with a glum expression. "I don't like it."

I shuddered as I recalled the fights we'd had with Aubrey and others with the Sapphire Resort group when they owned The Beach House Hotel for a short time. They had wanted to convert it into a "hip" hotel more suited to South Beach in Miami Beach than the upscale inn we had created. "If I didn't know both Brock and Aubrey and how they were so eager to destroy what we'd built, I wouldn't be so worried. But these men don't play by the rules." Every nerve in my body went on high alert.

"Yep. That's exactly the way I feel about this. I don't know how they're going to do it, but they're going to try to hurt us."

I nodded, wishing I could deny those feelings. "Any idea what they're going to call the hotel?"

"Bernie heard they're naming it The Sand Castle Hotel, a Playground for the Hip."

"If that's the route they're going, it shouldn't hurt us too much. Our guests are completely different," I said with a note of hope.

Rhonda frowned. "That's what I think. But I'm still nervous about it. We have older guests who want a quiet time. That's for sure. But we also have younger ones who want a good time, a lovely wedding, a nice honeymoon, or simply a great vacation with fantastic food."

"You're right. Those guests like it here, but they might be talked into something different. Especially if comparisons are made between the two properties. And I have an awful suspicion that Brock and Aubrey will try to go after our guests."

I wondered how the day could get worse when our intercom buzzed. I picked up the phone.

"You have special guests waiting to speak to you and Rhonda in the lobby," said one of the young women at the front desk.

I glanced at Rhonda. "Okay, thank you. We'll be right there."

CHAPTER TWO

When Rhonda and I arrived in the lobby, I saw a petite young woman with straight, shoulder-length blond hair wearing jeans and a blue-and-white striped maternity top. She was gazing around the lobby, looking a little lost. Next to her stood a tall young man with dark-brown curly hair. As I got closer, I saw that the girl had large blue eyes which reminded me of paintings of waifs by Margaret Keane. The man beside her wore a look of concern as he stood nearby as if to protect her.

"Hello," I said cheerfully. "How may we help you?"

"Did Amelia Swanson send you?" asked Rhonda.

The girl nodded. "She said she'd send you the information. We arrived earlier than we thought." She smiled at the young man. "Jax drove through the night to get me here."

I extended my hand. "I'm Ann Sanders, and this is my business partner, Rhonda Grayson. And you are?"

"Oh, sorry," said the woman shaking my hand. "I'm Amanda Rogers. But you can call me Mandy."

"We're very pleased to have you here with us," I said and turned to her companion. "Jax?"

He nodded. "Jax Thomas. A ... friend of Mandy's." His dark-brown eyes glowed as he said her name, and I knew the connection between them was special.

"We have a room for Mandy," I said to Jax. "Will you be staying too?"

Mandy and Jax glanced at one another. "At least for

tonight. We're from Virginia, but I'm looking for a job here."

"What kind of job?" asked Rhonda smiling at the two of them.

"I'm studying law by night and have been working at a landscape company by day," Jax said.

Rhonda and I glanced at one another. We'd just learned that Manny's nephew Paul was moving out of town, and we'd need someone to take over for him.

"I'll tell you what," said Rhonda. "If you're interested in working here at the hotel, we can set up an interview for you later this morning. It would be a full-time assistant position." She grinned. "I just knew looking at you, that you were meant to come here today. I sometimes have those special feelings, you know."

I was as surprised as Jax looked. Rhonda and I hadn't discussed needing someone, and she'd never mentioned such an ability before. Was she already thinking of what she claimed was her matchmaking ability?

Rhonda winked at me.

"I'd like that," said Jax. "I need the work, and I want to be sure Mandy is all right."

"He's a really good friend," said Mandy, her eyes shiny with tears.

Rhonda studied them both. "Yes, I see that."

"You look exhausted," I said to Mandy. "Why don't we show you to your room? You'll be pleased to know that it is more private than some of the others."

"Thank you. Ms. Swanson told me you'd help me, but I had no idea I'd be staying in a beautiful place like this."

I smiled at her openness. "Once you're settled, we'll give you a tour of the property and figure out how best to arrange things for you."

"Thank you both so much," said Mandy, her voice

trembling with emotion.

"I'll bring the luggage in." Jax gave us an apologetic smile. "I left my truck in the front circle. Hope that's all right. There's quite a bit of luggage. We didn't know how long we'd be here." He gazed at Mandy's stomach. "The baby's due in a few weeks."

Mandy caressed her baby bump but didn't say anything.

"Why don't you both follow us to Mandy's room?" I said, waving them forward. "The luggage can come later."

Rhonda and I led them down the long hallway to the last room on the first floor. It was the same room Tina Marks had once used as a hideout.

From the ground-floor room, guests could step out to a nice-sized patio and onto the beach beyond. Lush landscaping provided privacy on both sides of the patio. We'd planned it that way, thinking it would be a room for honeymooners before we created the Presidential Suite.

Mandy walked through the room, checked the bathroom and the fact that we had a small refrigerator and microwave available, and then went outside. "It's so peaceful," she murmured, stifling a yawn.

I pulled down the bedspread on the king-size bed, patted the pillows, and turned to her. "Why don't you take a nap? We'll talk later."

Mandy waddled to the bed and sank onto the edge of it, testing the mattress. "This is perfect!"

"C'mon, Jax, I'll help see that your truck gets unloaded and parked," I said.

"Sweet dreams!" Rhonda called to Mandy, closing the door behind us.

"How do you know Mandy?" I asked Jax. I hoped I wasn't intruding, but Rhonda and I needed a lot more information about these new guests.

"She and I grew up in the same little town in West Virginia. Her father is still a minister there, which is why she couldn't go back home after ... after she found out she was pregnant."

"The baby's not yours?" asked Rhonda, sounding surprised and bringing a smile to my face. Guess her special powers weren't working.

"No, Ma'am. That baby isn't mine. Mandy wants us just to be friends."

"I see, but how about ..." Rhonda began.

I elbowed her. No matchmaking ideas now. The poor guy looked as exhausted as Mandy.

"We can talk later," Rhonda said to Jax, not to be deterred.

As we walked with Jax across the lobby, Bernie appeared. We introduced him to Jax, and Bernie said, "Let me get a bellman to help you. Then we'll find you a parking space."

One bone of contention with Aubrey of the Sapphire Resort group had been his insistence that only expensive, luxury cars be allowed to park in the front circle. I wanted each guest in whatever vehicle they chose to feel special.

I walked to the front door, looked out, and stifled a chuckle. Aubrey would've had a fit seeing Jax's truck parked right in front. The older model red truck looked as if it had seen plenty of use and sported a few scrapes, along with a dented bumper.

Bernie and Jax moved past me, and I turned to Rhonda. "We'd better go see if Amelia has sent us any information."

We rushed to the office, anxious to fill in a lot of blank spaces about our two newest guests.

Rhonda checked her email. Sure enough, there was a short note with an attached document that would fill us in on Mandy's story.

She printed it off, and we sat side by side to read it.

After we finished, Rhonda and I looked at one another and sighed together.

"What a sad story," said Rhonda. "Her parents turned her away, disowning her, leaving her on her own."

"Worse still was the way it all happened. Just think about this. Senator Worthington's staff holds a party, someone slips her a roofie, she doesn't remember anything until the next morning, and people tease her about being drunk. No wonder she doesn't know who the father is and why she felt she couldn't file a complaint because everyone would say she was simply drunk, not drugged." I clasped my hands to my cheeks.

"But what's worse is that Mandy's parents didn't care. They still kicked her out!" said Rhonda. "What's wrong with those frickin' people?"

Tears stung my eyes. "No wonder Amelia stepped in to help her. Now, it's our turn. That poor girl! What if something like that had happened to Liz or Angela?"

"I'd hunt down any guy who ever did that to Angela," said Rhonda. "No wonder Mandy doesn't want the baby."

"I wouldn't say that. Did you notice the way she was cradling her stomach when she was walking along with us?"

"Okay, Annie. I'm going to say it right now. Those two are getting married and probably right here at the hotel. I just know it. They might be young, but there's something mature about their relationship."

"Ordinarily, I'd place a bet that you were just making this up, but I'm not going to do that. I want any bit of happiness that can come to Mandy to happen right here."

"Are you saying you believe in my powers?" Rhonda asked, wide-eyed.

"Nope, I'm just saying that this young woman is due for

something good to happen to her." I knew if I agreed with her, she'd never let me forget it. "Now we'd better talk about that job for Jax. Are you thinking what I'm thinking?"

Rhonda grinned and nodded. "We've been trying to get Manny to slow down for months. We're going to have to be careful about not hurting his feelings, but Jax might be the one to help us."

"Guess we'd better go talk to him now," I said, already trying to think of a way to approach it.

We walked outside into balmy air refreshed from the onshore breeze. I took a moment to look around. In the course of converting Rhonda's Beach House into a hotel, we'd added on to the six-car garage and built comfortable apartments above it for Manny and Consuela and for another staff member from time to time. We also had placed a professional laundry on the ground floor there, along with the small spa and exercise facilities that Troy operated for us. Behind the building were two composition tennis courts and to the side, an area for horseshoes and bocce ball.

While Consuela was at work in the kitchen, I hoped we'd be able to talk to Manny alone. He and his nephew, Paul, worked together on landscaping and other maintenance projects at the hotel. As we rounded the front of the hotel and walked into the side garden, we saw Manny on his knees weeding the flower bed surrounding the gazebo.

"Morning, Manny!" said Rhonda.

He slowly got to his feet and faced us with a smile. His tan face beneath the floppy straw hat he was wearing appeared younger than his late-sixties age. But after being in a car accident a couple of years ago, his body hadn't kept up with that image. We didn't like seeing him work so hard, but his pride had kept us from being too firm about it. Now, maybe we could step in and help him.

"Buenos dias, señoras," Manny said. "What can I do for you?"

Rhonda turned to me for direction.

I cleared my throat. "We have a special guest in the hotel. Someone Amelia Swanson asked us to help. A friend brought her here, and he's looking for work. We thought maybe you could train him. With Paul leaving, we don't want to have you without help. And if he works out, we can arrange for you to have more time off."

"Yeah, you're always here working," said Rhonda.

Manny held up his hands and shook his head.

I quickly added. "If you trained him, he'd be able to find work elsewhere, if necessary. He's had some landscaping experience, but not in Florida. We'd like you to meet him and decide for yourself. What do you say?"

Manny studied us. "You're not making me retire?"

"No, Manny," said Rhonda. "You'll always be my Manny around the house."

He laughed. "Okay. I'll meet with him and we'll see."

"Thanks. His name is Jax Thomas, and he seems like a reliable guy," I said. "Where's Paul?"

"He's taking the day off," said Manny.

"Then this is a perfect time to have someone else around, if only for training," I said, giving Manny a quick hug. He was a dear man.

Rhonda and I left him before Manny could change his mind.

Inside, we went to Mandy's room and knocked softly.

Jax opened the door and placed a finger across his lips.

I waved him into the hallway, and Rhonda and I told him that Manny would talk to him about perhaps doing some

14

work at the hotel.

"He thinks he'd be only training you, not hiring you to come on board. That's how we have to play it because he and his nephew have always done the work themselves," said Rhonda.

"And he's afraid we're asking him to retire, which is never going to happen," I said. "He's been a loyal worker for us from the beginning and for Rhonda before that."

"Okay, thanks. Show me where to go, and I'll talk to him," said Jax. "It would be great if this worked out. Then I could keep an eye on Mandy."

"Let's do it," I said.

"Go ahead," said Rhonda, "I promised Angela I'd check in with her. She was going to try to arrange a hair appointment, and I said I'd help out with the children."

Jax and I left her, and I led him outside, hoping the men would get along. I already admired Jax for his attention to Mandy and his ambition to get ahead. It would all depend on how Jax handled Manny.

As we drew close, Manny turned to us and stopped watering the new plants he's put into the ground.

"Manny, this is Jax Thomas, the young man Rhonda and I told you about."

Jax bobbed his head and held out a hand. "Pleased to meet you."

Manny shook hands with him, studying his face. Then with a barely perceptible nod to me, he said, "My pleasure. Come let us talk."

Manny led Jax inside the gazebo and motioned for him to take a seat on one of the built-in benches.

Satisfied that things were off to a good start, I left them thinking another change was about to take place at the hotel. Guests were expected to come and go in the hotel business.

But we worked to keep personnel in place. Luckily, our staff remained loyal with a few exceptions at the lower-paid levels.

When I returned to the office, I looked again over the information Amelia had sent regarding Mandy Rogers. Reading how she'd been rejected by her own family, how helpless she felt to find out more about what had happened during that party, I felt anger all over again. I might have said we wouldn't allow the hotel to be a home to troubled young women, but I was glad Mandy was here.

A little while later, Jax knocked at the door and entered.

"How'd it go?" I asked him.

"Okay. Manny said he'd teach me all he knew so I could find a job elsewhere." He smiled. "You were right. He's afraid I'll want to take over. I tried to tell him I don't even know how long I'll stay. I'm just taking things one day at a time."

"The fact that he's doing this says a lot about you. Thank you for your understanding. When are you going to start?"

"Tomorrow. I have to meet him at 7 A.M. I explained I'd been driving all night and needed time to get settled."

"That'll work. It gets too hot in the afternoon for outdoor work if it can be avoided. What can I do to help you?"

"If you don't mind, I just need to get some sleep. And where is the nearest coffee shop?"

"Let me introduce you to Consuela, Manny's wife. She handles the kitchen in the morning. And not only do we have great coffee, we have the best cinnamon rolls around."

"Sounds great," said Jax, following me into the kitchen.

After introductions were made, Consuela took hold of Jax's arm. "Come with me. I'll see that you get a decent breakfast."

Smiling, I left them. Rhonda and I had always tried to make our staff feel as if they were part of a family—our hotel family. Even though I wasn't sure taking in Mandy and Jax was going to work out the way I hoped, I was happy to see Manny and Consuela on board. In many respects, they were the heart and soul of the operation, having helped us put the hotel together before the doors even opened.

CHAPTER THREE

Before I left the hotel to go home, I decided to check in with Mandy and Jax. Rhonda had left early to watch Angela's kids, and I wanted to make sure our new guests were nicely settled. It would also give me a chance to make an unexpected inspection of housekeeping services as I made my way to their room. Bernie did a great job of managing the property, but as owners, it was wise for Rhonda and me to check things for ourselves. At the far end of the hallway, I gently knocked on the door to Mandy's room.

Mandy opened it. "Hello, Ms. Sanders. Come on in."

As soon as I crossed the threshold, Jax came in from the patio. "Hello."

"I don't want to intrude; I just wanted to make sure you're comfortable and have everything you need."

"Jax got us some groceries," said Mandy.

"All expenses will be taken care of for you. Feel free to order whatever you want for in-room service or come to the main restaurant for meals. The gourmet restaurant requires reservations."

Mandy brushed at the maternity top she was wearing. "I don't have nice enough clothes to go into the restaurants. I'd feel more comfortable here. But thank you."

"You're fine," I said, but I noticed the top was stained and made a mental note to tell Rhonda. Maybe some of Angela's maternity clothes would fit Mandy. The two women were about the same size, and it would seem a friendly gesture, not charity.

I noticed also that a pillow and blanket sat on the couch. "Would you like to have a cot brought into the room?"

A look of relief crossed Mandy's face. "That would be nice. Jax slept on the couch, but I think a cot would be more comfortable for him."

Jax nodded silently.

I took a moment and then spoke. "Amelia suggested you might want to talk to Barbara Holmes, a psychologist who has worked with a couple of other guests of ours. I highly recommend her and agree that it would be helpful for you to talk." I handed her Barbara's card. "I hope you call her. Again, all expenses will be taken care of. And we can make arrangements to take you to her office and back."

Mandy bit her lip and took the card.

"It's a good idea, Mandy," said Jax.

She looked at him and nodded. "Okay. I'll call her tomorrow."

Jax smiled at me. "Anything else?"

"You'll need plenty of sunscreen and a hat," I said to Jax.

He saluted me. "Already taken care of."

"Great. I'm leaving to go home now. We'll see you in the morning."

I left them wondering what the story was between them. It was obvious Jax was into Mandy and took care of her. But Mandy was clearly relieved when I mentioned the cot.

After I placed an order for a cot for the room, I left the hotel thinking about Mandy's background. On a whim, I drove to Bits 'N Bytes, the store Chad and Liz owned. It was where Chad ran his IT consulting business, providing computer services to businesses and individuals in the area.

Liz looked up from behind the counter with a look of surprise when I walked into the store. "Mom! What are you

"I just had to see my daughter today," I said cheerfully, knowing she was struggling with disappointment.

"That's nice, but I'm okay," Liz said. "I'm working on jewelry for the hotel. I'm getting so busy I'm trying to hire someone to help me."

"That's great!" She was designing beaded charm bracelets and necklaces for wedding parties and spa packages at the hotel and was doing better than anyone had thought. But then, her taste was excellent, and hers weren't ordinary beads or charms.

"Do you know of anyone who could help me?" Liz asked.

My thoughts flew to Mandy. I had no idea if she was talented at that sort of thing, but if she was, she could earn a little money and keep her mind off her troubles. "I think I may have someone in mind. Let me tell you a little about her."

"Let's go in the back. How about a cup of coffee or a bottle of cold water?"

"I'll take the cold water," I said following Liz into the back.

We sat at her desk in the room behind the front of the store. After knowing how Mandy's parents had treated her, I thought how sad it was for Mandy and for her parents too. I treasured these moments with Liz, moments when we could sit and talk about almost anything.

"Amelia Swanson asked Rhonda and me to help a young woman she's been talking to."

"The vice president is asking you for another favor? Does Vaughn know?" She gave me a steady look. Vaughn had been very upset that Rhonda and I had been placed in danger by doing a favor for the vice president.

"This isn't the same thing," I replied a little bit

defensively. "There's no danger with this one. Sadness, but no danger."

I told her the story, not mentioning that Mandy was thinking of giving her baby away. I couldn't do that when Liz was trying for one. Especially when I had the feeling that this wasn't what Mandy really wanted. Just an intuition of mine. But I wasn't ready to talk it over with Rhonda just yet.

When I was through telling Liz the story behind Amanda, Liz reached over and squeezed my hand. "I sometimes forget how lucky I am to have you for a mother. Poor Amanda. Having a baby should be a joyful time."

"Usually," I said. "But you can imagine all the feelings that Mandy must have."

Liz nodded solemnly. "If she's clever at working with her hands and wants to help, I'm willing to see how well she does."

"That makes me happy. I'll speak to her about it and let you know if she wants to meet with you. Now, tell me what else is going on with you and Chad."

"Well, I've repainted a couple of rooms in the house and we ordered new furniture for the lanai. The old furniture you gave us is wearing out."

"I'm glad you got use out of it," I said, pleased that Liz was focusing on other things than the empty bedroom she planned to use for a nursery.

Chad came into the store through the back door. I watched his face light up when Liz smiled at him. They were such a cute couple. I hated the thought that the stress of trying for a child might ruin the connection they so clearly enjoyed.

"Hi, Ann!" He kissed me on the cheek. "What brings you here?"

"Just seeing how Liz is doing," I said. "I may have some

help for her in the jewelry business."

"That would be terrific! She's been working into the evenings trying to complete orders. I'd help her, but I'm busy on my own."

"We'd do better if we didn't have to manage the store," said Liz. "But we're not ready to make a change just yet. But we're seriously thinking of it."

I felt my eyebrows rise. "Really? I thought you were doing well."

"We are, but we could be doing better. We have a lot of lookers, not buyers," said Chad. "Customers are going direct to the manufacturers. I don't blame them, but it makes it tough to beat those prices."

"I didn't realize that," I said, understanding why Liz was so intent on making the jewelry business work. First thing tomorrow, I'd talk to Mandy about it. She, like Jax, could test out a new job. "I'd better get home. Robbie's day camp is having Parents' Night, and we have to eat early."

"When does Vaughn get home?" Chad asked. "I'm wondering if I can talk him into going sailing."

I laughed. "Vaughn needs no excuse to get out on the water on his beloved boat, *Zephyr*. He was going to try to make it home for the school activities tonight, but I haven't heard from him. Call anytime."

I hugged Liz goodbye and got to my feet glad I'd stopped by. Though we lived in the same town, with our busy schedules, we didn't see each other enough. It was always good to have face-to-face conversations.

When I pulled into the driveway of my house, anticipation built inside me wondering if Vaughn had made it home from New York. When Trudy, my beloved black-and-tan miniature dachshund, didn't race to greet me, I had my answer.

Smiling, I entered the house and walked outside. Vaughn, Robbie, and Trudy were down on the dock by the boat.

When Trudy noticed me, she barked and trotted up the hill on her short legs wagging her tail.

Laughing, I gave her pats on the head and then walked down the lawn to say hello to Robbie and my man. Tall, with dark curly hair, dark eyes that drew you in, and an easy, sexy smile that still set my heart aflutter, Vaughn was an extremely handsome man.

The look of delight that crossed his face as I approached was something I'd carry in my heart for a long time. It still sometimes surprised me that the man on television in the soap opera, *The Sins of the Children*, the man other women swooned over, was mine.

"Welcome, home!" I threw my arms around him and hugged him tight before turning to Robbie.

"Hi! Did you have a good day at camp?" I asked him, realizing how brown, how fit, how tall he suddenly seemed to me.

"We got to make animals out of shells. I made one for you," Robbie said proudly.

"How sweet." I gave him a quick hug. "Thank you. Are you guys going sailing?"

"Not tonight. Rain is predicted," said Vaughn. "Maybe tomorrow."

"Chad asked about going for another sail. You might want to give him a call."

"Excellent," said Vaughn. "I want to talk to him about a new computer." He gave me a questioning look. "Everything okay there?"

I shrugged. "Nothing new. I have lots of other things to tell you."

"I'll walk you up to the house. We're through here."

Robbie and Trudy raced ahead of us. Watching them, I smiled at such a peaceful scene. Then I thought of some of the news I had to share with Vaughn and sobered.

While Robbie watched one of his favorite television shows, Vaughn and I sat on the lanai with glasses of wine. I loved this time of day when Vaughn was home, and we could catch up on news. His input on some of the problems we faced was important to me.

After I told him about Mandy and Jax, he was quiet. "I think it's nice that you're helping them out, but I don't like the fact that Amelia is asking you for another favor when the last one almost got you killed."

"I know. I felt the same way, but when you meet Mandy and Jax, you'll understand why Rhonda and I are happy to help them. In many ways, they represent so many of the problems facing young people today. We're lucky with our kids, being able to help them. But so many others don't have that kind of support."

"I see your point," said Vaughn. "What else is going on?"

I set down my wine glass and faced him on the couch. "Brock Goodwin has joined forces with Aubrey Lowell and others to buy a hotel up the beach. They're calling it 'The Sand Castle— a playground for the hip.'"

Vaughn choked on his sip of wine and quickly covered his mouth. When he could get a breath, he said, "The two of them together? That's trouble just waiting to happen. How'd you find this out?"

"Bernie told Rhonda. I've been so busy with Mandy and Jax that I haven't had time to think about it. But you're right. It feels like big trouble to me."

"There's never a dull moment for you and Rhonda," said

Vaughn.

"How about you? How are things going on the set? Any more trouble from Simon?" Simon Merrill, one of the producers of *The Sins of the Children*, had been sexually harassing Vaughn's co-star Darla Delaney, who'd just married the love of her life, Meredith Wilkinson.

"Funny you should ask. He's been fired. If guys like Simon continue to abuse their positions to take advantage of others, their days are numbered."

"I'm glad he's gone. I heard from Meredith recently. She and Darla are thinking of buying a house in the area."

"Great. It'll make things easier when everyone wants to get together," said Vaughn.

I loved that he was as open about extending our family as I was. Having grown up an only child, I was delighted our family was growing in unexpected ways.

"Time for dinner," I said. "I have a steak or chicken breasts in the refrigerator. Your choice. Then we'll have to get ready for our meeting."

He grinned. "I'll grill the steak if you make one of your romaine salads."

"Deal," I quickly said, wanting to go in and check on Robbie. With an active imagination, he was content to play on his own building spaceships and racing cars or whatever else he dreamed up. But I liked to connect with him and hear about his day. Other mothers had warned me that boys tend not to share too much information as they grew older. I wanted to take advantage of Robbie's willingness to talk with me. I also intended to give him hugs for as long as I could.

When I walked into his bedroom, he was sitting on the floor building something with his Legos. He looked up at me and smiled. "Don't get too near this spaceship. It's about to take off." He jumped to his feet, holding a multi-colored collection of plastic pieces, and zipped around the room with Trudy at his heels.

I couldn't help the smile I felt spreading across my face. Robbie's camp counselor, an elementary grade teacher during the school year, told me that Robbie was very bright and might one day grow up to be an engineer of some kind. Having an adult daughter, I knew well enough that plans like that would change more than once.

"Want to tell me about your day at camp?" I asked.

"It was fun," he said. "I went swimming." He stopped talking to me and ran out of the room holding his creation aloft as he and the dog ran down the hall, away from me.

I chuckled to myself, aware of how fast he was growing up.

CHAPTER FOUR

When I went into the hotel the next morning, I checked in with Bernie.

"Hi, Ann. I'm glad you caught me. I was about to go to a meeting of the SW Florida Hoteliers group. I wasn't sure I'd be able to make it, but when I heard Aubrey Lowell was going to make a presentation, I cleared my schedule. We have to be diligent when it comes to him and that new project of his."

"Absolutely," I said. "Listen carefully and report back to us on not only his presentation but how the other hotels feel about this."

He smiled and gave me a little salute. "Already planned to talk to a few people about it in private."

"Thank you," I said, letting out a soft sigh as I headed into the kitchen. A second cup of coffee might give me the energy to face the thought of our having to deal with the situation.

Rhonda was already in the office when I walked in.

"Hey, Annie. I want to talk to you about Manny."

My heart thumped with worry. "Manny? Is it bad news?"

"Not really. He just wanted me to assure him that we weren't about to replace him. It seems Paul is thinking of moving to Arizona because his girlfriend wants to move there."

I set my cup down on my desk and faced her. "How does Manny feel about that?"

"He's not happy about it, of course, because they have a close working relationship."

"But now he has Jax to train," I said.

Rhonda nodded. "But I don't think Jax speaks Spanish. That could be a problem."

"Manny knows English, and I'm sure Jax can follow directions," I sputtered.

Rhonda held up her hand. "I know, I know. I told Manny he couldn't make any decisions until he and Jax had worked together for a couple of weeks. And Paul will stay to help train Jax."

"Okay. It seemed such a simple solution. I hope Jax can pull it off."

"Me, too," I said. "I just spoke to Bernie. He's off to a meeting of hotel people. Aubrey is making a presentation to them."

"That slimy bastard," said Rhonda. "What he says and what he means are two different things."

"Bernie is as worried about him as we are," I said. "Not that it gives me any comfort." I sat in front of my computer. "How are we doing?"

"You're the numbers person," Rhonda said, "but for this time of year it looks as if we're holding steady."

I opened my computer and set to work going through our reservations, restaurant sales, and other data. As we often told ourselves, things could change in a heartbeat. One hurricane could blow our sales projections to bits.

A little later, I stretched and said to Rhonda. "I'm going to see how Mandy is doing. Liz is thinking of talking to her about the jewelry business, and I promised I'd speak to her about it as well. I'm also going to ask her if she's thought about seeing Barbara Holmes."

"You go ahead. I'm going outside to see how things are with Manny and Jax."

I left and walked to Mandy's room. Outside the door, I

could hear talking and wasn't sure if I should go away. Before I could decide, the conversation stopped, and I took the opportunity to knock.

When Mandy opened the door, it was clear she'd been crying. "Is everything all right?" I asked.

She shook her head. "The couple I've been talking to about adopting the baby are pushing me to sign an agreement. I told them I can't. We all kinda freaked out because we couldn't agree."

I took a deep breath. "Okay, why don't we talk about it bit by bit and go from there."

Mandy waved me inside the room and out to the patio.

I watched as she maneuvered her swollen body into a chair, cradling her stomach as if to protect it.

Sitting opposite her I said gently, "What's really going on?"

"Up to now, I haven't committed to giving up the baby. And now I'm not sure I want to. Not as we get closer to her due date."

"Her? It's a girl?"

Mandy shrugged. "I don't know for sure. It's just a feeling I have. Everyone suggested I don't find out the sex if I was planning on giving the baby away."

"Why don't we call Barbara Holmes and make an appointment for you to speak to her? She's a professional and can give you far more help than I can. But, as a new friend, I don't like the idea of more stress for you from the adoptive couple."

"Okay, let's call the psychologist. I'm so mixed up right now."

"I'll get her on the phone, and then you can talk to her alone. When you're through I have something pretty exciting to talk to you about."

Mandy's young face brightened. "Okay."

I called Barbara's number, told the receptionist why I was calling, and handed the phone over to Mandy.

While she talked, I walked out onto the beach, pleased with the idea it was so late in the morning I'd miss Brock Goodwin. I took off my sandals and walked to the water's edge. The lacy edges of the Gulf water caressed my feet and pulled away drawing sand around my feet with it, making me feel as if I was on unsteady ground when I was perfectly still.

Little sandpipers and other birds bustled past searching for food. Their tiny footprints in the sand were proof of their existence before a wave washed them away. Observing the bird's footprints so easily erased, I was reminded of what little time we had to live and love and enjoy one another.

My thoughts flew to Mandy, and I stared out at the water moving in a rhythm as old as the beginning of time. No wonder she was confused. I already knew she was attached to her baby. No one should force Mandy into a decision she wasn't ready to make, no matter how willing she'd been to consider it earlier.

I heard the sound of jogging behind me and then the steps slowed.

"Ann?" came a voice I dreaded. I turned around and faced Brock Goodwin. A handsome man with gray hair and a trim body, he was the most annoying person I knew.

I sighed. "Hello, Brock. Aren't you a little late for your run this morning? You're usually so early."

His chest puffed out and his smile was what I could only call a smirk. "I had a meeting to attend. You may not have heard, but I'm a hotel owner now."

"As a matter of fact, I did hear that you're a shareholder in Aubrey Lowell's new hotel."

Brock shook his head. "Always trying to put me down."

"Nonsense. Just keeping it real," I said.

"What's real is that our hotel is going to become the newest, best hotel along this coast. The Beach House Hotel won't be the same. People are going to understand that it's a boring place. The young and hip, and the older and more sophisticated people will want to stay with us."

"I'm not worried about it," I said. "There's room for both businesses."

"We'll see about that. I can't wait for you and Rhonda to get your comeuppance."

"Tell Aubrey we wish him nothing but the best," I said, crossing my fingers as I moved away from Brock. I wasn't lying outright, was I?

I returned to Mandy's patio, curious to know if she'd signed up with Barbara. Barbara had been a huge help to Tina Marks and was still helping Lindsay Thaxton cope after divorcing her husband and enduring the trauma of his abuse and failed murder attempt. Mandy smiled at me as I approached, and a little of the tension that Brock had caused eased a bit from my neck and shoulders.

"Thank you for suggesting my meeting with Barbara Holmes. We talked briefly, and I like her already," said Mandy.

"She's a lovely woman," I said. "When are you going to see her?"

"She's squeezing me in tomorrow morning."

"I'll make arrangements at the front desk for someone to drive you there and pick you up," I said. She wasn't the only guest we'd helped with appointments in the past. What Brock didn't understand was that a guest at The Beach House Hotel could expect personal services like that.

"That would be terrific," said Mandy. "Jax started his trial job with Manny today, and I don't want to disrupt that."

I sat down facing her. "I hope I'm not intruding, but what exactly is your relationship with Jax? Anyone can see that he adores you."

Mandy sighed and shook her head. "He deserves someone far better than me. My parents have told me over and over again that until I come back to my father's church, I'm not worthy of any man. Even Jax, who isn't in the church."

"Is that why you keep pushing him away?" I asked softly.

Mandy's eyes filled. "Like I said, he can find a woman who would help him in his law career, be an upstanding wife to him. I already know I can't do that. And me carrying someone else's baby was the final straw. My parents have told me I'm no longer welcome in the family."

"What did you do in Washington?" I asked, gently changing the subject.

"I was an intern on Senator Worthington's staff. I thought if I had a better understanding of legal matters, I'd be good enough for Jax. Now, I know I'm not." She wagged a finger at me. "I'm not about to mess up his life. His future is bright. He's smart. As nice as it is that he's going to be working for you, he deserves to complete his courses and go into law like he's wanted since I can remember."

Feeling helpless to say anything that I thought could be helpful, I said, "Barbara is someone who may be able to help you sort out your feelings." I reached over and took hold of her hand. "I'm glad you're here, Mandy. You've got a lot to think about."

She gave me a shaky smile. "Ms. Swanson said it would be wise for me to come here. I can have privacy and peace. She's right. I already know it."

"How are you working with your hands? Have you done any craft work?" I asked, sending a look of surprise to her face.

"I've knit and I've sewn. Part of the churchwork my mother directed. Why?"

"My daughter, Liz, designs jewelry. Mostly putting together beads and charms in interesting patterns, doing custom work for bridal parties, baby showers and births, and the like. She's getting so many orders she needs help. I was thinking it might be a little boring for you after a while to be here without anything to do."

"Really? I could do that while waiting for the baby to come? I would love it. 'Busy hands are happy hands', as my mother used to say."

"I'll call Liz and perhaps we can stop by the store after your appointment with Barbara tomorrow morning. She and her husband, Chad, run the Bits N Bytes store downtown."

"Interesting. Thank you for thinking of me." Mandy smiled and for the first time, I saw a light of happiness in her pretty blue eyes.

I left her with the promise that I and not someone from the hotel would drive her to her meeting with Barbara and then we'd meet Liz and go to lunch.

Excited about how things were coming together, I went to the office.

Rhonda was at her desk frowning at her phone.

"What's up?"

"We just got a text from Bernie. He's going to be gone the rest of the day. He and a couple of other hotel managers are getting together privately to talk about what to do about Aubrey and friends. Aubrey announced that no local hotel is safe from their campaign to build theirs into the best-ever Gulf Coast hotel. He said that hotels on the Gulf Coast have been mediocre at best, that after seeing how The Beach House Hotel is run, they're confident they can do better. Bernie goes on to say he and his friends are going to consult with a lawyer about the possibility of libel, that Aubrey is so full of himself that he isn't about to listen to any talk of cooperation among the hotels." Rhonda made a face. "How do you like them apples?"

"I don't," I said, sliding into my desk chair and facing her. "I met Brock down at the beach."

"Yeah? What did Mr. Asshole have to say?"

"He can't wait for our 'comeuppance'." Remembering my earlier conversation with him, I shuddered. He was a nasty man, but Aubrey was sounding even worse. What an awful way to start a new business. And Rhonda and I weren't the only ones worried about it.

Rhonda and I spent the rest of the day going over our ad campaign, which centered on focused service, outstanding food, a luxurious setting, and a prime location.

Studying it, I said, "We're not competition for what I understand Aubrey is planning. So, I don't know why he's badmouthing us and the other hotel people. No one else is talking about a playground for the young and hip. That's South Beach talk."

"Our coast is considered the quiet one. That's how we want to keep it," said Rhonda. "Anyone can go to Miami and beyond to get more action."

"Precisely. Let's wait and see what Bernie has to say before we even think of how we're going to react. Aubrey is a pretty classless guy." Thinking back to prior confrontations with him, I started to laugh. Rhonda had once told him, "If I weren't such a lady, I'd wring your fucking neck." I smiled at the memory. Only Rhonda could get away with saying something like that.

Still, I was both encouraged and discouraged by the day's events.

CHAPTER FIVE

When I arrived home, Vaughn, Chad, and Robbie were down on the dock washing the boat from the day's sailing trip. It did my heart good to see the three of them together. Chad was a nice guy who loved Liz dearly, but I had the feeling he wasn't as anxious for children as she. Maybe because he ran his consulting business pretty much by himself and worked long, hard hours. I first met him a couple of years ago when he installed some computer and electronics systems for the hotel. With strawberry-blond hair and blue eyes, he and Liz were adorable together. I couldn't wait to see what any child of theirs might look like. She was as blond as he and had the same sparkling blue eyes.

Vaughn, who got along with anybody, particularly liked Chad, probably because Chad tended to be quiet and thoughtful. Trudy saw me standing outside the screened-in lanai and raced up the lawn to greet me. Vaughn noticed and gave me a wave.

I waved back and headed into the kitchen to put together some appetizers I knew they'd appreciate. There was something about being in the salty air, skimming across the water in a sailboat that built a healthy appetite.

Inside the kitchen, I got out cheese and crackers, olives, and a bowl of nuts and was cutting up carrot sticks when Liz appeared.

"Is my hubby still here?" she asked, giving me a quick kiss on the cheek.

"Yes, and I'm about to serve appetizers and drinks. Care to join us?"

"Absolutely. I can't wait to tell you and Chad about a certain visitor I had at the store. I'll wait until we're all together."

"Any more famous actors like we had last week?"

Liz shook her head. "Not really. But you'll be interested just the same."

Vaughn and Chad came into the kitchen, followed by Robbie and Trudy. Liz and Chad embraced.

"Ah, that looks delicious, hon," said Vaughn snitching a carrot stick as he kissed me on the lips.

"Mom, can I have some juice?" Robbie asked.

"Of course," I answered, checking Trudy's water dish to make sure she had enough.

After getting Robbie his juice and finishing up the tray of appetizers, I headed out to the lanai where Vaughn, Chad, and Liz had already taken seats.

I offered the tray of food to everyone and then set it down on the table.

Sitting on the couch next to Vaughn, I accepted the glass of pinot noir he handed me and took a sip. It, and being here with my family was so pleasant.

"Okay," said Liz. "Now that we're all together, let me tell you who came into the store this afternoon. Aubrey Lowell."

"What did he want?" I asked, uneasy already.

Liz turned to Chad. "He wants you to do the entire Bluetooth network for his new hotel, along with installations of any computer programs they may need."

Chad's eyebrows shot up. "Really? That's a lot of work. What did you say to him?"

Liz gave us a smug smile. "I told him we'd need more information."

"And?" Chad said.

"And that's when he got nasty. He told me you'd better hurry and put in a bid but not to make it too high because someone he knew told him we were not doing that well and might need the job." Liz glanced at me.

"Brock Goodwin," I said.

"I'm pretty sure," said Liz. "The only thing is he doesn't know the truth. The store isn't that busy, but Chad's consulting business that's run out of the store is very successful. We don't need to grovel for any job."

"I'll talk to Aubrey tomorrow and see what he wants. I'd want to tour the property before I even considered any job there. It can be a real nightmare to try to update an older property. Besides, I know very well what it's like to work for him. He may not remember, but he tried to get out of paying a monthly fee for my services at The Beach House Hotel before I changed the name of my company."

"He's not to be trusted, but I'd be anxious to learn anything you can tell me about the hotel. Bernie is concerned about a negative advertising campaign they intend to conduct touting their hotel as the only viable one on the Gulf Coast. It sounds silly, but Bernie knows as well as Rhonda and me that Aubrey wouldn't hesitate to do it."

"The fact that Brock Goodwin is even associated with it tells me a lot," said Vaughn. "Too bad he has no ethics."

"I don't understand why people don't get rid of Brock as president of the Neighborhood Association," Liz said.

"He has a group of friends who like thinking they're an important part of the community. Retired CEO types who like to feel as if they're in control," said Chad. "Besides, who would want that job?"

"Someday Brock Goodwin will get his comeuppance," said Vaughn.

"That's exactly what he said about Rhonda and me," I said. "He hates that we've bested him time after time. Frankly, it's a little scary."

"I'll always protect you whenever I can," said Vaughn. "I don't like that man."

Robbie, who'd been sitting at the edge of the pool, kicking at the water with his feet, said, "Can I go swimming now, Mom?"

"Sure. I'll watch you." I waved Liz over, and we both sat at the shallow edge of the pool, cooling our toes in the water. "I want to talk to you about Mandy."

"Oh, nice! Is she interested? I got another email order, and I need the help."

"Mandy knits and sews and does craft projects. I'm guessing she'll be helpful. She was thrilled with the idea. I told her we'd come to the store so you can meet her and talk to her about it. And then, if possible, we can have lunch together."

"That sounds great. Thanks, Mom."

"Mom! Lizzie! Look!" Robbie called to us and then did a head stand in the pool, his legs moving rapidly to keep his balance. As he came to the surface, we both clapped.

"Super job, Robbie!" cried Liz, grinning. "Do another!"

Without hesitation, Robbie took a breath and ducked under the water again.

Liz turned to me. "He's growing up so fast. Hard to forget the shy, unhappy little boy he'd been when Dad died."

"We've been good for him," I said.

Liz's eyes filled, and I squeezed her hand, understanding where they'd come from. I sometimes thought her eagerness to have a baby came from the fact that when she had been designated as guardian for two-year-old Robbie after his parents' death, she'd been too young to take care of him and had agreed for Vaughn and me to adopt him.

Chad and Liz joined us for a simple meal of grilled hamburgers and a tossed salad and then left to return home. I then sat outside for a while just letting my thoughts flow. Robbie was due to go back to school the following week even though Labor Day had yet to arrive. First grade was a big deal—the beginning of years that would fly by.

Vaughn came out and joined me. "Penny for your thoughts."

I turned to him and smiled. "Just thinking of the months ahead. It's going to be busy."

"I hope you're not going to let Aubrey and Brock weigh you down with worry."

"I'm not," I said, realizing how much I meant it. Life was too short to let people like that interrupt my plans for doing well both at the hotel and at home.

"Good. Because I was thinking we might want to have a private getaway. Even if it's for only a long weekend. We haven't done that for a while."

I smiled. "Are you thinking of The Palm Island Club?"

He laughed. "Maybe. How does next weekend sound?"

"Lovely," I said. "Absolutely lovely." The Palm Island Club was on a little island right off the southern shoreline of Sabal. Since we could reach it only by a short boat ride, I always felt as if I were worlds away on another honeymoon when we stayed there.

Vaughn squeezed my hand. "Okay, I'll set it up. I've already asked Liz if she'd take Robbie for us."

"Well, aren't you the clever one," I said, giving him a teasing smile.

"I'll prove just how clever as soon as we go to bed," he

replied, his eyes twinkling.

"I'll do the dishes while you see that Robbie has a bath."

"No problem. Robbie's done. He got in a swim while you and Liz were talking. How fast can you do dishes?" he said, grinning. I laughed, but I intended to work quickly.

The next morning, I picked up Mandy for her appointment with Barbara Holmes and realized that, though it had been laundered, she was wearing the same striped top as she had for the last couple of days.

" 'Morning!" I said cheerfully as she entered my car in the front circle of the hotel. "Are you all set for Barbara?"

"Yes," said Mandy, smiling. "I think you and Amelia are right. It'll be good to talk things over with her."

"I spoke to Liz and she's excited to meet you. After that, we can go to lunch."

"Okay," said Mandy shyly, folding her hands in her lap in front of the baby bump that took up most of it. "I've made an appointment with Dr. Benson as you suggested. I'm meeting with her tomorrow. Rhonda helped me set it up."

"Ruth Benson delivered both of Rhonda's young children. I think you'll like her."

"You've both been so kind to me. I really appreciate it." She smiled at me and then gazed out the window.

"How old are you, Mandy?" I asked. She seemed so young, so unsophisticated.

"I just turned nineteen," she said. "I was selected for the intern program through my high school and our national Congressman's office. My parents didn't want me to go, of course. And now I've proved to them that I shouldn't have left."

"What happened isn't your fault," I said.

"As far as they're concerned, I should've known better than to go to a party. At home, I wasn't allowed to dance or sing. Those are sinful things to them."

I bit my tongue so I wouldn't say what was on my mind. I reminded myself everyone should be able to choose the life they wanted. But I thought it was wrong to keep children from doing the same.

We were both quiet as I pulled up to the front entrance of the building where Barbara Holmes practiced.

"I'll return for you in one hour, and then we can visit Liz."

"Thank you. See you then," said Mandy.

I watched her make her way to the door, and a plan formed in my mind.

Pulling up in front of Angela's house, I was amused by the sight of the tricycle and the baby stroller parked by the front entry. One of the benefits of living in Florida was the ability for children to be outside a lot of the time. At this time of year, mornings were a great time for her to walk the baby with Evan peddling his bike close by.

I knocked on the door, and Angela answered it, holding her baby in her arms. Almost four months old, Sally looked like a cross between both her parents with dark hair, brown eyes, and pink cheeks I wanted to squeeze. However, Reggie's mother, Katherine, insisted she looked exactly like her father. Something that annoyed Rhonda no end.

"Hi, sweetie!" I said, giving both Angela and the baby a quick kiss on the cheek. I'd always felt close to Angela. At five foot three inches, she had fine features, dark hair, and brown eyes that shined with humor.

"Come in, Ann," Angela said smiling. "I haven't seen you in a while."

"I have a question for you," I said, following her into the living room where Evan, her four-year-old, was building something with a set of wooden blocks.

"Excuse the mess," said Angela. "Evan, can you say hi to Auntie Ann?"

"Hi." He smiled at me and went back to his project. Seeing him like this, so calm, reminded me of how needy he'd been when Sally was first born and when Angela's mother-in-law, Katherine Smythe, was in charge.

"Guess what!" Angela said as if she'd heard my thoughts. "Katherine is flying down here at the end of the week. She says she can't bear to be away from the children."

"Does your mother know?" I asked. Rhonda and Katherine did not get along.

"No, and I'm not going to tell her until I'm ready to pick up Katherine at the airport. That way, Mom won't worry about Katherine not accepting her." Angela shook her head. "Katherine can be mean, but I think her last visit helped her to understand that Reggie and I have the right to make our own decisions, and that my mother is a decent person."

"Rhonda was kind to her," I said, defending my best friend from a woman who had little softness within her.

"I know and I appreciate that, but I have to keep trying with Katherine. For Reggie's sake. What did you want to talk to me about?" said Angela. "Something at the hotel?"

"Some*one* at the hotel," I answered, taking the seat on the couch that Angela offered me.

I told her about Mandy. "I'm wondering if you'd be willing to lend her any maternity clothes. She looks to be your same size. I've seen her in only one top. She has a few more weeks to go, but it would be nice if she could change up her wardrobe a bit."

"Sure. I was saving some things for Liz, but I'm certain

she won't mind." She turned to me. "If you watch the kids, I'll go get a few things." She laid Sally on her back on a blanket on top of the carpet and handed her a plush ball to play with.

I sat on the carpet by the baby, observing both children. Angela was a wonderful mother. How would Rhonda react to having Katherine here in the house with the kids again? It hadn't worked well before.

Sometime later, Angela returned carrying several items of clothing. "A lot of my stuff was for winter, but I brought out a couple of cooler tops Mandy can borrow, along with a sleeveless dress. I don't have any maternity shorts."

"These will be great. I can take her shopping after lunch and pick up a couple of things. I don't want her to believe we think she's a charity case. Though she's been through a lot, she has pride."

"I'll try to get over to see her and say hello. Mom told me about her, but I haven't had the chance to get away."

"I think she's going to help Liz with the jewelry business," I said, making conversation.

"Really? Nice. Liz asked me, but I can't. By evening when these two are finally in bed, I'm too tired to do much of anything. I know it'll get better, but not for a while."

"It's a good thing Liz has this business to keep her busy. She's enjoying it, and it gives her something to do when she has to tend to the store." I checked my watch. "I'd better go. I don't want to be late to pick up Mandy."

"Next time, I hope you can stay longer. I didn't even have the chance to offer you anything cold to drink," said Angela, giving me an apologetic smile. "Promise you won't tell my mother about Katherine?"

"I promise, but you know we all have a hard time keeping things from your mother. Thank you for the clothes. Love you," I said, kissing her. She might not look like her mother, but Angela was every bit as generous.

CHAPTER SIX

Mandy was sitting outside on a bench when I pulled up to the medical building where I'd dropped her off. Alarmed to see her out so early, I braked the car and waited for her to make her way to it, aware that she'd been crying.

"Hi, Mandy! You're out a little early."

She gave me a shaky smile. "I got pretty emotional, and Barbara thought we should stop. She gave me a notebook to write down my feelings every day so we can talk better next time." Mandy faced me. "I'm so angry. Why did this have to happen? It's not my fault somebody drugged me. Why should I end up like this?"

"I'm sorry," I said. "It doesn't seem fair."

"Seem fair? No, it doesn't seem, it *is* fucking unfair," she said, sounding like Rhonda. I remained quiet, studying her as I drove away. Mandy had appeared almost waif-like when I'd met her, but I was beginning to see the fire inside her.

"No matter what I choose to do, I'll regret it the rest of my life," said Mandy, heaving a loud sigh and staring out the window.

"I like Barbara's idea of writing down your thoughts each day," I said, hoping to give her some comfort. There was so little I was qualified to say. Going forward, I vowed to be more present for Mandy. Hers wasn't the only life in jeopardy.

"I thought after lunch, I'd take you shopping for a few things for you. My treat."

"No, no, I can't let you do that," said Mandy.

"No worries," I said. "It gives me such pleasure to do this for you. In the meantime, Rhonda's daughter, Angela, has chosen some things you might like to use. She'd planned to lend them to Liz, but that isn't yet a possibility."

Mandy frowned. "What do you mean?"

"Liz and Chad have been trying for a baby, but so far, no luck."

"Oh, I'll remember that when I meet her," Mandy said, looking thoughtful.

I placed a hand on Mandy's shoulder. "I'm sure it's going to happen for them soon, but I'd rather not mention it."

"Yes, of course. I'm excited to meet her and learn more about her business," said Mandy. "And I want to meet Angela too. It's very sweet of her to lend me some clothes. I've been out-of-work, and I can't ask Jax to help me any more than he's done."

"He seems like a great guy," I said.

"Yes," Mandy said.

I found a parking spot not too far from the store. Mandy and I studied the windows of a couple of clothing shops as we headed down the block to Bits 'N' Bytes.

Liz was behind the counter talking to a customer when we stepped inside. She smiled and waved. And then, after she rang up a purchase, she walked over to us.

"Hi, you must be Mandy," Liz said, holding out a hand, carefully avoiding staring at Mandy's round stomach.

"Yes, and you must be Liz," Mandy said, beaming at her. "I can't wait to see your jewelry."

"Me, too," said Liz, motioning us to the back of the store. In her office, she'd set up a special worktable on top of which was a sizeable stacked set of small, clear-plastic storage boxes filled with colorful beads. A goose-neck desk lamp brightened the area.

"This is where I work," said Liz. "Orders are flying in from the website I set up as well as custom work for Mom's hotel. I need all the help I can get. How are you at doing something like this?"

Mandy studied the worktable and turned to Liz. "I'm used to working with my hands, and I need to earn some money, so I'm very interested in doing this."

"Okay, have a seat. Let's see how you do. I'd like a silver bracelet with three different colors added."

"You want me to make anything I choose?" asked Mandy. A smile crossed her face as she sat down.

While she worked, Liz and I moved to the front of the store where I told Liz about my visit to Angela, and that Katherine would be returning to Florida at the end of the week.

"Does Rhonda know?"

I shook my head. "Angela will tell her the morning of Katherine's arrival, so Rhonda isn't worked up with worry beforehand. I don't know why Katherine has such an ability to shake Rhonda's self-confidence."

Liz made a face. "I don't blame Rhonda. Katherine's been totally rude and disrespectful to her in the past, acting as if Rhonda was way beneath her. I don't know how Angela manages to deal with her."

"Katherine's difficult for sure," I too disliked how she treated Rhonda.

Mandy appeared and handed Liz a bracelet.

Liz studied it and then looked up at Mandy with a broad smile. "I love how you used blue, green, and orange together. It reminds me of a setting sun over the Gulf waters."

"Yes," said Mandy proudly. "That was my thought."

"I would love for you to come work for me. Let's go out

back to discuss the details."

"I'll wait here," I said, eager as always to look around at the array of technical items on display. Now that I knew they might consider giving up the store, I could see how much inventory they were required to carry and better understood their desire to be free from that debt.

Liz and Mandy emerged from the back, chatting happily. It pleased me to see them so excited.

"Chad is working on a big job on Marco Island, so Elena is coming to watch the store for me while we have lunch."

As soon as the words were out of her mouth, Elena walked inside. "Am I late?"

"Right on time. Thanks," said Liz, making the introduction to Mandy.

"If we have time before I have to meet Robbie at the camp bus, I need to talk to you," Elena said to Liz. "It's about Troy's plan to open another spa. I'm still worried about it."

Liz nodded. "We can talk anytime you wish."

As we left the store, I liked the idea of how Elena and Troy were fitting into my family. Elena had babysat Robbie since we first got him, had met and married Troy at the hotel, and now was like a daughter to me. It was sweet that her sister, Rita, was a close part of Rhonda's family.

We decided to go to André's. It was a favorite of mine, a small French restaurant with outdoor seating tucked in a little alleyway along with a dress shop I loved and a silversmith who did fantastic work. Often, we sat outside. But today was warm, and with Mandy so pregnant, I thought she might not be comfortable in the heat and asked for seats inside. The small restaurant was filled with a lovely aroma of butter, mushrooms, onions, and seasonings I couldn't name.

But they already were prompting me to order a mushroom crepe, for which André's was well-known.

We were seated at a table by the window, which allowed us to look outside as well as to study the interior. I loved the bright-yellow painted walls and the blue and red accents in the material of the tablecloths from Provence. Blue-rimmed water goblets and tiny vases filled with silk flowers in bold colors added to the French décor.

"Smells delicious," said Liz, looking over the menu she'd been handed. Our waitress, Margot Durand, was Andre's wife and co-owner of the restaurant. I'd met them before through Jean-Luc.

"*Bonjour,* Ann," said Margot. "How are you? So nice to see you here."

"Thank you. It's my pleasure," I responded smiling.

Margo returned my smile. "And how are Jean-Luc and his girlfriend? We have not seen as much of him as usual."

"They seem to be doing very well. Lindsay has moved in with him, and they both seem happy." After the trauma of her ex-husband attempting to kill her, Lindsay had decided she liked the life-style of Southwest Florida and most especially liked the relationship she had formed with Jean-Luc. I didn't know if they were ready to take things to the next level, but I had a suspicion that another wedding at the hotel was in the future.

"*Ah, si bon!* For you ladies, I recommend the mushroom quiche, the croque-monsieur, our signature French onion soup, or any of the crepes. Our signature salads are a staple. We have received some fabulous, fresh assorted mushrooms. What may I bring you to drink?"

It took no time for us to order. Iced teas for all, quiche and salad for the girls, and a mushroom crepe for me. With Vaughn gone again, I'd just nibble for dinner.

After Margot placed our orders, she returned to the table. "I have only a minute, but wanted to tell you about a visit we had from Aubrey Lowell. I understand he's opening a new hotel, The Sand Castle."

"Yes," I said, wondering what Aubrey was up to now.

"He came to understand very quickly we were not interested in working at his hotel. But we have found out he's been trying to bribe our sous chef away."

I made a face. "That doesn't surprise me. He's not to be trusted, as you well know from Jean-Luc."

"Pierre, our sous chef, turned him down after Aubrey said he wanted to change up the idea of a French restaurant, combining it instead with Caribbean cuisine. 'Real food for real people,' he called it." Margot's nostrils flared with indignation. "Can you imagine?"

"I can't," I said. "Aubrey's an interesting person. He is in a position to have a very successful career in his family's hotel business, but he has proven he isn't as knowledgeable as he claims. Bernie explained to me that this new hotel isn't and will not ever be part of the Sapphire Resorts. That, in itself, tells me Aubrey will make his own rules."

"I don't like it," said Margot.

"Me, either," I said and watched Margot hurry off to seat new customers.

"Mom, is Aubrey going to try to ruin The Beach House Hotel all over again?" Liz asked.

"He may try, but for all the talk about an exciting new property, we and most of the hotel owners in the area understand that Aubrey is not to be trusted." I noticed Mandy sitting quietly and remarked, "I'm sorry to talk business."

"No, go ahead. Believe me, I've heard all kinds of things while working in Washington," she said. "This sounds a lot like it."

Liz leaned closer to Mandy. "Tell us more about your time there. I stayed in D.C. for a couple of months when I visited Nell, my step-sister, a few years ago."

While we ate our meal, which was every bit as delicious as I'd hoped, Mandy regaled us with stories about some of the Senators and social events.

As she talked, I wondered how a girl from a small, poor town in West Virginia had made her way to the country's capital. When I asked, she simply replied, "I was the valedictorian of my class and knew I wanted a different life from the time I first realized there was a whole, better world out there. My father is well-known in the area because of the church, but in the real world, he'd be nothing."

I heard the bitterness in her voice but remained quiet.

"This friend of yours, Jax, how does he fit into the picture?" asked Liz.

Mandy smiled and set down her fork. "Jax is my best friend. He grew up a few houses down the street from me. He's smart, and he won a football scholarship to the state university. He graduated in June in business, but he's been taking online courses in law to see if that's what he really wants to do. His parents own a business in town, but he isn't sure he wants to join them. He'd rather live somewhere else. When he heard what happened, he called and came to help me until I left D.C. to come here."

"Wow! What a guy. Sounds like he's really serious about you," said Liz. "Like something out of a romance novel."

"He can do much better than being with me. I owe him that," said Mandy, her eyes welling with tears.

"But ..." Liz persisted.

I held up my hand. "I understand what you're thinking, but don't push, Liz."

Liz glanced at me and then at Mandy. "Sorry."

"How about dessert?" I said brightly to lighten the mood. "All the pastries are delicious."

Before we could order, Margot brought a small tray to our table filled with tiny portions of several desserts. "From André," she announced proudly. "Our sample dessert tray."

"Thank you," I said, delighted. It was a generous gift. Jean-Luc occasionally sent members of his kitchen staff to Andre to teach them a few secrets to creating French pastries.

As we left the restaurant, I turned to Mandy. "I'm aware you left home with only a few of your things. I'd like to take you to the mall so you can fill in some items of clothing. As I said earlier. It makes me so happy to do this for you."

Mandy gazed at me, her eyes filling. "That's so nice of you. I wish I could do it on my own, but I don't need much, I promise."

"We'll get whatever you need. It's going to be so fun!"

"I'll pay you back after I do some work for Liz," said Mandy, smiling at Liz.

"It's not necessary, but whatever you wish." I turned to Liz. "Thank you for taking the time to have lunch with us. I'm delighted you and Mandy are working together. Hopefully, it will be a huge help to you."

"I'm happy with what I've seen," Liz replied. "Thanks, Mandy. I'll see you tomorrow."

Mandy and I returned to my car, and then we headed to the mall.

After I dropped Mandy off at the hotel and made sure she

had help with her packages, I drove around to the back and parked my car. After a morning off, I wanted to check in with Rhonda. In the office, she looked up at me and smiled. "I've been going over our ad campaign and want your input. But first, tell me how this morning went."

I told her about how Angela had lent some of her maternity clothes to Mandy. Even though I wished I could tell Rhonda about Katherine's visit, I didn't mention it. A promise was a promise. "Liz is very excited that Mandy is going to help her with the jewelry business. She's been overwhelmed by orders. I think it'll be helpful for both of them to work together."

Rhonda gave me a worried look. "What do you think is going to happen to Mandy after the baby is born?"

I let out a sigh. "I have no idea. I thought maybe she and Jax would stay together, but she insists she owes him the chance to get to know other women, that she's not good enough for him."

Rhonda's eyes widened. "Doesn't she see how he looks at her? It's clear that he loves her. And though they're young, they're not the babies some kids are at that age."

"At lunch, Liz started to press Mandy on it, and I could see the panic rise in Mandy's eyes. She's under too much stress right now to push that idea. Alone in the car with me this morning, she allowed her anger to show. And then at lunch, it was clear there are anger issues with her father. Poor girl! Barbara has her keeping a diary of sorts to track her feelings and thoughts. Maybe that will help." I shook my head. "Her parents sound awful. You'd think a minister would be understanding."

"In the meantime, Manny is very happy with Jax's help, though he won't come right out and say it." Rhonda beamed at me. "I think it's going to prove to be a great move on my part to suggest hiring him."

"Whoa! Wait a minute! I suggested it," I grinned. "Okay. Okay. We both came up with the idea."

"Agreed," said Rhonda, "though the minute I heard he'd done some landscaping I was already thinking about it."

I laughed. Rhonda was a little competitive, but I loved it. It kept me on my toes.

"If Jax should agree to take the job with Manny on a permanent basis, we could put him in the other apartment over the garage," I said. "At least until he found something permanent."

"Great idea," said Rhonda. "But I've already requested housekeeping to go through it and make sure it's ready for him."

"Ah, great minds think alike," I said.

Rhonda elbowed me. "Some faster than others."

We laughed together.

I followed Rhonda outside to where Paul and Jax were working.

"How's it going?" I asked.

Both men turned to us and nodded.

"Okay," said Paul.

"*Bueno*," Jax said, grinning. "Paul's teaching me some Spanish so Manny can tell me what to do."

Paul chuckled. "This guy knows plenty already."

"Can we talk to you privately?" I asked Paul.

"Sure. Where do you want to meet?"

"Why don't we go to the gazebo. We can talk there," I suggested. "Will you excuse us, Jax?"

"*Por supuesto*," said Jax, looking to Paul for approval.

Paul gave him a thumbs-up sign and followed us across the front lawn to the side garden.

We took seats in the gazebo, which had become a lovely

location for small weddings. Liz had been married there almost nine months ago.

"We understand you intend to move to Arizona as soon as it's convenient. Is that right?" said Rhonda.

"Yes, my girlfriend's family is there, and living close to them is important," said Paul. "It'll be good for me, too. I've been offered a partnership in a landscape company there."

"Sounds perfect," I said. "A chance for you to grow. How soon do you plan to move?"

"I promised Manny I'd stay until I trained someone to take my place. My cousin was all set to take over for me, then Jax appeared. But I like him, and he's smart. A hard worker, too. Later, if there's room for my cousin, that would be great."

"Are you comfortable about our hiring Jax full-time? Is Manny okay with that idea?" I asked, looking to Rhonda.

"Manny told me he liked him," said Rhonda. "But I want your opinion about it working out for the long haul."

Paul thought a minute and slowly nodded. "Manny will make it clear what he wants, and Jax is willing to learn Spanish. I think it'll be fine."

"Me, too," I said. "Now, we'll see if Jax is open to the plan. If not, we'll have to talk to your cousin right away."

"Will you ask Jax to come here?" said Rhonda. "We'll talk to him about the position now." She smiled. "Best of luck to you, Paul. We'll miss you."

"But we're happy for you too," I added.

Paul gave us a little salute and left.

Rhonda and I gazed at one another, and I realized a new chapter was about to begin. Paul was just a kid when he'd started working with Manny. Now he was an independent young man about to start his own business far away from us. It felt like losing a member of the family.

Judith Keim

Rhonda sensed my dismay and reached over and clasped my hand. "He's been a great worker, but Jax will be fine too. You'll see."

"If we can give him stability, perhaps he'll stay, and so will Mandy," I said, realizing how beautifully that could work for everyone.

Jax strode toward us.

I studied him as he moved. He was taller and stockier than Paul but walked with the grace of an athlete. Like Paul, he was a handsome man with a kind manner about him. Lord knew he'd been wonderful to Mandy.

"You wanted to see me?" Jax asked as he took a seat on the bench opposite us.

"Yes," said Rhonda. "Paul is going to be leaving for Arizona in a couple of weeks, and we're wondering how you'd feel about taking over for him permanently?"

"It's a full-time position that requires you to be available on a regular basis," I said. "But we're able to provide living quarters for you for the next several months until you're acclimated to both the job and the area."

"But that comes with a commitment from you to stay at least a year," said Rhonda.

"And as you already know, we provide benefits," I said.

"We'll give you some time to think about it, and if you're serious, we'll work out the details," said Rhonda. "We know you have Mandy to consider."

Jax took off the straw hat we'd given him and rubbed a hand through his dark curls. "Thank you for the offer. I'll let you know for sure after I talk to Mandy. I can't leave her now, but I want her to know if I take this job, she can always stay with me."

"She loves you, ya know," said Rhonda.

Jax's head jerked up and his eyes fastened on her face.

Rhonda shook her head. "Anybody can see you guys love each other."

I placed a hand on her knee to stop her. "Why don't you report back to us tomorrow morning with your decision. We'll talk about particulars then."

"Okay," Jax said. "Thanks." He stood, and all but ran away.

I glared at Rhonda.

She placed a hand on her hip. "What? They love one another. Any fool can see that. Why mess around?"

"They each have a lot to think about. We don't need to be pushing them into something they're not ready for."

Rhonda let out a long sigh. "You're right, Annie. But I can't stand it when people can't make up their minds. Drives me crazy."

I nodded, knowing very well if she hadn't pushed me, I might not have the life I had.

CHAPTER SEVEN

The next morning, I was in the office with Rhonda and Dorothy Stern, who'd worked for us from the beginning doing odd jobs that we didn't have time to do ourselves. We loved Dorothy for many reasons, among them the ability to put Brock Goodwin in his place during the Neighborhood Association board meetings. Barely over five feet tall, retired from operating her own business, Dorothy wore thick-lensed glasses that did nothing to hide her ability to see problems she could help solve. In our case, she'd stepped in to help with mailings when the hotel first opened and kept us apprised of any dirty moves Brock had in mind for us. In return, she felt needed and appreciated. She'd become a beloved member of the hotel family.

At the sound of a knock at the door, Rhonda and I glanced at one another.

"Come in," I called.

The door opened and Jax stood there. "Hi, I've come to talk to you about the job."

"We can talk here. We're almost finished." I turned to Dorothy. "This is Jax Thomas, who's been working with Manny."

Dorothy held out her hand. "Hello, I'm Dorothy Stern. Such a strapping young man. I'm sure Manny appreciates your help."

Jax grinned. "He's a fair boss and makes me work hard."

Dorothy said. "I'll go to give you all some privacy. See you next week?"

"Yes," said Rhonda. "I'll let you know ahead of time what project we want you to work on."

Dorothy beamed with pleasure. "Okay. See you then."

"Please sit down," I said to Jax.

Jax took a seat in front of my desk. Rhonda pulled up a chair next to him and sat, forming a comfortable circle.

"What did you decide?" Rhonda asked eagerly.

"After a lot of thought, I've decided to take the job. It may lead to an opportunity to have my own business in the area someday. I like working at a hotel, getting to know the operation. And I'd like to take you up on your offer of housing. Later, if things work out, I may want a place of my own, but in the meantime, I'm very happy to stay on the property."

Rhonda leaned forward, a gleam in her eye. "Is Mandy..."

I coughed and glared at her.

Jax looked from me to her. "If that's what you wanted to know, Mandy is going to remain in her room." The glum expression on his face told a story of its own.

"When you're ready, gather your things, and we'll show you your new home," I said.

"They're in the hallway," Jax said.

"Okay, then, let's go," I said.

We left the office and headed over to the two-story building that used to be a multi-stall garage. Aubrey had wanted to tear down the building and put in another new wing of the hotel, eliminating the spa. Thankfully, we hadn't allowed that to happen.

We climbed the stairs to the second floor and then I opened the door to the apartment next to Manny and Consuela's.

By the expression on his face, I knew Jax was pleased with the apartment. It was well laid out, with one bedroom, a study, a combined living and dining area, a compact but well-equipped kitchen, and a large deck off the living area that provided lovely views of the grounds behind the building.

"This is great," Jax said.

"And later, if Mandy decides to move in, there's plenty of room," Rhonda said, smiling as she moved away from me, aware that I was about to stomp on her foot.

Jax sighed. "Maybe someday she will."

I sent Rhonda a warning look to keep quiet.

"We'll leave you now. I'm sure Manny is anxious to know of your plans. We'll write a new employment agreement, which you can sign in our office during a break."

Jax bobbed his head. "Thank you very much. I appreciate it."

We all shook hands, then Rhonda and I left.

On the way back to the office, I turned to Rhonda. "I know we think Jax and Mandy would be good together, but we've got to stay out of their business."

"I know, I know, but did you see how Jax looked when I asked about Mandy? I'm ready to tell that girl she'd better wake up. Jax loves her. And when she doesn't know anyone is looking, I see how much she loves him."

I stopped and held up my hand. "Enough matchmaking!"

She made a face. "You're right. I just have to give them time to realize they can't live without the other."

I emitted a long sigh. Rhonda was Rhonda. She wouldn't give up. To divert her, I said, "What about Jean-Luc and Lindsay? You should be concentrating on them."

Rhonda's face lit. "That's right. They need to be thinking ahead. Jean-Luc has never looked happier. We should pay a visit to Lindsay."

"Maybe next week. Tomorrow Vaughn and I leave for

Palm Island for a few days, and Katherine ..." I choked on my last word and stopped, silently chastising myself for giving away Angela's secret.

Rhonda stopped walking and faced me. "Katherine? What about her?"

"Nothing. Just a slip of the tongue," I said, trying to make it sound as if it was a simple mistake.

Rhonda placed her hands on her hips and stared at me. "Annie, you're the worst liar ever. Something's going on. You'd better tell me now."

"Oh, all right. I wasn't supposed to mention it, but tomorrow Katherine is coming for a visit."

"A visit? Where is she staying?" Rhonda's lips thinned. "With my daughter?"

Caught, I could only nod my head. *Forgive me, Angela!*

"And my daughter didn't tell me? What the fuck is going on?"

Shuddering at the word I would never use, I tried to smooth things over. "Angela didn't want you to worry about it. She knows what you think of Katherine and how she makes you feel ..."

"Like shit with her snooty ways," Rhonda said, twisting and marching ahead of me.

I hurried to catch up to her. "Listen, Angela simply didn't want you to get worked up by another visit so close to the last one. She's trying hard to make things better between Reggie and his parents."

"Did Angela invite her, or did Katherine invite herself?" Rhonda asked, and I knew how important my answer was.

"Katherine called and invited herself."

Rhonda sighed. "At least that part's right." She shook her head and sighed again. "I've tried my best with that woman, but she makes it plain as day how she feels about me."

"I'm not so sure anymore," I said.

"What do you mean?" Rhonda asked.

"She really appreciated your hug after the horrible scene with Reggie's father. That's another reason she wants to return to Sabal. She wants to make sure nothing will keep her from her grandchildren. I'm sure you can understand that."

Rhonda sighed. "It's just that Katherine drives me crazy."

"And that's exactly why Angela was waiting to tell you. You were sweet to her before. You can do it again."

"I guess."

I knew that behind Rhonda's apparent confidence and her joy for life was a young girl who'd been bullied growing up in her tough neighborhood. And Katherine was a pain in the butt.

"But she better not pull any of that bullshit about having the kids move up north to be with her," said Rhonda. "If she does, I won't even try to be nice to her."

"I think you know that isn't going to happen. That's why Reggie's father tried to disown him."

"Yeah, poor Reggie. Both of his parents are terrible. Good thing he has Will and me."

"Absolutely," I said, meaning it. Working with Will had changed Reggie into a kinder, more thoughtful, humbler person. And Rhonda didn't like bullshit from anyone. Even after winning one hundred eighty-seven million dollars in the lottery, Rhonda was who she'd always been—a kind, generous person to all. Maybe that's why she found it so difficult to deal with Katherine's lack of appreciation for others.

By the time we were back in the hotel, I was grateful to be able to go into the kitchen and grab a cup of coffee for a little pick-me-up.

Rhonda went to see Angela, and I decided to go check on Mandy. At the sound of voices from inside her room, I hesitated and then realized one of the voices belonged to Liz. I knocked.

Mandy opened the door. "Hi. Come on in. Liz brought over some work for me to do. She's showing me now."

"Great. I just wanted to check to make sure that you have everything you need now that Jax has moved out."

A fleeting expression of sadness crossed Mandy's face. She swallowed, looked away, and then turned to me with a smile I thought was forced. "He's very excited about his new job."

"And we're pleased to have him," I said.

Liz joined us and gave me a quick hug. "I'm so glad you introduced me to Mandy. We're going to make a great team. I love some of her ideas."

"That's nice to hear. I'll leave you two so you can work. Mandy, let me know when you need a ride to Barbara's office."

"Thanks. Not until next week. In the meantime, I've been writing in my journal."

"Okay, see you later," I said, hesitant to keep them from their work.

"Have a wonderful weekend!" said Liz. "Elena and I have the babysitting for Robbie covered. Enjoy Palm Island."

"Thanks," I said, loving the idea of a minivacation with Vaughn. Just the two of us.

When I picked up Vaughn from the airport that afternoon, I didn't know who was more excited—Robbie, Trudy, or me. The smile on his face as he came to the car filled me with joy. As exciting as it was to visit him in New

York from time to time, these homecomings were what we liked best.

I got in a quick kiss before Trudy licked Vaughn's face and Robbie tugged on his arm to tell him about something that happened at school.

"Ready for our getaway weekend?" Vaughn asked me when things quieted.

I grinned and nodded. I'd even bought a new bikini to wear. And the nightgown? Let's just say I counted on not needing it at all.

Vaughn's gaze roamed over me, and I felt a thread of anticipation weaving through me at the thought of the next two days alone with him. I'd already packed a suitcase for each of us.

At home, Vaughn changed his clothes into shorts, a golf-shirt, and deck shoes, checked his suitcase, and then said. "All set to go."

"Elena should be here any minute," I said, watching Robbie and Trudy run around in the backyard chasing a volleyball. "Liz is going to help out so Elena can go with Troy to look at the place up the coast he's considering to buy."

"You and Rhonda have worked out a deal to continue running the spa at the hotel even if he opens his own?"

"Yes. Thank goodness, he has a superb manager lined up at the hotel, and Elena is going to help out too. Funny, the minute you think everything is set at the hotel, plans and personnel change. One of the defining facets of the business."

Vaughn wrapped an arm around me. "But you and I will never change."

I leaned against him, loving the feeling of security I felt whenever we were together.

My cell rang. *Rhonda.*

"Hi, what's up?" I asked. "Katherine get here all right?"

"Yes," said Rhonda, "but, Annie, she looks terrible. Something's horribly wrong. I just know it."

"Did you ask her about it or mention anything to Angela?" I asked. Rhonda sounded very upset.

"Though she did say hello to me with a smile that was really big of her, I can't ask Katherine. And I haven't had a chance to talk to Angela privately."

"What do you think is wrong with her?" I asked.

"I'm not sure. It's been only a couple of months since I've seen her, but she looks as if she's lost a lot of weight, and there's no color in her face."

"If you're this worried, find a time to talk to Angela or Reggie. Let me know if I can do anything. Vaughn and I are just about to leave for the Palm Island Club."

"Oh, right, right. Go and have fun. And get out of bed once in a while," Rhonda added letting out a raucous laugh that made me smile every time.

"What's going on?" Vaughn asked.

I told him about the conversation, including Rhonda's last remarks.

He chuckled. "There's only one Rhonda." He winked at me. "But she does have some intriguing ideas about how to spend vacations."

Laughing, I shook my head at him and turned as Elena walked into the kitchen.

"Ready to go?" she said. "It looks like a perfect weekend. No storms just yet."

I shuddered. Hurricane season had been quiet so far. But early fall was a time of year we Florida residents stayed tuned to weather reports.

After hugging Robbie goodbye and patting Trudy on the head, we climbed into Vaughn's jeep and headed to the dock downtown. That's where we'd pick up a boat ride to the small island off the coast. Arriving by boat was part of the charm of Palm Island Club. Another was the fact that well-known people like Vaughn could have some privacy, much like the assurance we gave to guests at The Beach House Hotel.

We parked the car in the private lot and waited at the dock for the launch boat to arrive and carry us over to the exquisite site. The trip itself took only minutes, but it was a relaxing way to start the stay.

Another car pulled into the lot. A young couple got out and dragged their suitcases over to us.

"Hello," said the woman. I guessed from the way she was dressed in high heels and a pretty pink sheath and the sport coat that her companion wore that they were visitors to the area.

"Honeymoon?" I asked her.

Blushing prettily, she smiled and glanced at the young man beside her. "It's our second day married."

"Congratulations," I said, turning at the sound of the Club's motor launch approaching.

We all stood by as the boatman stowed our luggage in the boat and then helped us aboard.

I sat beside Vaughn, relieved he was barely recognizable with the baseball hat he wore on his head and the sunglasses that hid his mesmerizing eyes. I'd never grown used to the idea of people wanting to speak to him, flirt with him, or ask him for his autograph when we were out on a date.

As we crossed the water, I listened to the sound of the boat breaking through the rolling waves and the cries of the birds swirling in the sky above us. The tangy salt of the air filled my nostrils and gave me a sense of anticipation. Time alone with Vaughn was a precious thing. Remembering what the last few horrifying months had been like protecting

Lindsay from her addict ex-husband, I needed this break as much as Vaughn. I squeezed his hand, and he squeezed mine back, giving me his famous smile.

I noticed the look of recognition on the young bride's face as she stared at Vaughn, but I chose to ignore it, selfishly keeping Vaughn close.

Two bellmen met the boat, picked up the luggage, and led us to the Main Lodge where we checked in.

In mere minutes, the bellman taking care of our luggage led us to our private cabin. To my delight, it was the same cabin where we'd spent precious time alone on an earlier trip.

We followed the bellman into our cabin, and I took a moment to gaze around. A vase containing a mix of tropical flowers sat on a low-slung table in front of a plush, tan couch. Next to it sat a welcoming bottle of champagne resting in a bucket of ice beside two tulip glasses.

"Nice touch," murmured Vaughn.

While the bellman settled our luggage in the master bedroom, I opened the drapes to view our private patio and small splash pool, its water bubbling as air was pumped through it.

After the bellman showed us all the conveniences, he left, and I went into the master bedroom to hang up my things.

Vaughn came up behind me and wrapped his arms around me. "As long as we're getting out of our clothes to change into swimsuits, I have a plan," he murmured into my ears. "A special 'welcome to vacation' plan."

I turned around and lifted my face for a kiss. He was such a sexy, practical guy.

CHAPTER EIGHT

Late afternoon, I sat in a beach chair next to Vaughn under a palm tree reveling in the sound of the waves lapping the shore, slowing the rhythm of the past few days. I wiggled my toes in the soft warm sand and watched shore birds sprint along the edge of the water in a continual search for food. In the distance, a couple strolled beside the water, hand in hand.

"It's so pleasant," I said to Vaughn. "Thank you for arranging this. It's always hard to get away from the hotel, but it's so wonderful when it happens."

He turned to me with a smile. "I keep wondering how much longer I'll be willing to do the show. Especially now that I'm cast in an old-man role. I'm not ready to quit acting. My agent is looking for a movie for me. Do you mind?"

"What? Mind? Of course not. I want you to be satisfied in your career." I meant it too. Being unhappy in a job was like slowly dying. Besides, Vaughn was a very talented actor. Something I had to get used to when I recognized certain phrases from the show when he spoke to me.

"We'll see what happens. I'm not in any rush," Vaughn said. "We've got so much going on in the family that I don't want to disrupt that."

"I got a call from Nell last night. I haven't had a chance to tell you that she's thinking of coming back soon. They'll be here for Thanksgiving." I smiled. "She's trying to talk Ty and June into joining us for that weekend."

"It would be great to see my kids together again," said

Vaughn. His son, Ty, had married June Chang and was more or less stuck out in San Francisco with his job and her family.

"I hope by then Liz and Chad are expecting. It would make the holidays that much more exciting."

"All in good time, Ann," Vaughn reminded me gently.

"You're right. It'll happen with or without my worrying. I'm sure of it."

He smiled. "That's better." He stood and held out his hand. "Ready for a stroll. The sun is beginning to lower in the sky, and it's a bit cooler with the breeze that's come up."

I rose and took his hand. It was doing simple things like this that made our relationship work. My ex, Robert, had never been able really to relax. He'd been too busy working, taking credit for my ideas in the business I'd created on paper and making them his own.

A shudder crept across my shoulder, and I warned myself not to dwell on those thoughts. My life was so much better now.

After our walk, we changed into casual clothes and decided to walk to the Main Lodge for dinner. Vaughn had called ahead and requested a corner table so he wouldn't have to deal with any fans.

The maître d' greeted us warmly. "So nice to have you here again, Mr. and Mrs. Sanders. We have your table ready." He signaled for a waiter to show us to our table and then made sure we were properly seated.

After being given a menu, I gazed around the room, admiring the rustic opulence of the lodge. It had been made to appear as if it were an ordinary beach house with wooden wall panels painted white and seafoam-green carpeting on the floor. Crystal chandeliers and wall sconces shed sparkling rainbows everywhere, adding to the shabby-chic atmosphere that had been created beautifully. The same ambience was true in the private cabins. I supposed some might call it glamping kicked up a notch or two.

"You're smiling," said Vaughn, reaching across the table and covering my hand with his broad fingers.

"It's so nice to be here, away from our work," I said. "Rhonda and I have decided to refurbish the guest rooms within the next year, and we're already working on a budget and schedule. With Aubrey touting his hotel as the best in the area, we thought it was time to spruce them up."

"Ah, I know how conservative you are with money, so I know it's a concern," Vaughn said.

"Yes, but you have to spend money to make money," I countered.

He grinned. "Like everything else you and Rhonda have done together, it'll work out. Just don't let someone like Aubrey rattle you. He's a total ass. As is one of his investors."

"Yes, he and Brock together can't be good. We're just waiting to see what kind of stunts they pull with us and the other hotels in the area."

"As long as we're talking about the year ahead, I've decided to look at a script my agent wants me to read for a part in a movie. If I like it, I may go forward with an offer to play the lead role. I think it would help my career. Right now, I feel as if it's facing a slow death."

"I understand. I want you to do whatever you want in your career as long as you come home to me," I said, not at all surprised by his remarks. I'd been present for the interview the producers had set up to make him seem more like a father figure than the sexy mayor of the town.

"I'll always come home to you," Vaughn said. "Even when I was in the airplane crash, my number one thought was making it back to you."

Tears made my vision blurry momentarily. In the few years we'd been together, so much had happened. Even now, the future was full of plans, some of which I knew would change.

The wine steward came to the table. "Have you made a selection?" he asked politely.

Vaughn chuckled. "Sorry, I was talking to my bride. How about suggesting a bottle to go with dinner? I know I'm having the sea bass with a lemon and caper *beurre blanc* sauce." He looked at me.

"I'll make it easy and have the same. It's one of my favorite dishes."

"Okay, a white wine," said Vaughn.

While he and the steward discussed choices, I gazed around the room. The tables were mostly full even at this early hour of seven-thirty. Here on the island, dinner came early because there was so little to do in the evenings, and people went to bed early.

I glanced at Vaughn and smiled at the memory of making love with him with the afternoon light coming in through the slats of the blinds washing over us. The first time we'd made love, I was nervous about Vaughn seeing my stretch marks and scars from delivering Liz. When he'd told me that he considered those imperfections badges of honor, I'd fallen in love with him all over again.

The wine steward left, and Vaughn smiled. "We selected a nice *pouilly fumé*."

"Lovely," I said. I'd come to relish a lot of different choices.

After the wine was tasted by Vaughn and poured for each of us, he lifted his glass. "Here's to us."

"To us," I replied, realizing "us" was no longer just two,

but included the others we kept adding to our family.

Following dinner, we strolled along the beach to work off the *crème brûlée* we'd shared for dessert. Then we headed into our cabin.

"How about a nightcap in the pool?" Vaughn said. "The hotel has left a small bottle of brandy in the room."

"Sounds delightful," I said, feeling decadent. The small splash pool outside was protected by carefully planted foliage to provide privacy. With no one else close to us, I stripped my clothes off, gathered a couple of towels, and headed outside.

'I'll bring the brandy," Vaughn said, opening the bottle.

A few minutes later, Vaughn appeared naked, carrying two snifters of brandy.

I took in the details of his body. No wonder he was fighting against the image of an older man. He was still in prime shape.

He set the glasses down next to the pool and climbed in, ducking underwater. When he straightened, the water came only to his shoulders. His dark curls hung in his face. With a toss of his head and a swipe of his hand, his famous face emerged.

I caught my breath, still sometimes surprised that with women swooning over him, he'd chosen me. But then, he was a down-to-earth guy. He had his family and me to remind him that being a television star did not make him a perfect man.

Vaughn swam over to me and pulled me up against him. I put my legs around him and we sat on the steps leading into the pool.

Facing him, I murmured, "I love you."

"Love you back and more," he said and placed his lips on mine.

My body responded and I reveled in his taste, his touch. When we pulled apart, we simply smiled at one another.

"Shall we?" asked Vaughn, reaching for the glasses of brandy while still holding me in his lap.

I took a sip and let the burning liquid coat my throat as it went down. The evening, my man, the drink, and the stars in the sky created a perfect moment.

The next morning when I awoke, the space next to me in bed was empty. I climbed out and padded to the window. Vaughn was sitting on the sand in a beach chair lifting his face to the morning sun.

I quickly carried out my morning routine and went outside to join him.

"Hello, sleepyhead," he said, smiling at me.

"I had a fabulous rest," I said, sitting in a chair beside him. "It's amazing what a little vacation can do."

"Yes. That and great sex." He winked at me.

I laughed. "That too. What have you got planned for the day?"

"Nothing but reading. Maybe a nap. I thought we might order food sent to the room for dinner, but that's up to you."

"It all sounds fine," I said happily. "How about some coffee? I'll bring some to you."

"Thanks," Vaughn said. "I'm enjoying just sitting right here."

Inside, I fixed us each a cup of coffee. Before I could carry it outside, my cell rang. *Rhonda.* My heart thudded with alarm.

"Hi, Rhonda."

"Annie, I had to call you. It turns out Katherine has been diagnosed with pancreatic cancer. That's why she's here. She wants to be treated at the Moffitt Center in Tampa, where she can be close to the kids." Her voice hitched.

"Oh, my word! She's about our age and far too young to die."

"I went to see her after Angela called with the news and have promised to help her in any way I can." Rhonda's voice wavered again. "She thanked me and then gave me a hug. Guess she no longer needs to be so snooty."

"I'll text Angela to let her know how sorry I am, and that I'll help in any way she and Katherine want. Thanks for letting me know," I ended the call feeling sick to my stomach. Vaughn and I had been busy discussing the future, but who knew what the future would really bring?

I carried the coffee outside, and taking a seat beside him, told Vaughn the news.

"That's sad," he said. "I'm sorry to hear it."

"Me, too. Vaughn, no matter what, we need to enjoy every day."

He nodded solemnly. "That's why it's important to do things like this."

I finished my coffee and got up. "I'm going to take a walk. Be back in a while."

I headed across the sand thinking how precious life was. I stepped into the frothy foam at the water's edge. The rhythm of the waves rolling onto shore and pulling away again like a shy child steadied me. The endless movement of the water was as old as time. Life would continue for each of us until it ended. How we lived it would make all the difference.

CHAPTER NINE

When we arrived home, Liz, Chad, and Robbie were out back of the house down by the dock. They were concentrating on building a sand castle together. The sight brought tears to my eyes. After receiving news about Katherine, I, more than ever, wanted to live well, to shower those I loved with support and affection.

Vaughn and I headed down the lawn to them. Trudy saw us, barked, and came trotting toward us.

I picked her up and kissed her, laughing when she wiggled into position and covered my cheeks with enthusiastic kisses.

"Hi, Mom! Hi, Dad!" called Robbie as Liz and Chad stood and faced us with smiles.

I met Liz halfway and threw my arms around her. "How did you do with Robbie?"

"Great." She beamed at me. "I did even better with something else." Her eyes filled. "I'm pregnant. We finally can tell you."

"Oh, how wonderful!" My eyes widened and joy flooded my blood stream. "Really?" I squealed with delight and hugged her tight, relieved for her. Then I turned to Vaughn. "Liz and Chad are going to have a baby!"

Vaughn wrapped his arms around Liz and hugged her tight. "Great news!" He turned away from Liz and clapped Chad on the back.

"Lizzie's growing a baby," said Robbie grinning. "In her tummy."

"I know," I responded. "I'm so happy!"

"Can we go sailing now?" Robbie asked.

Vaughn checked the sky and his watch and said, "Everyone up for it?"

Liz looked at me with uncertainty, and I knew she wanted to stay behind and talk over her news with me. "Why don't you men go ahead? Liz and I will stay behind."

"Okay," said Vaughn understanding. He'd been through moments like this before with his wife and with Nell.

"Have fun!" I called. I wrapped an arm around Liz's shoulder, and we walked up to the house.

"How far along are you?" I asked.

"I figure four or five weeks. I have an appointment with Dr. Benson next week."

"So that would place the time of birth somewhere next April or May?"

Liz smiled and nodded. "A perfect time before the hot weather sets in. And that will give us time to sell the store and set up an office for Chad in the same building as Will's finance office. We've already looked into it."

"You've done a lot of work in preparing for this little one," I said, squeezing her shoulder. "Does Angela know?"

Liz's expression grew solemn. "I told her yesterday not knowing that she'd just received the news that Katherine is battling cancer. She was thrilled for me but sad about Reggie's mom."

"Life's pattern is like that. As one person leaves, another comes into being. But don't let that take away your joy in having this baby. If you want me to help you, just ask."

"Well," Liz said smiling. "I thought you might like to go to Dr. Benson's office with me. I need someone to take down information in case I freak out and don't remember all that she says."

"I'd be delighted to do that if you're sure it's what you

want," I said, pleased. "What about Chad? Doesn't he want to go with you?"

"No, he'll go with me at other times. You've listened to me cry every month; you deserve to hear the good news too," Liz said, and I knew why I loved her so much.

After the men returned from a short sail and we'd had a simple meal of grilled chicken and a salad, I took a moment to go into my bedroom to call Angela.

She picked up right away. "Hi, Ann. We're all in a funk here, but tomorrow I'll call the doctor's office that Katherine will be using and get a better idea of the routine going forward. She's already had two chemo treatments, which were difficult. That's why she wants to be here with Reggie and me and to see the kids."

"I'll help in any way I can. If you need to go to Tampa, I'll arrange a limo service for you."

"Too late," said Angela, and I could hear the smile in her voice. "Mom has already taken care of that. She also promised to send any food over that sounds tasty to Katherine. She's been really sweet about it."

"Your mother is one of the most generous people I know," I said. "How's Reggie doing?"

"He's very angry at his father right now," Angela said. "Arthur hasn't been as supportive as he should be. I think he's been in denial because Katherine is usually the strong one."

"Give Katherine my best, and my love to you and Reggie and the kids. Being near them may help Katherine's spirits."

"I know. And speaking of that, I'm thrilled about Liz's news. Sally and the new baby can grow up together."

"Wouldn't that be lovely," I said, excited all over again by

Liz's happy news.

We said our goodbyes, and I hung up the phone, fighting emotion. Life, sweet life, could be so damn difficult.

Later, after I'd tucked Robbie into bed, I phoned Rhonda.

"Glad you called," she said. "Congratulations on Liz's pregnancy! I'm so happy for her and you!"

"Me, too," I said, "though she's not sharing the news with anyone else but our families until she's seen the doctor."

"Understood," said Rhonda. "Liz called to tell me but asked me not to say anything until you were home and heard the news from her first. It's been killing me not to say anything."

A smile crossed my face. Rhonda and I and Liz and Angela were as close a family as anyone could imagine.

"I was waiting to ask you, but I was talking to Jean-Luc, you know, checking on the status of things with Lindsay and him, and I've invited them to dinner. I'd like you and Vaughn to come too. Will you?"

"Let me double-check with Vaughn, but I'm going to go ahead and say yes. You're not pushing too hard on the romance, are you? I know you think you're a matchmaker ..." I let my voice trail off.

"I'm working behind the scenes. That's all," Rhonda said. "It makes me feel better after hearing the awful news about Katherine. She and I never got along, but I'd never wish something like this to have happened to her."

"Of course not. I understand you've already promised to help with the food, a limo, and anything else."

"Funny, how something like this can tear people apart or bring them together. Who would've thought we'd end up as friends?

"It's surprising, but nice," I said.

"See you at work and then for dinner tomorrow. Seven o'clock sharp. I'm cooking for Jean-Luc, and it's going to be delicious."

"Can't wait!" I said happily. Rhonda was a marvelous cook.

The next morning Rhonda and I were discussing various color schemes for our rooms' renovations when Bernie walked into the office and slapped a newspaper down on my desk.

"Better read this," he said.

I picked up the Sabal newspaper folded to the society section.

"A New Hotel! A New Gulf Coast!" was the title of a full-page article written by Terri Thomas. Rhonda came over to me, and with her looking over my shoulder, we read the article together.

As I read one sentence after another, a knot formed in my stomach. "Time for something different from the upscale snobbery of The Beach House Hotel," Terri had stated. "Even the cinnamon rolls don't taste as fresh as they used to," she'd continued.

Rhonda slapped the top of my desk. "The fucking traitor! Terri Thomas is not getting sweet rolls from us ever again. How many has she eaten over the last few years? Plenty. She got a whole bagful each time she came here to do an article on us!" Tears formed in Rhonda's eyes. "How can she say stuff like this?"

"Hold on. Let's read the rest of the article," I said, fighting the sting of tears.

Terri went on to describe the plans for The Sand Castle

Hotel and how it could bring new life to the area. Included in the article were photos of the new lobby which was under construction but whose walls were painted a dark aquamarine. Fish and other colored sea life were painted on the walls, making one think of being inside a fish tank. A large sandbox with seating around it was the central feature in the off-lobby bar.

"Fun, fun, fun!" declared Terri in her article. There was a picture of her and Aubrey together, holding small, red-metal buckets filled with chips in one and peanuts in the other.

Aubrey's smile was more a smirk which made me want to shred the newspaper.

The article ended with a quote from Aubrey. "We're here to provide vacations for discerning individuals who no longer want to wallow in their wealth but to give everyone a chance to have plain fun, all of us together."

I finished reading and glanced at Bernie and Rhonda, as upset as they visibly were.

"I'd like to wring his fucking neck," said Rhonda. "Hers, too."

"Terri Thomas is a fool if she thinks she can print something like this without a thought of libel?" Bernie said, his voice cold with anger. "I suggest we get in touch with our lawyer and have him give her a call. Whether he thinks we should pursue it any further should be decided later."

I nodded, my mind whirling. "I think you're right, Bernie. Why don't you take care of that? If later, Rhonda and I need to be involved, we'll gladly take it on. In the meantime, we need to come up with some reinforcements. I suggest we have Dorothy Stern gather support in the neighborhood, start a campaign on the editorial page to decry the article, and get people behind The Beach House Hotel. Our guests are not snobbish and don't wallow in wealth."

"Knowing the kind of wealthy background Aubrey comes from, his words burn my ass. Is this some kind of vendetta against his own family?" asked Rhonda, gripping her hands together so hard her knuckles were white.

"I don't know," I said. "But I think we shouldn't answer Aubrey directly because he won't play fair."

"He's just been waiting to get back at you two for disgracing him," said Bernie. "He's nothing but a ... a *dummkopf*." When Bernie spoke German, I knew he was really upset.

"Okay, I'll call Mike Torson now," said Bernie "and see what he suggests we do initially. I'm sure he'll want to talk to the two of you if there's any further action to be taken."

"I'll call Dorothy," said Rhonda.

"And I'll work on a letter to the editor," I said, furious to have been put into the position of protecting the hotel's reputation from someone like Aubrey Lowell. "First I'm going to take a walk on the beach to tame the words I'd like to say."

"I'll go with you, Annie. I hate mornings to start like this," said Rhonda.

As we made our way onto the sand, I thought back to when I'd first seen the home Rhonda called The Beach House. Spread along the beach like a lazy pink flamingo, it had a natural beauty and character that I'd loved even then. The hotel we made of it was upscale, as the setting and building deserved. But we'd always prided ourselves on treating each guest with excellent service and genuine warmth that came from gratitude. That couldn't be faked.

I took off my sandals and wiggled my toes in the warm sand, exuding a sigh that came from deep within me. By my side, Rhonda did the same. An onshore breeze caressed my cheeks as we crossed the sand on tiptoes to the cooler water's edge. There, as I so often did, I faced the moving water, slowing my breaths to match the timing of the waves rolling into the shore. I couldn't let someone tear down what Rhonda and I had worked so hard to build, but I also knew playing Aubrey's game could ruin us.

"Okay, spill. Tell me what you're thinking Annie," said Rhonda. "I see how upset you are."

"I know you want to fight back, but if we do, we might end up losing. We have a classy place with an excellent reputation. That's how we have to play it."

"Yeah, I guess you're right," said Rhonda, kicking at the sand with a bare toe. "You know me, I'd like to blast that guy in the balls. And Terri? She doesn't even deserve a hello from the two of us."

I placed a hand on her arm. "Let's let others fight our battle. Later, if we have to step in, we will. Deal?"

"Deal," said Rhonda.

We strolled down the beach, stopping now and then to pick up a shell and toss it back for someone else to find.

Rhonda clutched my arm. "Look who's headed our way."

I glanced ahead and let out a groan. "Sorry. I can't face Brock right now." I turned around and headed back to the hotel, Rhonda at my heels.

We'd been walking a few minutes when I heard the sound of running behind me and turned to face Brock.

"What do you want?" I asked, not hiding my irritation.

"Just wanted to make sure you saw the article that Terri Thomas wrote about The Sand Castle Hotel. It was great!"

"For whom?" Rhonda asked, her eyebrows rising above her sunglasses.

"For us. Aubrey and me and the others. It's about time

things were shaken up here," he said. "Of course, you may not like it when your business suffers. But then, you made my business suffer when you canceled the contract with my company for decorative objects for the hotel."

"You know perfectly well that the supposed sale was all part of a bribery scheme you and Aubrey cooked up to convince the city to approve additions to the hotel before we took it back," I said through clenched teeth. I couldn't help but wonder why Brock continued to be such a source of aggravation to us. Did it have anything to do with the way I'd rejected him years ago? If so, it was a foolish gesture that had made many enemies for him.

Rhonda took my elbow, and we walked away from Brock, arm in arm.

"You and your hotel are going to be taken down," called Brock. "You deserve it."

Rhonda's body stiffened.

I held onto her. "Just keep walking." Rhonda had grown up in a tough neighborhood where it wasn't unusual to settle disagreements physically. When somebody like Brock threatened her or her family, she was more than ready to react.

"I swear ..." Rhonda began.

"Breathe," I said. "He's not worth it. Our best revenge is succeeding."

"You're right. Some guys in business just like to make it miserable for others. Maybe that's why he and Aubrey have become such close friends."

"They're snakes," I said, telling myself to draw a calming breath.

When we got back to the hotel, Bernie came into the

office. "I talked to Mike. He'll call Terri Thomas and warn her that the owners of the hotel are mulling their legal choices. He said that should worry her without going forward with any legal filings."

"Thanks," I said. "We don't want to get into a huge pissing contest with her, Aubrey, or any of his investors. Ours wasn't the only hotel they spoke against. Others will be in touch too, which lifts the burden from us."

"Clever thinking," said Bernie. "Aubrey is a foolish young man who doesn't realize how important it is to cooperate with others in the business. I think he'll be surprised by the lack of support for his project."

"I'd feel better if we updated the security on our computer systems," I said. "He messed with our reservations before."

"And he'd be happy to do it again," said Rhonda.

"I'll call Chad," said Bernie. "Maybe changing a few passwords and a few other moves would be smart."

I smiled. Having Chad work on the computer systems at the hotel and my house was how Liz had met him. And he was excellent at his job.

CHAPTER TEN

That evening, as Vaughn and I drove to Rhonda's house, my stomach growled in anticipation. Rhonda was a fabulous cook who'd spent the afternoon away from the hotel preparing dinner. Jean-Luc enjoyed well-prepared food, and though he wasn't overly particular about it, having him eat at your home was always a little nerve-wracking. Fortunately, he liked Vaughn's grilled steak, my standard scalloped potatoes, and special fruit and green-leaf salads.

After experiencing some of the competition between Jean-Luc and Rhonda when we'd first hired him, I knew Rhonda's meal would include a few of her mother's Italian family recipes.

When we arrived, Jean-Luc's car was already in the driveway. Vaughn parked beside it, and we got out.

As we walked to the front door, it burst open, and Willow and Drew came racing toward us. "Auntie Ann! Uncle Vaughn!" cried Willow, holding out her arms to us.

Vaughn picked her up while I hugged Drew to me. When I'd first met Rhonda, she'd given up all hope of having a second family, and these two little ones were precious to all of us.

Rita was standing by the door. "All right, Willow and Drew, you've said hello. Now it's time to come with me."

Willow's happy expression morphed into a defiant frown. She glanced up at me, then turned to Vaughn for help. When neither of us responded, she said, "Oka-a-ay."

Drew, the faithful little brother that he was, followed Willow inside and then the three of them climbed the stairway to their rooms.

Rhonda rushed over to us, standing in the front hallway. "You're here! We're out back by the pool for cocktails. It's too nice to be indoors. Believe it or not, there's a whisper of fall in the air."

"Sounds great." Fall in Florida was discernible to natives. Not so much for visitors. But even the slightest dip in daytime temperatures gave a hint of what to expect. For now, the weather pattern was stable. That more than anything in the hurricane months is what mattered.

Jean-Luc and Will rose as we entered the lanai. Will greeted me with a hug. Jean-Luc, handsome in his sophisticated way, with his gray hair tied in back of his head, kissed both my cheeks in the French way. I turned to Lindsay. With her auburn hair and classic features, she looked very much like her sister, the vice-president.

"How are you? You look lovely," I said, pleased by the aura of health and happiness that surrounded her. She looked nothing like the broken woman who'd arrived at our hotel a few months ago.

"Thanks," Lindsay said, casting a glance at Jean-Luc. From the looks they exchanged, I thought Rhonda didn't need to even try any matchmaking. It had already taken place.

Will mixed us drinks, and we sat in a group, chatting easily.

"Lindsay is going on a vacation with her sister," Jean-Luc announced. "But she has promised to come back to Sabal."

"To stay with you," Rhonda said, giving nods of approval. "Any time you want to make arrangements at the hotel, we'll be glad to set something up." She looked at me and smiled.

Jean-Luc shifted in his chair.

"I like staying with Jean-Luc," said Lindsay. "I feel very safe and happy there. But we like the status quo, don't we?" she asked Jean-Luc.

He smiled and nodded. "It is *parfait.*"

I could see that Rhonda wanted to say more and sent her a warning look. It was much too soon to think of anything else. "Where are you going on vacation?" I asked.

"We're going to the south of France," said Lindsay. "I want to see where Jean-Luc grew up and enjoy some downtime there. Amelia has arranged to rent a villa."

"That sounds lovely. When are you leaving?"

"Not for a few weeks. Amelia's waiting to get a personal issue settled. She's helping a senator and his wife adopt a baby from one of the women she's working with in her foundation."

Rhonda and I looked at one another.

"Are you talking about the young woman Amelia sent here?" I asked.

"Yes," Lindsay said. "Senator Worthington hired her as an intern. Now he and his wife want to adopt her baby."

Goosepimples ran across my back. No wonder Mandy was unsure about giving her baby to them. Senator Worthington was a powerful man who had a horrible reputation with the way he treated women.

"Is he the one paying for Mandy's stay?" asked Rhonda, looking as concerned as I felt. *Was being here at our hotel a kind of bribe to Mandy?* The thought made me queasy. I knew Mandy had felt pressure from the prospective parents, but this put new light on the pressure Mandy must be feeling. And I didn't like it.

"Have you met Senator Worthington?" I asked Lindsay.

"Yes. I don't much care for him, but his wife, Cassie, is

lovely. I know they've been trying for children for a couple of years. We've talked about it."

"To be honest, I hope Amelia isn't pushing Mandy to give up the baby. Mandy's very torn about it," I said.

"I think Amelia's come to realize that and is concerned that everyone realizes it is a choice, not a requirement for Mandy. I promised Amelia I'd meet Mandy soon."

Feeling only a little better, I leaned back in my chair and took a sip from the glass of prosecco wine Will had handed me.

The men began talking about sailing, and I took a moment to mull things over. Senator Worthington was an imposing figure, had been Mandy's boss, and was paying for her stay with us. All those things formed a trio of pressures that I thought was unfair to Mandy, a naïve young woman who'd suffered for years from her parents' treatment of her.

"We'll help her," Rhonda said quietly, understanding my emotions.

"I can see you're upset," said Lindsay. "I'll pass that on to Amelia."

"She should've given us the details," Rhonda said.

Lindsay shook her head. "She couldn't. For all the reasons she doesn't want Mandy to feel unwarranted pressure about any decision she makes."

"I guess you're right," I said. "But I don't like it."

"Let's not ruin the evening," Rhonda said. "I've been cooking all afternoon."

"And it smells delicious," I said. Rhonda was right. There was nothing we could do about Mandy's situation but support her in every way we could while she wrestled with the biggest decision of her life.

Later, seated inside at the dining room table, I sipped on a red Barolo Italian wine between the antipasto course and the

Italian Wedding Soup that Rhonda announced was next. She'd glanced at Jean-Luc as she'd said it.

He laughed and I did too, remembering the fight that had broken out in the hotel kitchen when Jean-Luc had told Rhonda he could make this soup as good as her mother's recipe.

Then the conversation centered on Lindsay's upcoming trip to France and Jean-Luc's childhood growing up with a grandmother who loved to cook and who'd encouraged him to use his talent professionally.

Following a course of veal piccata and then a refreshing salad, the conversation died as we faced a raspberry topped panna cotta dessert. Though we'd been served small portions with every course, we were challenged by the delicious-looking ending to the meal.

"Fantastic, Rhonda," I said, patting my full stomach.

We all smiled at one another, including Jean-Luc who was as pleased by the meal as the rest of us.

"Whenever I decide to retire, you can take over as chef at the hotel," he said to Rhonda graciously.

She raised her glass of wine. "Here's to good food and fun people to enjoy it!"

We all lifted our glasses. It had been such a pleasant evening.

After sitting outside for a while to settle our meals, the group broke apart. Tomorrow was another workday for Jean-Luc and me.

Later, after I got ready for bed, I climbed beneath the sheets, my thoughts still on Mandy.

Vaughn reached for me, and I nestled against him, molding my body to his. The weight of him next to me and the way his arms held me close made me feel protected against what sometimes felt like a turbulent life.

"What do you think about the senator and his wife wanting Mandy's baby?" I asked him. "It seems a little weird to me. Almost as if it were planned."

"Whoa," said Vaughn, sitting up and staring down at me. "That's an awful thought. I wasn't happy when you announced you were helping Amelia Swanson again because of possible political ramifications. This is a case in point, though I don't think it was planned. Worthington no doubt feels he's owed the baby for all he's doing for Mandy. He's a powerful man used to either getting his way or fighting those who are against him. This situation makes me uncomfortable. I think you and Rhonda should stay out of it."

"I won't get involved with Amelia or the senator, but while Mandy is here with us at the hotel, I'm going to do all I can to help her."

"Agreed," Vaughn said. "I know you too well to believe otherwise."

"I'm scheduled to take Mandy to Dr. Benson's tomorrow. And I'm going to invite her and Jax to dinner so we both have a better idea of what's going on."

"Make it sooner rather than later because I have to get back to New York. Now let's talk about something else."

He settled beneath the covers and I cuddled up against him again. "Isn't it fantastic news about Liz? I'm totally thrilled for them. And very pleased that she's asked me to go to the doctor's office with her. Chad has agreed because this appointment is just to confirm she's pregnant."

"It's great that she has you around," said Vaughn. "It was hard for Nell not to have Ellie here, but she was very appreciative of your support during the pregnancy and birth of Bailey." He cupped my face in his hands and placed his lips on mine. "Love you."

I reveled in his touch and focused on what he and I shared, telling myself to let my worries go, that happy times were ahead.

CHAPTER ELEVEN

The next morning my worries about Mandy returned. I decided to head over to the hotel for my early walk hoping I'd have a chance to talk to her. She'd told me she wasn't a late sleeper. It would also give me a chance to check on Jax.

I dressed, left Vaughn and Robbie eating breakfast, and drove to the hotel, parking behind it. From there, I could easily walk onto the beach without getting caught up in the business. I strolled onto the sand, and, as always, took a moment to breathe in the salty air and gaze out at the water. At this early time of day, the beach was lined with shell seekers bent over like shore birds searching for tasty tidbits.

I headed up the grass to Mandy's room. She was sitting on her patio with a glass of juice in her hand.

"Hello!" I said, waving.

She looked up and smiled. "Hi. Glad to see you. Dr. Benson's office called to reconfirm my appointment at two o'clock. Are you sure you don't mind going with me?"

I sat down opposite her and smiled. "I'm delighted you asked. Dr. Benson is a wonderful doctor. I think you're going to be very happy with her."

Mandy lifted a notebook from the table beside her chair. "I've been keeping a daily log of my feelings like Dr. Holmes asked. Doing this has made it even more difficult to try to sort my thoughts."

I studied her. "I've learned that Senator Worthington and his wife are the people who want to adopt your baby. I know he was your boss. Does that affect your decision?"

"Maybe," she said. "The thing is my parents told me I'll never be a suitable mother because I've stepped away from the church." Her voice became bitter. "They don't want me around to remind their precious church members that I'm a sinner." She stopped and drew a deep breath. "They said I shouldn't have been at a party, and that's why I got pregnant, that I deserved the life ahead of me."

I was too stunned to say anything for a moment. Such hatred for a child. "They don't understand about the drugs given you?" I finally asked.

"It's worse than that. I disobeyed my parents by taking a job in Washington D.C. And now they'll never forgive me."

"Your father is a minister?" I said, unable to stop myself from sounding incredulous.

"He and my mother both are preachers," Mandy said, looking miserable. "But I could never do what they do, ask for money all the time. That and the way they try to make people believe the only way to get to heaven is through them."

"I understand your feelings," I said as gently as I could while wanting to scream at the horrible way they had treated their daughter. "You're lucky to have a friend like Jax to help you."

Mandy gave me a shaky smile. "He says he loves me, but I know I'm not right for him. Not when my own parents despise me."

"Barbara Holmes is an excellent listener," I said, having used her myself after Robert had left me in such a mess.

"Yeah, she's been great. I've told her I wouldn't be a good mother for the baby, but we're working on that too." Mandy rubbed her stomach. "It's a girl, as you know. And I already love her. Secretly, I call her my little Belle, after Beauty and the Beast. Pretty silly, I know, but I had to call her something. We've been together all this time."

"It's sweet, not silly," I said, touched by her words.

A movement behind me drew my attention. Jax stood there. Wearing a straw hat and holding a pair of garden clippers in his hand, he smiled at us and focused his gaze on Mandy. "Hey. How are you doing?" He indicated the blue sky above with a wave of his arm. "It looks like it's going to be a nice day."

I saw the flash of love in Mandy's eyes and how she'd quickly looked away as if steeling herself against such feelings.

"I'm glad to see you, Jax," I said. "I'd like to invite both you and Mandy to dinner at my house tonight. It's a last-minute invitation because Vaughn will be heading back to New York, and I wanted him to meet you both. I hope you'll come."

Jax and Mandy looked at one another and nodded.

"That'd be nice," Jax said. "I'm pretty tired of my cooking, and I can't ask Mandy to cook for me every night."

"We'll keep it simple," I said. "Come around five o'clock and bring your bathing suits if you'd like a swim before dinner."

"That sounds great," said Jax. He gave me a little bow. "See you then."

As he walked away, Mandy said, "I try to cook dinner for him, but I'm not the greatest in the kitchen, so Jax often is the one cooking for us."

"You're spending your evenings together?"

"Most of them. It gets pretty boring here in the hotel room. I don't have anything to do." Mandy's eyes grew wide and she clapped a hand to her mouth. "Sorry, I didn't mean to make that sound so bad."

"It's fine. We certainly don't want you to feel like a prisoner. I understand it was Senator Worthington's idea for you to come to The Beach House Hotel to give you plenty of rest before delivering your baby."

A frown creased Mandy's brow. "Yeah. He's paying a lot of money for me to stay, but after Vice President Swanson told him about this place, he thought it was a smart idea. I guess that means I owe him."

"You haven't signed any papers to that effect, have you?" I said, seeing how easy it would be to make Mandy believe she had to pay them by giving them the baby.

"No, neither Ms. Swanson nor Jax wanted me to do that. But Senator Worthington believes we have a deal." She sighed and looked down at her stomach. "I had nowhere to go, and this seemed like a perfect solution. At first."

I reached over and took hold of her hand. "You have a lot to think about, I know, but, Mandy, you have to follow your heart."

She lifted her face and looked at me with eyes swimming with tears. "I wish I could believe I'd be a really great mother."

I let out a soft sigh, wanting to say so much, knowing I shouldn't. If Rhonda were here, she might want to push the idea of marrying Jax, but as much as I wanted to, I wouldn't. I got to my feet.

"Guess I'd better get to work. I'll meet you in front of the hotel at 1:45. In the meantime, how are you doing helping Liz?"

A smile brightened Mandy's delicate features making her beautiful, not that she'd believe it. "I love working with her. It's so much fun. She's lucky to have you as a mother. I see how you are with one another and realize I never had that kind of loving relationship with mine."

"Both Liz and I are happy you've come here. I have a feeling that things will work out for you if you let them."

Mandy's smile disappeared. "I'm in such a mess."

"One day, one thing at a time," I said, and waved goodbye.

Heading down to the sand once more, I strolled along the water's edge deep in thought. I'd had a strict, somewhat sterile upbringing with my grandmother after my parents were killed in an automobile accident. But I'd known I was loved. I couldn't imagine the hurt inside Mandy. I heard my name being called and looked up to see Rhonda standing by the gate to our hotel next to the beach. I went over to her.

"Hi, there! Thank you again for dinner last night. It was delicious."

Rhonda grinned at me. "I couldn't let Jean-Luc think I'd forgotten my mother's family recipes. We may have had some hard times in my childhood, but my mother always made sure there was tasty food on the table. 'Course having the butcher business helped."

I returned her smile. Life was so unpredictable. She was now a multi-multi-millionaire. I told Rhonda about my conversation with Mandy. "She and Jax agreed to come to dinner. It won't be fancy like yours, but if you and Will want to join us, you're welcome to do so."

Rhonda shook her head. "Thanks, anyway. But I'm cooking for Angela's family."

"How is Katherine? I've left messages for her, but no answer."

Rhonda checked her watch. "Why don't we go visit her now? We won't stay long, but I want you to see the situation for yourself. Maybe you can help with suggestions. Katherine and I are now friends, but I have to be careful what I say." She sent a text to Angela and waited for a reply. "Angela says it's a good time to come. Sally is down for a nap and Evan is playing outside."

"Okay. I've wanted to be able to speak to Katherine, to give her my support." I found my sandals, and we walked up to Rhonda's car.

As we drove to Angela's house, we talked about the letter to the editor I was waiting to send. 'I think Bernie is right, that we should let others support us while we keep a low profile," I said to her.

"As much as I'd like to be very clear how I feel about the whole thing, I agree with Bernie," sighed Rhonda. "But if I see Aubrey, I won't hold back. That little prick is due for some trouble from us."

"All we have to do is keep on succeeding at The Beach House Hotel. That's sweet revenge in itself."

Rhonda pulled into Angela's driveway.

We got out and looked at one another.

"Here goes," said Rhonda.

I understood her nervousness. Katherine had hurt Rhonda deeply in the past. The fact that Rhonda was reaching out to her was sweet but still wasn't easy.

Angela greeted us at the door, holding a finger to her lips. "Hi, glad you're here. Sally's sleeping. I don't want to disturb her. Come on inside."

I followed Rhonda through the doorway. "Where's Katherine?"

"Out on the lanai resting." Tears filled Angela's eyes. "She's failing so quickly. I think if she'd gone to the doctor earlier, she'd have a better chance of surviving. As it is, she's been told that it's a matter of months. She doesn't want to continue with chemo or do anything else about it. She says she's too tired. That could make it weeks."

"How does Reggie feel about that?" I asked. As difficult as Katherine could be, she'd always loved her son. That's why she was here. Her husband had told Reggie he wasn't welcome in their homes up north. Another family rift.

We walked quietly out to the lanai.

I held in a gasp when I saw Katherine stretched out on a lounge chair dozing. The woman who'd been such an imposing figure was a ghost of her former self.

Sensing us, Katherine opened her eyes and smiled. "Ah, the dynamic duo," she said softly.

Rhonda sat in a chair next to her and lifted her hand. "How are ya doin', hon?"

"I'm still here," Katherine said, trying unsuccessfully to smile. "Arthur's coming tonight. He had no idea how sick I am. He thought it was just a way for me to get his attention. The joke's on me."

I bent down and kissed her cheek. "I'm so sorry to hear this, Katherine."

She looked up at me. "How's that handsome husband of yours?"

I gave her an indulgent smile. She loved telling her friends she was a "close" friend of Vaughn's. "He's heading back to New York after a long weekend."

"Even though the show has made him more of a father to the schoolteacher, my friends think he's still perfect."

I pulled up a chair on the other side of her and took a seat opposite Rhonda. "I want you to know I'm available to help in whatever way I can. I was wondering if you'd enjoy some light massage therapy. I remember how Rhonda's ex-husband enjoyed that."

"That might feel soothing."

"Gentle, not rough," I said. "He found it helpful after lying around so much."

"Thank you, Ann," said Katherine. She turned to Rhonda. "And thank you for all the food you've been preparing. The custard you made yesterday tasted so delicious. Strange how certain foods sound delicious and others not so much."

"Whatever you want, I'll fix you," said Rhonda, patting her arm gently.

"I know we haven't always been friends," said Katherine, "but I'm glad we are now. Just don't let my grandchildren forget I was here."

Tears escaped Rhonda's eyes. "Of course not, Katherine. Evan knows you. And very sweet that Sally Kate has your name, huh?"

I held back a sob. When Sally Kate had been born a few months ago neither Rhonda nor Katherine was happy that both family's names had been used. Now it seemed appropriate that they had, and that Rhonda and Katherine had accepted it and each other.

Angela joined us carrying a glass of water and holding something in her other hand. "Katherine, time for your medication."

Katherine sat up. I could easily see how thin she'd become in a few short months. She'd always been thin, but now she was almost skeletal. Not wanting to overstay, I waited until she'd swallowed her pills and then stood and kissed her on the cheek.

"I'll make arrangements for you to have a massage anytime you want. You can let Angela know when you're ready, and we'll send someone from the hotel. I think you'll enjoy it."

"Thanks, dear," Katherine said.

I stepped aside to give Rhonda a chance to say goodbye. Watching the two of them embrace, I thought how nice it was for Reggie and Angela to know they'd become friends.

"See you later," Rhonda told Angela. "I'm doing dinner for you, an old-fashioned pot roast like Katherine wanted."

"Thanks, Mom," Angela said giving her mother a hug. "You don't know what it means to have your help. The smell of food cooking has been nauseating for Katherine, and we all enjoy your cooking."

"Your mother outdid herself for Jean-Luc and Lindsay last night," I said. "It was delicious."

Angela grinned. "Some of Nonna's recipes?"

Rhonda nodded. "Good old Italian food. Wouldn't dare go French cuisine for Jean-Luc."

I joined in the laughter, though sadness over Katherine lingered in all of us.

CHAPTER TWELVE

When I picked up Mandy in front of the hotel, I was touched to see her wearing one of the tops Angela had lent her and a pair of shorts I'd bought her. Her face shone with health, and I realized that having this time to relax and rest was helping her.

"All set?" I asked as Mandy slid into the passenger seat of my SUV.

"Yes, I'm excited to meet Dr. Benson. Now that I'm drawing closer to delivery, I imagine I'll be seeing quite a bit of her."

"As I've told you, she's an excellent doctor."

It was quiet as I drove the short distance to Dr. Benson's office. Ruth Benson was a popular OB-GYN, which is why Mandy hadn't been able to get right in to see her. I found the last remaining spot in the parking area next to her building and pulled in.

I got out and waited for Mandy to join me so we could walk into the waiting room together. Inside, I took a seat, placed my purse on the empty chair beside me, and waited for Mandy to finish checking in with the receptionist.

While she filled in paperwork beside me, I gazed around the office. Walls painted a bright yellow were covered with several framed collages of babies Dr. Benson had delivered. Cherubs with an array of skin tones gazed out at me. I said a silent prayer of thanks that Liz was pregnant. She and I had wanted it so badly.

Mandy's name was called.

She touched my arm. "Will you come in with me?"

"Sure," I said. "I want Dr. Benson to know you're a guest at the hotel."

Ruth Benson was a short, gray-haired woman who carried the bulk of weight well. Her eyes, a mesmerizing blue, seemed to miss nothing as she studied Mandy and turned to me with a smile. "Hello, Ann. I'm surprised to see you here."

"Mandy is staying at the hotel with Rhonda and me until she delivers her baby. I wanted you to know that in case you might need that information."

Dr. Benson nodded and turned to Mandy. "Let's sit and talk for a while before I examine you."

Mandy and I took seats in the two chairs in front of Dr. Benson's desk.

After she settled behind the desk, she smiled at Mandy. "You look nice and healthy. How are you feeling?"

"I'm okay." Mandy's face crumpled. "I just don't know what I should do."

"Maybe I'd better explain," I said, and gave Dr. Benson a brief synopsis of what was going on. I put my arm around Mandy's shoulders. "Rhonda and I support her, no matter what decision she makes."

"I see," said Dr. Benson. "Why don't I take a look at you, Mandy, and we can talk about timing and what to expect as far as delivery routines. I assume you'll have Ann or Rhonda with you at the time of delivery."

"And maybe my friend, Jax," said Mandy, blushing prettily.

"Okay, that's your choice," said Dr. Benson. "My nurse will show you to the exam room. I'll meet you there."

Dr. Benson rose, opened the door, and called for a nurse.

A pretty young woman, pregnant herself, introduced herself to Mandy and led her away.

After they'd gone, Dr. Benson spoke to me. "It sounds like Mandy is having a tough time. But I want you to know I, as her doctor, make no recommendations as to whether a patient should keep a baby or not. I leave that up to the woman herself, even when my feelings are strong. It would be unprofessional for me to do otherwise."

"I respect that," I said. "I'm trying to do my best to remain as neutral as you. But it's plain to see that she loves that baby and that her friend, Jax, would like to be more than that. Barbara Holmes is working with her now."

"Barbara is as helpful as they come," said Dr. Benson. "Are you planning to come into the examination room?"

"No, not this time. But when I see you in a couple of days with Liz, I'll do it then," I said, breaking into a huge smile.

"Okay!" said Dr. Benson. "I look forward to seeing you both then. I'll send Mandy out with some information about the hospital and procedures there. In the meantime, I'll be seeing her each week until delivery. Her paperwork said her delivery date was four weeks away."

I left Dr. Benson and went to the waiting room, my mind spinning. By this time next year, my grandchild might be ready to begin crawling.

By the time I'd finished a few chapters in the book I was reading online, Mandy appeared in the waiting area wearing a smile and holding sheets of information in her hand.

I stood. "Ready?"

She nodded and headed to the door.

I followed her. We left the building and walked out into the fresh air. Above us, clouds raced across the sky reminding me to keep a better watch on the weather. Even though named hurricanes were cause for concern, most never hit Sabal directly. Still, wind damage could cost us, which is why we did a better job of securing patio and beach furniture at the end of each day during these times.

"How did you like Dr. Benson?" I asked Mandy as we headed back to the hotel.

"She's very nice, so kind. She says my baby girl is doing well. I told her I've been eating well and exercising by walking along the beach a few miles each day."

"That's wise," I said. "If you take care of yourself, it makes a big difference after the baby is born."

"Thanks, Ann, for everything. Having you and Rhonda help me makes me happy. Dr. Benson can't say enough nice things about the two of you."

"Amelia Swanson knew we'd do everything we could to make you comfortable," I said, realizing it was true.

"She helped me a lot when I first found out I was pregnant," said Mandy. She stared out the window and turned back to me. "And later, when I returned to D.C. after visiting my parents."

I wanted to say something about her parents but kept quiet. Still, it bothered me how hypocritical they were preaching about kindness and showing none of it in their own house with their daughter.

I dropped Mandy off in front of the hotel and then drove behind it to park the car. Inside, I grabbed a cup of coffee in the kitchen on the way to the office.

Jean-Luc waved to me.

I went over to him. "How's it going?"

"We're sold out for tonight. The state hospitality group is holding a meeting here and we're setting up the library for a special dinner for them."

"Bernie told us about the meeting. What are you planning for dinner?"

"Cold Poached Salmon with a dill-yogurt sauce, sugar snap peas, and a cold smoky *salmorejo* soup."

"Sounds delicious. I love that soup. It's a blended version of gazpacho."

Jean-Luc smiled. "And with a bit of smoky olive oil."

"You're wonderful," I said, meaning it. Having Jean-Luc join us after we were first up and running was a stroke of genius. People came from all over to eat at our restaurant. I left him and walked into the office.

Rhonda looked up. "How'd it go with Mandy at Dr. Benson's?"

I plopped down in my desk chair and faced her. "Mandy burst into tears when Dr. Benson asked how she was doing. That poor girl is so stressed, I can't help but wonder what pressure is being put on her from up north."

"You mean by Senator Worthington?"

"Yes," I said. "I know she talks to him and his wife from time to time. I'm not sure it's such a smart idea. It doesn't seem fair."

"When is the baby due?" Rhonda asked.

"Four weeks from today unless she goes early," I answered. "It doesn't give Mandy much more time to make a decision. I just hope she isn't being rushed into one. I'd like to speak to Senator Worthington myself."

"You may get the chance sooner than you think," said Rhonda. "I checked the VIP sheet for the month, and he and his wife are scheduled to arrive next week for a short stay."

"Oh, I don't like the sound of that," I said alarmed by the thought of having even more pressure placed on Mandy.

"Me, either, though I'm curious about them as a couple. At least Lindsay had something nice to say about the wife." Rhonda let out a long breath. "Who knew we'd become so attached to some of our guests?"

"I think that's what Amelia Swanson was counting on. Mandy's very grateful for our support."

"Talking about support. I have to leave soon. I'm cooking for Katherine tonight. She wanted pot roast, now she wants lemon meringue pie. Weird how she's craving certain things, but I'm happy to do that for her." Rhonda clasped her hands together and gave me a worried look. "It could be you or me dying. It scares me to think of it."

"I'm glad you and Katherine have the opportunity to settle your differences. I'm sure Reggie appreciates it as much as Angela."

"I'm hoping I miss Arthur's arrival. I thought he was the easier one to take of Reggie's parents. Now, I know he's not."

"Go and cook. You'll feel better," I said. "I'm keeping it simple for dinner tonight with Mandy and Jax."

"Let me know everything about the evening. Wish I could be there too."

"I'll be anxious to see how Mandy and Jax act together," I told Rhonda. "That will make a big difference in my mind as to how this situation is going to end."

"Mine too. By the way, did you tell Dr. Benson about Liz?" Rhonda beamed at me.

"Yes. She was pleased to hear the news."

"Not as pleased as the rest of us," said Rhonda. "I've already ordered a bunch of things for the baby's room. Liz told me they've painted it a soft gray and are going with an elephant theme."

"We haven't talked about that yet. I'm hoping that when Liz and I see Dr. Benson later this week, we'll follow up with lunch and a shopping trip. It's sometimes hard to find privacy at the house with Robbie and Vaughn around." I loved that Liz was as close to Rhonda as I was to Angela.

That evening, I waited anxiously for Mandy and Jax to

arrive. They'd confirmed they'd not only drive themselves, but they'd bring their bathing suits for a swim in the pool. Vaughn was grilling both chicken breasts and beef filets while I was filling in with potatoes and two salads—romaine and a fresh fruit mélange.

When I heard the sound of Jax's truck pulling into our driveway, I went to the front door and walked over to greet them.

"Nice neighborhood," said Jax as he carefully helped Mandy out of the truck.

Vaughn and Robbie appeared, and I made all the introductions.

I noticed Robbie staring at Mandy's round stomach and said, "Mandy's going to have a baby."

"Why? Babies cry a lot," said Robbie. "Bailey was really loud."

After a moment of surprise, we all burst into laughter.

"Babies are worth the crying, son," said Vaughn, ruffling Robbie's dark locks of hair.

"Come on in," I said. "I'm glad you brought your suits. It's a lovely evening for a swim."

Mandy and Jax stood a moment in the front hall gazing around. "It's so beautiful," murmured Mandy.

"Thank you. Let me show you to one of the guest rooms. You can change there. I've already laid out beach towels for you."

Jax and Mandy followed me to the guest wing and their room.

"Thanks," Jax said, closing the door behind them.

I returned to Vaughn who was in the kitchen marinating the chicken. He smiled at me. "I see what you mean about wanting to take care of Mandy. With those big blue eyes of hers and her fragile looks, she could use a friend or two."

"She's stronger than she believes, but she needs all the friendship we can give her," I said. I took appetizers outside and set them on the table on the lanai.

Robbie was sitting by the pool dangling his feet into the water. When he saw me, he said, "Okay, can I go into the pool now?"

"Yes, I'm here to watch you." It was a strict rule of ours that Robbie could never swim in the pool alone without someone nearby to watch him.

Jax and Mandy came out to the lanai. Jax was in a swimsuit but Mandy was still dressed, though she held a towel.

"You're not going swimming, Mandy?" I asked.

She shook her head. "I couldn't get into my bathing suit. I'll sit and watch with you."

I smiled and patted the chair next to me. "The guys can all swim together."

Jax dove into the pool and came up out of the water with a smile. "That feels great!"

"Daddy!" cried Robbie when Vaughn walked out to the lanai. "Come join us!"

Vaughn chuckled. "Be right there, son! Give me a minute." Vaughn took off his T-shirt and tossed it on a nearby chair. Then, he stepped to the deep end of the pool and dove in.

"I did a little research before we came," said Mandy. "I didn't realize who your husband was. It must be so exciting to be married to someone famous like him."

"Vaughn and I have a strong marriage in spite of it," I said. "He likes his work, and that's important. We don't spend a lot of time with actors beyond his work in New York and here helping at the community theater when he has time."

Mandy was quiet and then said, "I also know Robbie is your adopted son. But you treat him like your own, and he obviously thinks of both of you that way."

"Of course. He may be adopted, but he's our child in every way that's important, and we love him," I said.

Mandy studied me thoughtfully and nodded.

Just then, Liz and Chad arrived.

I got to my feet to greet them and turned to Mandy. "I forgot to tell you I invited them to join us. Thought it would be nice for you two gals to have some fun together away from your work."

"Thanks," said Mandy, smiling as Liz approached her and gave her a hug before turning to me. "Mom, I intended to buy a dessert to bring with me, but we were running late and didn't stop at the store."

"No problem. You know I keep ice cream on hand when Vaughn is home. That'll do."

Liz introduced Chad to Mandy and greeted Jax. Then, while the men swam, we women sat in a circle and chatted about the jewelry business. Listening to Liz and Mandy talk, I realized they were fast becoming friends.

Later, after the men changed their clothes, we all sat on the lanai sipping drinks, sampling cheese and crackers, and generally enjoying one another.

I carefully watched how Jax and Mandy interacted, more like a married couple than friends, and listened to Jax explain how he hoped to set up his own landscaping business one day, apparently giving up on the idea of law at this time. Chad talked about the pros and cons of owning your own business, and Vaughn explained that he was actually in business for himself as well.

"And I'm in business for myself," said Liz proudly. "It's small now, but I hope to have it grow. Eventually, Angela and I will take over the hotel, but not for some years. Right, Mom?"

"Right." As much as Rhonda and I sometimes wanted to ease ourselves away from the hotel business, we knew it would only happen when our daughters were ready to take over our roles. Besides, with Robbie going to school full-time and Liz grown, I had time on my hands I needed to fill. Neither Rhonda nor I were women who liked to lunch and shop all the time.

"So, when are you guys getting married?" Chad asked Jax and Mandy, surprising us all.

"You're so perfect together," Liz added.

Jax shifted in his chair and gazed at Mandy. "I'm ready any time, but I have to convince Mandy."

"Oh, I'm sorry ... I didn't mean ..." Liz said.

"It's all right," said Mandy. "I love Jax, but we're not getting married. It wouldn't be right."

"She thinks I can do better," said Jax, looking uncomfortable. "I'm hoping to convince her otherwise. But first things first," he continued, glancing at Mandy's extended stomach.

"Well, I'm hopeful things will work out for the best," I said, giving them both a smile. If Mandy were my daughter, I'd want to shake her for not accepting herself as loveable. But Mandy was not my daughter, and she had enough to overcome that I wouldn't burden her with more negativity. As I'd often thought, Mandy's parents should be punished for what they'd done to her self-esteem.

"How about another round of drinks?" asked Vaughn. "Mandy and Liz, more fruit punch? Guys, another beer?" He smiled at me. "Another pinot noir?"

After we'd all placed our orders, Jax and Chad followed Vaughn inside.

'I'm sorry," Mandy said to me. "I know I hurt Jax's feelings, but it's complicated."

"There's nothing wrong with letting love grow if that's what you want," I said gently. "But I understand you've got a lot to figure out. Just take it step-by-step."

"He's really into you," said Liz. "And he seems like a very nice guy."

Mandy let out a long sigh. "I know. That's what makes it so hard. I owe him so much for helping me to get away from my parents."

Liz and I exchanged glances, and then I said, "Do you have plans for after the baby comes?"

Mandy looked to Liz. "I was thinking of staying in the area and maybe working with you."

"Really? That would be awesome," said Liz, her eyes shining with excitement. "That would mean I could expand the business. I've been talking to a silversmith in town."

The men returned with our drinks, and the conversation moved to the growth in the area.

Bored playing by himself while we talked, Robbie climbed up onto the couch next to me and leaned his head against my shoulder. I wrapped an arm around him loving his closeness, well aware that he was growing fast, and times like this were limited.

I noticed Mandy staring at us and smiled at her. She smiled back, but I saw the confusion in her expression.

That night as I lay next to Vaughn, I said, "What did you think of Mandy and Jax? Nice young people."

"Yes, but I'm not sure they're ever going to be a couple.

Mandy really shot down Jax. He was upset but was a gentleman about it."

"I'm hoping she can forget what her parents made her believe about herself and move on," I said. "They'd make such a darling couple."

"Whoa! Now you're sounding like Rhonda. Don't go there, Ann. They have to work it out for themselves." Vaughn drew me closer. "I know you want everyone to be happy, but it's not your job to see that they are."

"I guess," I sighed. "But I feel so sorry for her. For them both to be stuck because of the emotional abuse she'd suffered at the hands of her own parents, the people who should have shown her unconditional love. Then I remembered how I felt when Robert dumped me."

"You're a strong person, Ann. I'm afraid Mandy might not be as strong as we'd want," said Vaughn.

"She may surprise us all," I said, hoping it was true.

CHAPTER THIRTEEN

The next day Vaughn packed to go back to New York. As I watched, I wondered how many more times this scene would play out. If Vaughn liked the script, it might end sooner than we'd thought. But then, he might be gone for longer periods of time. It was a life lesson, reminding me to enjoy the time we had together.

On the way to the airport, silence reigned in the car until my cell rang. *Tina Marks.*

"Hi, there!" I said, speaking into the online system. "How are you? When are you coming to Florida with that adorable little boy of yours?"

"That's why I'm calling. I have a few days free and am wondering if I could come later this week? If so, any chance of staying at the guesthouse at the hotel?"

"Great news! I'll work some magic and make sure you can have the guesthouse, but you're always welcome to stay with me."

"Thanks, but I'm bringing a nanny and need space of my own. But I want to spend some time with you. Also, I want to talk to Vaughn about a script I'm reading. He'd be perfect as one of the characters."

"Vaughn's with me now. I'm driving him to the airport. Go ahead and talk to him."

"Hi, Vaughn," said Tina through the car's speaker. "There's a role in the movie I'm going to do that would be perfect for you. It would be as a favorite uncle of my character—a younger, hip version of one that you could pull off. Not the stodgy figure they're trying to portray you on the show."

"You didn't like the PR for Darla Delaney and me?" Vaughn said to her.

"No, it's bullshit and you know it. You're the kind of man most women in their twenties and up want. They're making you seem as if you have one foot in a geriatric ward. You're not ready for that, are you?"

Vaughn glanced at me. "I'm getting pretty close to that mark, but no, I don't feel my age and frankly, I didn't like what was happening. Darla is a decent young woman, and I wanted to give her a chance for something better."

"Always a sweetheart," said Tina. "I'll have my agent send you the script and see if you like it. I must warn you though that Matthew McConaughey and others are looking at it."

"Send it right along. And thank you, Tina. I appreciate it and your remarks. I was beginning to think I might not have much of a chance to make a change."

I glanced at the look of happiness on Vaughn's face and filled with love for him. In so many ways, some of which only I knew, he was not ready to be considered old.

At the airport, we quickly kissed, then I waited while he removed his suitcase from the backseat and walked away. He turned and waved, and I waved back before heading into the traffic and to my life without him.

On the way to the hotel, I called Bernie and told him we needed to have the house available for Tina.

"No problem. The couple who was supposed to stay there has canceled. I have a feeling they are staying at The Sand Castle instead."

I let out a worried sigh. "I suppose we'll lose a few guests to them for a while until everyone figures out The Sand Castle isn't the fine hotel they represent."

"It's a problem, but I'm keeping my eye on it. I called our PR people and asked for suggestions. Hopefully, I'll have something soon to show you and Rhonda."

"Thanks. Situations like this can snowball out of control. We don't want that to happen. Thank goodness our wedding business looks strong for the fall."

"And like we talked about earlier, our guests are discriminating people, those who like quality."

"See you soon. I have an errand to take care of, and then I'll come in."

"Okay. See you later," said Bernie, and hung up.

I drove to Angela's house and got out, eager to see Katherine. I'd asked Vaughn to write her a short note. Knowing how proud she was of knowing him, I couldn't wait to give it to her. And now that Arthur had arrived, I wanted to see if there was anything I could do for Angela. Arthur's earlier visit had not been pleasant.

I knocked on the door and waited for a few seconds before it opened, and Reggie stood there.

"I have something for Katherine. May I come in?"

"Of course," Reggie said, his lips curving into a smile that didn't reach his eyes.

"How's it going?" I asked softly, stepping into the front entrance.

He shrugged. "It's not a happy time, but I think my parents are working things out. And my dad and I are talking."

"I'm glad," I said, giving him a quick hug of encouragement.

Angela joined us. "Hi, Ann. What's up?"

I held up the note. "Vaughn wrote Katherine a sweet note and I wanted her to have it."

Angela's face lit with pleasure. "Oh, she'll be so pleased.

She's lying down on the couch in the family room watching television with Evan."

When Katherine saw me, she gave me a weak smile.

I leaned over, gave her a quick kiss on the cheek, and handed her the envelope. "Vaughn wanted me to give you this."

Katherine clapped a hand over her heart. "For me? Really?"

"He knows you've told your friends that you are a friend of his. Here's proof of it."

Tears escaped Katherine's eyes as she handed it to me. "Why don't you read it to me?" She moved over to give me space to sit.

I lowered myself onto the edge of the couch, opened the envelope, and began reading the note.

"My dear Katherine, I was sorry to learn of your illness. As your friend and a family member of sorts, I want you to know I'm thinking of you. If you tune into the show in the upcoming week, I'm going to figure out a way to use your name in my dialogue as a special message to you. Best, Vaughn."

"Oh my!" said Katherine. "He's going to mention me?"

"Your name, yes," I said. "We'll all watch the show and listen for you."

A long sigh escaped Katherine. "That's so sweet. You married a treasure, Ann."

"After a bad one," I said honestly. "But you're right. Vaughn is a good man." As I said the words, I looked around, but Arthur wasn't in sight. I hoped he was over his anger with Reggie and Angela and had returned to the upstanding gentleman I'd first met.

Katherine noticed and said quietly, "Arthur is more like himself. I think he's learned that a parent can't live his child's life, no matter how much he loves him."

"A difficult life lesson," I said.

"Especially when he'd planned it for so many years," said Katherine. "I was angry too with Reggie's choices, but I see now how wrong I was. Too bad it took me so long."

I took hold of her hand and squeezed it. "At least you've resolved it. That's so important."

Katherine nodded but stayed silent.

I stood. "Well, I've got to go. I'm glad we had this moment, Katherine."

Arthur walked into the room, wearing shorts, a golf shirt, and sneakers. "Hello, Ann. Sorry to have missed you earlier. I was at the beach for a walk before it got too hot."

"It's a beautiful morning for a walk," I said, smiling at him.

He smiled. "Yes, I'm hoping to take Katherine for a ride, get her out of the house, and give the kids a break."

I smiled at everyone gathered together. "Sounds like a lovely plan. If you need anything, please let me know."

"Let me walk you to the door," said Arthur.

He followed me outside. "I owe you and everyone else an apology for my behavior during my last visit. I understand now why Reggie and Angela have chosen to remain in Florida and why Reggie has opted to work with Will instead of me. I'm not happy about it, but I will support them both. They've been terrific about having Katherine here with them." He looked away and when he faced me again, his eyes were watery with unshed tears. "I had no idea Katherine was so ill. I can't imagine why she didn't mention not feeling well. Like she told me, she was too upset about the kids being away from us, she thought it was making her sick." He shook his head. "We've more than learned our lesson."

"Are you all right with Katherine staying here until the end?"

He kicked at the driveway with a sneaker and looked up at me. "Yes. We've already called hospice. They're meeting with all of us later today. I've told the kids I'm covering all expenses of having her here and will reimburse them for any they've already covered."

"I'm sure they appreciate it," I said, knowing how uncomfortable he was.

"It's the least I can do after asking them for forgiveness." He drew a deep breath. "I also told everyone I want to get to know Will better."

"Oh?" I hid my surprise. He'd acted so superior to Will because Will's financial advisory services practice was much smaller than Arthur's international company.

"I bet that pleased Rhonda," I said, knowing how protective Rhonda was of Will or anyone else in what she considered her family.

He chuckled. "Yeah, she made sure I knew there'd better not be any bullshit."

"That sounds like her. Well, good luck, Arthur. I'm glad to see you've settled things here in Sabal."

"Thank you. My apologies again." He turned and walked inside, leaving me outside thinking more than one miracle had occurred here in the last few days. Too bad such sad circumstances had caused them.

"What happened?" Rhonda asked the minute I walked into the office. "Angela called me all teary, saying something about how we had to watch *The Sins of the Children* all week long. She couldn't take the time to explain because Evan needed her."

I filled her in on my visit to Angela's house.

Rhonda smiled and shook her head. "That was so nice of Vaughn."

"He was happy to do that for Katherine. As she said, I married a good guy."

Rhonda snorted. "After marrying that ass, Robert."

I laughed. "I more or less said the same thing."

"I'll set the timer on my phone, so we don't miss the shows this week," said Rhonda grinning. "Remember how we got hooked on them when we first met Vaughn?"

I laughed and nodded. I'd been as star-struck as anyone, never imagining I'd end up being married to him. Working in the hospitality industry, Rhonda and I had met many interesting people. Even now, I thought of some of them, like Lindsay Thaxton and Mandy, as members of my extended family.

Thinking of that, I told Rhonda about Tina's upcoming visit.

She, like I, was excited to see her again and meet her baby boy for the first time.

CHAPTER FOURTEEN

G reeting Tina at the hotel was even more exciting than welcoming Amelia Swanson. Tina stepped out of the limo, as regal as a queen. Her self-confidence was a pleasure to see. The first time Tina had come to The Beach House Hotel she'd acted like a spoiled brat when she was, in reality, dealing with the trauma of past abuse by her own mother, an unrelenting stage mother who'd tried to offer up Tina to get a coveted role.

As Rhonda and I walked down the front steps of the hotel, Tina jogged up to us and hugged us both. "Come see Victor!"

An older Asian woman with lovely gray hair emerged from the car holding the baby.

"Thanks," said Tina, taking the baby from her and holding him up for us to see. A smile lifted the corners of his lips, creasing his chubby cheeks. He waved his arms in the air with excitement. He had a tuft of dark hair, and as I got closer, I saw that his eyes were a light brown.

"He's adorable," I cooed as I took him in my arms.

"Give him to his Auntie Rhonda," said Rhonda, holding out her arms. I gave Victor a loving squeeze and handed him over.

Tina and I embraced again. "I'm so glad you could make it," I told her. "I've wanted to see Victor for myself and, more importantly, find out how you were doing. Vaughn seemed pretty excited about the possibility of a role in your movie."

"The producers are pretty excited about it too. You look beautiful as always, Ann."

"Thanks. That's sweet of you to say. It's been hectic, but life is good."

"I heard about some fancy new hotel not far from here called The Sand Castle. What's up with that?"

"Hopefully you'll be able to join Rhonda and me for margaritas this afternoon. I'll tell you all about it then."

"Sounds delightful! I'm going to rest from the flight and have some time with the baby in the pool. After that, it would be perfect."

Rhonda handed Victor back to Tina. "He's beautiful! And you look great!" she said to Tina.

"Not like some of the actresses that look as if they'd never had a baby, but I've been careful. I don't want to have the same problem I did when we first met."

"No worries," I said, smiling at the memory of how we'd had to hide Tina at the hotel until she lost some weight for a movie role.

"How's Jean-Luc? I've been thinking of a few of my favorite things to eat," said Tina.

"Jean-Luc is in love, though they're being careful about keeping it on a friendly basis at the moment."

"I'm predicting a wedding before the end of the year," said Rhonda. "And you know how excellent I am at that."

I couldn't help rolling my eyes. "Rhonda thinks she's a matchmaker. But this time, it's already a done deal."

"I'm so happy for him," said Tina.

Victor started to fuss. "I'm going to get settled in the guesthouse, and I'll be in touch later. Bernie told me I was pre-checked into the hotel when I called from the airport. I just wanted to see you first."

After Tina handed Victor to the nanny, we exchanged hugs all around, and then Rhonda and I stood aside as Tina returned to the car. We watched the limo enter the driveway to the guesthouse and turned to one another with smiles.

"She looks and seems great," said Rhonda.

"I thought so too," I agreed.

"We sure have had some adventures with our guests, huh?" said Rhonda as we climbed the stairs to the hotel's entrance.

"Yes, indeed. I wonder how long it will take for news to get out about Tina's visit," I said.

"Hopefully not long. I can't wait to put a certain someone in her place," said Rhonda.

I grinned. It was an idea Rhonda had come up with over coffee earlier that morning.

Late afternoon, Rhonda and I met Tina in the lobby bar. She was seated in the corner but stood when she saw us, causing more than one glance her way. Wearing a short sundress and high-heeled sandals that enhanced her long, shapely legs, she looked every bit a star.

Rhonda and I went over to her.

At a signal from me, the bartender came right over to us. He smiled at me. "The usual?"

"How about a margarita?" I asked Tina.

"Just one," Tina replied, "then bubbling water for me."

The bartender's gaze stayed on Tina a moment longer than was necessary, then he bobbed his head and left.

"So, tell me what's been going on with you two," said Tina. "And I want to know more about The Sand Castle."

"First of all, I'm ecstatic to tell you that Liz is going to have a baby. I'm going to the doctor's office with her to confirm the date and all." My vision blurred. "She was so worried she'd never get pregnant, even though it's been less than a year of trying. I had difficulty getting pregnant. I think that's why she was so concerned."

"Great news," said Tina. She turned to Rhonda. "And I got a notice about Angela's baby just about the time I had Victor." She smiled. "The family is growing."

"And how! Nell had a baby girl too," I said. "Bailey's a couple of weeks older than Sally Kate."

Our drinks came, and Rhonda told Tina about the situation with Katherine.

Tina shook her head. "What a sad story. Now, tell me about that hotel."

I set down my drink, drew a deep breath, and began. By the time Rhonda took over the telling of the story and how Terri Thomas had turned on us, I was furious all over again with Aubrey and his underhanded attempt to ruin us.

"And to think Aubrey and Brock are working together on this. What a gruesome twosome," said Tina shuddering dramatically.

"That's a nicer way of saying it than I would," said Rhonda. She looked across the room and her eyes widened.

I turned to see Brock walking toward us. "Oh, no!" I muttered. "Could this story get any worse?"

Smiling and keeping his eyes on Tina, he picked up his pace.

"What are you doing here?" said Rhonda. "I thought you'd be over at The Sand Castle with your buddy Aubrey Lowell."

"It's wise to see what the competition is up to," he said. His eyes lit with pleasure as he turned his attention to Tina. "Hi, Tina! Do you remember me? Brock Goodwin."

"Of course, I remember you." She settled her gaze on him. "But not in a favorable light."

His smile left his face. "I thought we had fun the few times we dated."

"A man old enough to be my grandfather trying to take

advantage of a mixed-up kid isn't what I'd call fun. Pretty sleazy, if you ask me."

"Come now. You married an older man," said Brock.

"Not as old as you and, fortunately, nothing like you," said Tina.

I watched the interchange with fascination. Both Brock and Tina were speaking in pleasant voices while their words stung.

"You'll have to excuse us," I said to Brock. "We're having a private meeting."

His nostrils flared, but he turned and walked away without saying anything more.

"What a total ass," said Tina. "Honestly, I don't know how you put up with him."

"We have to," said Rhonda. "He has some influence with the city and in the neighborhood. If that wasn't so, I'd have had some people from back home find him."

I laughed with Tina, but I wondered how true that might be someday. Brock continued to be a constant pain to us.

We finished our drinks, made plans for lunch tomorrow, and then Tina left to return to the guesthouse, and Rhonda and I went back to our office.

We sat, discussing the upcoming visit from Senator Worthington and his wife when my cell rang. *Terri Thomas.*

"Hello, Terri," I said, watching Rhonda's lips thin at the mention of her name.

I listened and then said, "Yes, Tina Marks is staying with us. I guess it didn't take long for Brock Goodwin to call you. An interview? Surely, you jest. After the scathing remarks you made in your feature on The Sand Castle, I must confess I admire your chutzpah. But, no, I'm not asking Tina to give you an interview. She's here for a rest and you know how we like to pamper our guests."

"Listen, Ann, I need your help," said Terri. "I'm in a whole lot of trouble for that article. My boss is furious with me. It's just that Aubrey was so generous with a weekend stay at the hotel, that I was forced to agree with him that it represents something entirely different."

"I have no problem with that. But you certainly understand the way you wrote about The Beach House Hotel and others in and around Sabal was hurtful and very unprofessional."

"Tell her no more sweet rolls at The Beach House Hotel," Rhonda snapped.

"It was a mistake," admitted Terri. "A huge one. Give me one more chance, Ann. I promise to do a better job for you."

"I'll ask Tina if she's willing to talk to you. But that's all. If she says no, that's it. Understand?"

"Yes, thank you. I'll call you tomorrow morning," said Terri. "I'm sorry for everything. You know I love The Beach House Hotel."

"I always thought so, which is why I don't understand what you did," I said coolly. "Talk to you tomorrow. No promises."

I ended the call and faced Rhonda, who was clearly upset. "Annie, why were you even pleasant to her? She's a frickin' traitor!"

"Because I have a plan. Maybe Tina can help us out in a way no one else can. We just have to give her an idea of what to say during her interview. Then it's Tina speaking. Not us."

A smile spread across Rhonda's face. "Okay! But Terri's not getting any treats from us. And we'll make it an early morning meeting held outside."

"Fine by me," I said, grinning at the thought. I called Tina, got her agreement, and called Terri back.

"Thank you," Terri gushed when she heard the news. "I'll

have a photographer take a picture of her, and then we can talk in the dining room."

"No," I countered. "We've decided to do a garden interview. Many of our guests use the garden for weddings or as a quiet space to rest and relax. It'll be the perfect place for you."

"Oh," said Terri, and I almost laughed at the disappointment in her voice.

I ended the call chuckling.

The next morning, I stood aside with Rhonda as Tina graciously talked with Terri.

Tina, an excellent actress, spoke lovingly of her time in Sabal, why she wouldn't stay anywhere else in the area, the New Mothers Program at the hotel, and her need to rest in a peaceful place where some of the finest food in Florida was served.

By the time, she was through, even I was ready to spend a couple of days at the hotel.

Terri finished taking notes and sat back in her chair. "Sounds like Ann and Rhonda told you what to say," she said, a smirk playing with her lips.

"Not at all," said Tina. "I am my own person, and as you may be aware, I continue to refuse all offers to endorse products. I don't need that. I want my fans to know I'm a happy mom and wife who's earned the right to enjoy elegant places like the Beach House, and that away from the work I do, I like to relax and be myself with my husband and baby. I'm allowed to do that here."

"I see. Tell me about your latest movie. What are you looking at now?" Terri asked.

I listened carefully as Tina told of a script that she was

looking at for a romantic suspense movie, the same one she'd mentioned to Vaughn. I hoped Vaughn would have the chance to work on it. The script sounded interesting, and it would be fantastic to have Vaughn and Tina work together, allowing me to visit the set and applaud them both.

Terri finished the interview. After the photographer took a few pictures of Tina in the garden, Terri left with him without any of the sweet rolls she loved.

Rhonda and I invited Tina inside the hotel for refreshments, but she turned it down. "I need to get back to Victor. I've given up breastfeeding, but I like to be there for his bottle anytime I can."

"Understood," I said, kissing her on the cheek. "You're such a great mom."

Tina's smile turned wobbly. "I never want to be anything like my own mother. That's why I try so hard."

"Well, it's working. Victor is a happy baby," I said, remembering how awful a stage mother Tina's mother had been, disregarding her child's sensitivity and even her safety.

Rhonda and Tina embraced, and as Tina walked away, Rhonda said, "Let's see what Terri does with that article. I have a feeling Aubrey isn't going to like it."

"Let's see how badly Terri wants those sweet rolls," I said, and Rhonda laughed.

That night, as I lay in bed talking to Vaughn on the phone, I told him about Terri's newspaper interview with Tina. "She described the new movie she's working on. It sounds very interesting. Have you heard anything more about it?"

"As a matter of fact, I'm reading the script now, and I like it. My role as the likable uncle is deeper than I thought because it's all about a brother relationship gone bad. So bad that one attempts to kill the other."

"Wow! A different kind of role for you," I said.

"Yeah. I really like that. It's being filmed in Canada, so that would make it an easy location to get to. There's a nice flight from Miami to Vancouver. I've already checked it."

"So, then you're going for it?"

"Oh, yes. I want it bad," Vaughn said. "I spoke privately to Darla and told her I was considering leaving the show, but I didn't want her to think I haven't enjoyed working with her; I only want to make a change in my career. I've done the one movie, but now I want to do more."

"She looks up to you, and I'm sure it meant a great deal to her to have that understanding between the two of you before anyone else could turn it into something untrue."

"By the way, I'm not sure how it happened, but an old picture of me and Lily Dorio turned up somewhere in one of those trashy supermarket newspapers. So far, nothing more has been said beyond questioning me as to where she is now. I have no idea, so I couldn't answer."

"Thanks for telling me. I'll keep an eye out for any gossip at this end."

We talked about Robbie's latest projects at school and my upcoming doctor's appointment with Liz.

"Hope everything goes well," Vaughn said. "Hard to believe you're a grandmother, Ann."

I laughed. "Hard to believe you're a grandfather."

"What happened to us, Ann?" he said quietly.

"Something wonderful. Don't let a label make you think otherwise," I said, surprised by his sensitivity to his age.

"You're right. I love you, Ann. You keep things real for me. Something I appreciate. Ellie used to do the same thing. Ah, I'm so lucky I found you."

I smiled. "Me, too. You've given me a reason to think I'm

loveable."

"What? Of course, you're loveable. And if you mean sexy, that too. What are you wearing?" he asked, his voice growing husky.

Playing this favorite long-distance game, I grinned. "Not much. Mostly lace and silky, see-through fabric. But I think I'll take that off."

"Hmmm," said Vaughn. "Imagine that."

We chuckled together.

It was some time before we ended the call.

CHAPTER FIFTEEN

T
he next morning, as I got ready for work, all I could think about was the upcoming appointment with Liz. Chad had been very gracious about having me go in his place. But he announced he'd attend any appointment Liz requested of him. Though it was just a normal doctor's visit, I was excited to do this with her. I liked and trusted Ruth Benson.

Rhonda called. "Annie, have you looked at your newspaper? Terri's article is there and it's a doozy."

"Hold on! I'll go look at it now."

I set down my hairbrush and raced into the kitchen where I'd placed the paper earlier before getting busy with Robbie. I opened it to the social page and stared at a picture of Tina sitting on the steps of the gazebo at Beach House Hotel. Glancing through the article I read Tina's comments about never staying anywhere else in the area and how The Beach House Hotel accommodated everyone with tasteful surroundings, food, and service.

"Excellent!" I said to Rhonda. Her words in quotes were non-confrontational, just honest. It was a subtle but true stab in the back to Aubrey.

"Yeah. It's a good thing she came through," said Rhonda. "The Sand Castle was never mentioned in the article, but those in the area will understand exactly what comparisons were made."

"See you later, I'm off to Liz's appointment," I said.

"I'm going to call Terri and thank her for the article. But

there'll be no mention of any cinnamon rolls!" Rhonda clicked off the call, and I rushed back to the bathroom to get ready.

When I picked up Liz at her house, she walked out to the car to greet me wearing a smile that lit her face. Studying her, I thought she looked even more beautiful than usual. Pregnancy gave a glow of health to some women. Liz was one of them. The soft cotton top she was wearing exposed a slight curve in her belly and I wondered if she, like me, would carry her baby out front. Otherwise, she was quite thin.

"Thanks for going with me, Mom. I thought later we could go window shopping. There's a cute little maternity store I want to check out."

"That would be fun," I said, a bit amused. No doubt she was counting on me to be as excited as she was about a few new things for her to wear during this time.

I parked at Dr. Benson's building, and we walked inside together.

In the office, women in varying stages of pregnancy filled the waiting room. Observing them, it was comforting to know that no matter how things were going in the world around me, making me concerned, new life was beginning.

While Liz registered, I sat down.

Liz soon joined me, and I smiled to myself when I noticed her studying the stomachs of the other women. One woman looked as if she was about to give birth any moment. She noticed Liz looking at her and patted her stomach. "Twins."

Liz turned to me wide-eyed. "I can't imagine having twins. I'm not sure Chad would like that. I know his mother wouldn't. She's already told us that though she's excited about our having a baby, she's not going to be able to be much help."

"Well, I wouldn't worry about it. You're going to have lots of help. And as for twins, there's no history of them in our family." I glanced at her stomach.

When the nurse called Liz into the back, she turned to me. "Will you come with me? I know you've been just as anxious about this as I have been."

"Sure. I'd love to."

Liz and I followed the nurse to Dr. Benson's office, where we took seats in front of her desk.

Dr. Benson came inside and closed the door behind her. Smiling at me as she sat behind the desk, she said, "Nice to see you again, Ann."

"Thank you."

Dr. Benson turned to Liz. "And you, young lady, are due for some congratulations. I know you've been worried about your family history and the difficulty you might have in getting pregnant. But it seems that's no longer a problem."

Liz beamed at her. "Chad and I and everyone I know are thrilled for us."

"Well then, let's talk dates and then I'll examine you. My PA, Jamie, will give you materials to take home with you, though I'm sure you understand the importance of diet and rest."

"Oh, yes. I've bought the book about expecting and," she looked at me with a smile, "I've got a whole lot of people willing to tell me what to do. If Mom can't answer something, Rhonda can."

I laughed with Dr. Benson. She knew how close Rhonda and I were.

After talking about the timing of Liz's baby and going over family history, Dr. Benson rose. "Everything sounds fine, Liz. Now, go next door and I'll come and examine you after

Jamie has taken your vitals and helped you prepare."

After Liz left the room, Dr. Benson said to me, "It's always so gratifying to see a young couple so excited about their baby. As you well know, that doesn't always happen. Any word from Amanda on her decision as to her baby's future?"

I shook my head. "No, and I'm concerned. The prospective parents are visiting her at the hotel and staying a couple of days."

"It's not an easy decision for a mother to give her baby away. Something I wouldn't wish on any woman. My heart aches for her," said Dr. Benson. "Let me examine Liz, and then we can talk about Liz's happy situation."

While I waited in Dr. Benson's office, I went through some emails on my phone, stopping when I saw one from Amelia Swanson. She asked if I'd be willing to entertain the senator and his wife, telling me it would be very beneficial to the hotel's business. I wrote back agreeing to it and suggested I include Lindsay.

A response came quickly. "Please don't. We're keeping Lindsay's whereabouts private for the time being."

I answered, assuring her I'd be quiet about Lindsay and made a mental note to tell Rhonda. She was so pleased that the "romance" between Lindsay and Jean-Luc was going well that she occasionally mentioned it.

Liz and Dr. Benson walked into the office, and I eagerly turned to them. Dr. Benson smiled at me and placed a hand on Liz's shoulder. "Liz is a healthy young woman, and I don't expect any problems. The due date may be off, though, and for that reason, I'm asking Liz to come back in two weeks to check her progress."

I frowned. "Is this out of the ordinary?"

Dr. Benson shook her head. "It's simply a matter of clarification. I will also have the opportunity to meet Chad."

She opened the door behind her, and I got to my feet.

"Thank you, Dr. Benson, and thank you, Liz, for allowing me to be here with you. I love the idea of becoming a grandmother to Liz's children."

"I have a long way to go to catch up to Angela, but we want our kids to be friends," said Liz, smiling and rubbing her stomach.

"See you later, ladies," said Dr. Benson. "Liz, stop by the check-out desk to set up your next appointment."

Though I wanted to ask Dr. Benson more questions, I knew we were being dismissed.

In my car, Liz turned to me with a grin. "I can't believe it. Sometime next spring I'll have a baby. I can't decide whether I want it to be a boy or, maybe, a girl. If it's a girl, she and Sally Kate could be close."

"Either way, I'm prepared to love and spoil your child."

"Chad says we're going to have to be careful so that this little one isn't too spoiled with our family and Rhonda's around. But, right now, I don't care. The idea of being a parent is too exciting."

"I agree. One step at a time. Shall we go shopping?" I asked Liz.

"Yes, I don't need anything now, but I want to look at all the maternity fashions. I've already noticed some of my pants are getting a little tight."

I chuckled. Liz was so excited about being pregnant. I just hoped that enthusiasm lasted through the months ahead.

We headed to a little shop called Mother's Delight.

Inside, I marveled at the new styles, the new fabrics, and the options in apparel pregnant women had today. When I was expecting Liz, maternity clothing styles were pretty unexciting. No wonder Liz was anxious to wear them. Comfort was the key.

After browsing, we picked out a few special things on sale and agreed we'd come back later for more.

As we left the store, I checked my watch. "Can we do lunch another time? I want to get back to the hotel. We have VIP guests arriving later today, and I need to make sure everything is set for them."

"Is this Senator Worthington and his wife?" asked Liz. "If so, Mandy is very nervous to have them here. I told her if she needs to escape, she can come to my house."

"Well, I certainly hope that won't be necessary. I've been asked to entertain them and am willing to do so because I want to get to know them better. It seems a little pushy of them to come to the hotel."

"I think so too," said Liz. "Did you know they made her promise she'd walk on the beach twice a day? I'll ride to the hotel with you because I want to check the designs Mandy is working on for me."

"Okay, and if you want to order room service for lunch, bill my account," I said, mulling over Mandy's situation.

When I walked into the office, Rhonda looked up at me. "How's Liz? How was the visit?"

"Fine. Dr. Benson said she's healthy. But she wants Liz back in two weeks to be certain of the due date. I thought it was odd, but Dr. Benson said it wasn't out of the ordinary."

"Dr. Benson's the best so I wouldn't worry," said Rhonda. "Did you get the message from Amelia Swanson asking if we'd entertain the Worthingtons?"

"Yes. That's one reason I wanted to talk to you. I'm suggesting we do a private dinner at the hotel. I mentioned inviting Lindsay, but Amelia asked me not to. What do you think we should do?"

"I like the idea of a private dinner. We can use the small dining room and keep it simple. I understand we want to welcome them, but at the same time, I'm worried for Mandy."

"Liz has told Mandy she can stay at her house if she'd be more comfortable," I said.

Rhonda shook her head. "Too late. As soon as the Worthingtons leave, Mandy is moving in with Jax. I saw him this morning. He told me they thought it would be safer for Mandy to be with him in case she goes into labor sometime in the night." Rhonda sighed. "Poor kid was positively beaming. I wish Mandy could give in to her wishes to simply love him without worrying about whether she'd be bad for him. It's very obvious he loves her."

"She's opening up more and more to us. Maybe she'll finally give in to what they both want," I said. It seemed so simple, but I knew it wasn't.

"Why don't we do the dinner for the Worthingtons tomorrow?" said Rhonda. "That'll give them a chance to settle in on their own tonight. It'll just be you and me and them. Right?"

"Yes. Vaughn isn't planning on returning soon. Believe it or not, he's seriously considering leaving the show."

"Really? What would he do? The movie with Tina?" asked Rhonda.

"He's hoping for the part in her movie. Other more famous actors are vying for it, but I think Vaughn has a good chance of getting it. I hope so. He's been a little down about the show lately."

Rhonda grinned at me. "Well, then, I'll keep my fingers crossed for him. He deserves the best." She sighed. "Angela told me this morning they're bringing in hospice for Katherine. Just to help out with medications, etc. She's not bedridden but spends most of her time sleeping. It's happening way too fast."

"What about Arthur? Is he going to stay for the duration?" I asked. "I know he regrets his earlier actions."

"He's flying to New York tomorrow," said Rhonda. "Then he'll come back here to stay. He's asked for space at Will's building. How do you like them apples?"

"Life is a bunch of circles. That's for sure," I said. It was hard to believe Arthur would deign to work in Will's small, simple office after being so haughty about his glamorous space in New York. But then, a lot had happened since I first met Reggie's parents at his wedding.

"The Worthingtons are due to arrive around four o'clock. I've asked our driver to notify us when they're on their way from the airport to the hotel," said Rhonda.

"Thanks. I want to make sure they get the special treatment Amelia has promised. She said it would be excellent PR for the hotel."

Rhonda made a face. "I don't like this whole deal. I can't help but wonder if Senator Worthington approached Amelia for help way before this incident with Mandy ever happened."

A long sigh came from deep within me. "I've had the same feeling about him. But I trust Amelia to do the right thing. She's helped women for a long time, and I hope she wouldn't get involved with anything shady."

"Maybe that's why I haven't said anything to Amelia about it. Still, I want to be sure Mandy isn't forced into anything," said Rhonda.

"We have to keep an eye on things without appearing to be involved." After seeing Liz so excited about her baby and how Mandy wasn't certain about the tough decision ahead of her, I wanted Mandy to make her own choice. She obviously loved the baby.

CHAPTER SIXTEEN

S ometime later, as we'd so often done since the hotel opened, Rhonda and I waited at the top of the front steps to greet our guests.

"How often have we done this?" said Rhonda, turning to me with a grin. "Each time, we meet interesting people."

"And some even become friends," I said.

Rhonda elbowed me. "Here they come."

Our white limo with The Beach House Hotel name and logo discreetly displayed on the side pulled up in front of us.

Rhonda and I walked down the stairway to greet them.

I was surprised to see Jax, not our regular driver, get out of the car and open the passenger doors for them. Senator Worthington got out and walked behind the limo to stand by as his wife emerged from the car. When they both turned to face us, I held back a gasp of surprise. Samuel Worthington, with his sandy hair and bright gray-green eyes, reminded me of Jack Kennedy. His wife, Cassie, was dark-haired like Jacqueline and moved with the same grace as she walked toward us smiling.

"Welcome to The Beach House Hotel," I said automatically.

"We're so happy to have you here," Rhonda said, as was our custom.

Senator Worthington's handshake was firm and his smile practiced.

"Thank you," said Cassie sweetly. "It's such a lovely place."

"It was Rhonda's seaside estate before we converted it to a hotel," I said.

"So, I read," said Samuel. "Amelia Swanson can't say enough nice things about it."

"You'll be staying in the Presidential Suite as you requested," I said.

"I think you'll be more than happy with it," said Rhonda. "Come this way."

"Your bags will be brought inside and sent to your room," I said, careful not to mention Jax's name. I didn't want the senator and his wife to associate Jax with Mandy in any way.

The senator walked ahead. Rhonda scrambled to catch up to him while I took Cassie's arm.

"I'm looking forward to our time here," she said. "I'm well aware that you know why we've come."

I nodded and waited for her to say more. But she merely smiled and looked away.

Inside, Bernie greeted them and offered to oversee the details of their arrival. Rhonda and I said our goodbyes and left them with Bernie.

In our office, Rhonda turned to me. "They are a handsome couple, but I noticed there wasn't a lot of love shown between them. Did you see him march ahead without bothering to see if Cassie was following?"

"Yes, I did. Cassie is sweet, though. I liked her."

"Thanks for not mentioning Jax. I assume you did that on purpose," said Rhonda.

"I did. The less they know of Jax, the more opportunity Mandy has to make her own choice." I shook my head, worried. "Now that I've met the prospective parents, I understand Mandy's dilemma. Poor kid."

"During my phone conversation with her, Amelia warned me not to interfere," said Rhonda. "I promised we wouldn't."

"It's not our business," I said glumly.

"Let's go say hello to Mandy," said Rhonda with a look of determination on her face I recognized.

"Okay," I answered, too restless to sit still. "Like you, I want to make sure she'll be all right." I shot her a look of warning. "But we have to honor Amelia's wishes."

Rhonda opened the office door, and we headed to Mandy's room.

Along the way, I thought of Angela and Liz and couldn't help being worried for Mandy.

Like Dr. Benson, I wouldn't wish a decision like hers on any young mother. Maybe staying with Jax for a little while would help Mandy understand he truly loved her, and the two of them together would make a great team.

Rhonda knocked on the door.

After waiting several seconds, Mandy came to the door and opened it.

At the sight of us, a breath left her mouth in a puff of air. "Whew! I thought you were Samuel and Cassie. Come on in."

My heart clenched with admiration at the sight of her carefully-groomed in Angela's dress, her hair sparkling, her skin glowing. "They just checked in, so I suspect it will be a few minutes before you see or hear from them," I said. "We just wanted to make sure you're all right."

"I ... I will be," Mandy said, her voice shaking. "I still haven't made up my mind though I might be forced to do it. There's no way I could pay them back for my stay here."

I frowned, confused. "You're not required to pay them back, are you? You said you didn't sign any papers."

"No, I'm not, but I wouldn't feel right about not following through if they pay for everything."

"Take a deep breath," said Rhonda. "Don't get caught up in details like that. If you need to, call us. We're here for you." She studied Mandy. "And Jax is here for you, too. Don't forget him."

I sighed at Rhonda's subtle matchmaking. If it came to a battle of will or wits, Rhonda was better than anyone I knew.

Mandy's shoulders straightened. "I know he'd help me if I asked."

"Good luck!" I said, checking my watch. "We'd better go."

The next day, I was sitting having breakfast with Robbie when my cell rang. Expecting a call from Vaughn, I picked it up. *Tina.* "Hello!" I said, cheerfully.

"Morning," Tina said. "I wanted to give you a call. I'm leaving a day early. Nicholas asked me to come home. Some sort of health problem." She stopped and then continued, her voice growing shaky. "It must be serious, or he wouldn't ask me to come."

"Oh, no! Please let me know how I can help."

"I have a feeling it's related to stress. He's been under a lot of pressure lately over the new film. And while he wouldn't tell me over the phone, I'm guessing the doctor has told him he needs to rest. He's already made arrangements to go to our ranch. I'll meet him there."

"I'm so sorry to hear this. Please keep me informed."

"Explain to Vaughn what's happened, so he'll know that any decisions on filling roles for the movie have most likely been delayed."

"Okay, I will. I'm wishing you the best with everything. 'Sorry we missed having dinner together."

"Me, too. But I'll call. Your friendship means the world to me."

"And to me," I said quietly as the call ended. Tina's husband, Nicholas, was quite a bit older than she, and I worried about her being left alone if anything happened to him. She'd come a long way since her first stay with us, but underneath the glamour and bravado, she was still needy in many ways.

I lifted the phone to call Vaughn, but his special chime was already ringing on the cell in my hand.

"Hi, sweetheart," I said. "I was about to call you. I just heard from Tina. Nicholas is having some sort of health issue, and she wanted me to let you know in case there's a delay in selecting actors for roles."

"Thanks for telling me. I was getting worried about not receiving a call. How's everything down there?"

"I'm sitting here with a darling little boy who wants to say hi," I answered, handing the phone to Robbie who was holding out his hand for it.

"Hi, Daddy!" said Robbie, and I filled with happiness hearing it. Robbie and Vaughn shared a special, close relationship. Funny, how the twists of life could sometimes make something like his situation so sweet.

When they were through, Vaughn and I chatted about his schedule and the Worthingtons' visit to the hotel.

"Don't become too involved with the situation, Ann. Especially if Amelia warned against it," Vaughn said.

"I know. I'll do my best. Talk to you later. Love you."

"Love you back," he said.

After we ended the call, I thought about Mandy. It was up to her to be strong. Aside from offering encouragement, there was nothing either Rhonda or I could do.

I was about to head out to the hotel when Liz called. "Hi,

Mom! Can you do a huge favor for me? Can you cover for me at the store for a few hours today? Rhonda called and suggested I ask Angela to go to lunch and do a little therapy shopping. Apparently, with everything that's going on with Reggie's family, Angela is depressed, but doesn't want Reggie or Katherine to know."

"Poor thing. I've wondered how Angela could manage. Sure, let me check in with Rhonda and Bernie, and I'll let you know when I can get there."

"Thanks. Having to be at the store daily is one reason we're thinking of selling the store or letting our lease go. Chad has already talked to Will about renting space in his building."

"Does he know that Arthur has asked for space there too?"

"No! Oh, boy! A family affair, huh?"

"I don't know how long Arthur will be there. I can't imagine he'll stay here after Katherine passes. He's got his company office in New York."

"Have you seen Katherine recently?" Liz asked. "Angela says she's not doing well at all."

"I haven't seen her for a few days. It's a shock that it's all happening so fast."

"Thanks, Mom, for helping out. Call me before you come."

"Okay, sweetie." As I set down my cell, I was saddened by the news of Angela's depression. She was usually a cheerful person, but I could imagine how difficult her present circumstances were. I was glad Liz was there to help her. They'd always been so close.

After checking in with both Rhonda and Bernie, I was pleased to hear that everything at the hotel was under control. Rhonda had worked with Jean-Luc on a menu for dinner, and Bernie's wife, Annette, would be in charge. At one time, it had been my job to oversee the staff serving dinner in the private dining room where important meetings took place that required absolute discretion. The staff serving those meals was carefully selected by Rhonda and me. Now Bernie took over that task, working with Annette to make sure these VIP dinner meetings went well.

I called Liz to tell her I was on my way.

The center of town was busy with tourists browsing in the upscale shops that lined the main street. Sabal was a unique seaside vacation spot that also was year-round home to people who enjoyed the weather and small-town, casual living.

Bits 'N' Bytes was as cute a storefront as the others lining the street. Chad and Liz had done a great job of dressing the window with interesting things, announcing their selections of electronic games, computers, and services. But their biggest source of income was from Chad's consulting to businesses and people in the area. He'd talked of perhaps hiring someone to help him, and if he did that, managing the store wouldn't be as important. I could understand Liz's desire to do business differently.

Liz was talking to a gentleman but greeted me with a nod as I stepped inside the store.

The man finished paying for his purchase and then, with a smile at me, left the store.

"Busy?" I asked.

Liz shook her head. "Not really. He was just picking up a new charger. Thanks for coming. Angela was ecstatic when I called her and told her what her mother and I had planned."

"It'll be good for you both to have some time together," I said. "Go and have fun. Still feeling all right?"

Liz shrugged. "A little tired, sometimes queasy, but I'm

not complaining." She placed her hand on her stomach. "Thanks for buying me these pants. They're so comfortable."

"You're wearing them already?"

"Why not?" she smiled. "I'm excited about it."

I hugged her. "Well, enjoy it. You have a long way to go."

We smiled at one another and then she turned away, grabbed her purse, and said, "Guess I'd better be on my way. Angela told me to hurry up and get there. She can't wait to escape."

I waved her off and went to the back office to stow my things.

At the sound of voices, I hurried back to the store.

An older man with gray hair, wearing a black shirt, tan slacks, and tasseled loafers, was looking at a display of an iPad. Next to him was a young woman with blond hair who was talking quietly to him.

He looked up at me and smiled. "Mind if I poke around while my bride goes next door to shop?"

I blinked in surprise as the woman turned to me. Her enhanced breasts were all but exposed in the tight, V-neck, sleeveless top she was wearing. She smiled at me and said, "I told Syd computers are boring, that I saw several things next door I'd like to buy."

"Go ahead," the man said. "Just leave me some money in the account. We're going to The Beach House Hotel for dinner."

The young woman pressed close to him and gave him a kiss on the cheek. "Don't worry, honey. You'll like what I buy."

He smiled at her. "Have fun. I'll be here or nearby when you're done."

"*Ciao*," she said, all but running out of the store.

He watched her leave with an indulgent smile while my

thoughts flew back in time to my ex, Robert, and Kandie, the voluptuous receptionist in our office. *Why were some men so stupid?*

"I heard you mention The Beach House Hotel. I think you'll like your meal there. Where are you staying?" I asked him.

"We're staying at The Sand Castle. It's supposed to be the latest and greatest. Suzie insisted we stay there. It's all right, but we won't come back."

"Oh? Why?" I said, pumping him for information.

He gave me a sheepish grin. "Guess I'm getting old, but I'd rather be in a quieter place and relax. Suzie thinks The Sand Castle is what she calls 'rad,' but the hotel seems a little tacky to me."

"How's the service?" I asked.

"Okay, nothing to write home about. Not for the cost," he said. "I forgot my iPad at home and thought I should look into getting another. Can you give me any advice?"

"A little," I said. "My son-in-law is the expert, but he sold me this one here, and I love it."

We talked about the iPad he was interested in, and I realized how much information I'd picked up listening to Chad and Liz talk about certain products.

A little while later, he left with the new iPad. I called Rhonda, told her the story, and asked her to see that he and his bride were given an excellent table and received our usual top-notch service.

"Glad you called. I'll take care of it. Also, when I spoke to Terri to thank her for the nice newspaper article, she told me Aubrey is furious with her, and that she's been directed by her editor to do another article about a different hotel, so it doesn't appear as if she favors one over the other."

"Interesting," I said. "Maybe that will calm things down

between Aubrey's hotel and ours."

"Let's hope so. Are you prepared to have a nice dinner with the Worthingtons? They've been pretty quiet here. I did see them on the beach with Mandy earlier but haven't seen them since. I don't dare go down to Mandy's room."

"Neither one of us can," I said. "After they've gone, we'll have the chance, but we can't give any indication of being involved."

Rhonda sighed. "You're right. But I hate to think of what that girl is going through. Is Mars in retrograde or something? Life is sure feeling complicated."

"I don't know anything about the alignment of planets, but it does seem as if things are very unsettled right now. But one thing at a time. Right?"

"Yeah, I guess. Will told me Chad is going to move into his office building sometime soon. Do you remember what it was like when we first met Will? He was so shy, so quiet. I never would've guessed things would work out the way they have."

A chuckle escaped me. "A few leaps of faith were involved."

"And still are," said Rhonda. "See you this evening. Everything is quiet here at the hotel. I met with Lorraine about the wedding coming up this weekend, and it's under control. Everything but the weather, that is. It's likely to be a rainy weekend."

"Or worse if Hurricane Alison decides to arrive," I said, and then wished I could take the words back. The hurricane was not projected to hit the U.S. coastline, but the idea of any possible tropical storm was worrisome. For our business as much as anything else.

A customer arrived and I quickly ended the call.

"May I help you?" I asked.

"Just looking," the man answered pleasantly.

"Sure, just take your time."

While he looked around, I checked the newspaper for movie listings. While Vaughn was away, I sometimes liked to take in a movie with Dorothy or Cyndi, my next-door neighbor.

"Excuse me," the man said. "Can you recommend a nice place for dinner?"

"Actually, I can. You might want to try the dining room at The Beach House Hotel. Their chef, Jean-Luc Rodin is well-known in the area."

"Thank you. Funny, when I asked at the front desk at The Sand Castle, that name didn't come up."

I gave him my best smile. "Well, I gladly give you my advice. Reservations for their gourmet restaurant are required though, so I'd call right away."

"Thanks. You wouldn't happen to have a menu, would you?"

"I do have one. We keep several on hand for visitors." I pulled it out from beneath the counter and handed it to him. "Those are just the basics. Jean-Luc prepares his meals with fresh ingredients, so the specials change daily."

"M-m-m, looks delicious. Thank you. I write a food column for my local newspaper up north. I'll be sure to give them a call."

"I feel certain you'll enjoy it," I said, hiding my anger at the underhanded way the Sand Castle was holding back information on our hotel restaurant. I knew Aubrey wouldn't play fair, but this pettiness had become ridiculous.

CHAPTER SEVENTEEN

L ater that afternoon, Liz burst into the store late carrying an armful of packages.

"Did you have a nice time?" I asked, knowing the answer from the happy glow on her face.

"It was so nice! Angela and I talked and talked. And then we shopped, just like old times. I've missed her so much!"

"Did you get some cute things?" I asked looking at the shopping bags.

"Mostly undergarments and things Angela suggested I'll want in time. She thinks I'm having a big baby. But then, Chad is over six feet, and I'm taller than she is, so it makes sense."

"Well, I'm glad you had fun together. Now, I'd better go. Things are quiet here. I sold an iPad and some charging cords. Everything is listed for you."

Liz hugged me. "Thanks, Mom! I really appreciate it!"

"You're welcome. Now, I'm off to get ready for dinner with the Worthingtons. First, I have to spend some time with your brother. I promised to swim with him when I get home."

"I think he's going to make a great swimmer on the local school team when he's a little older."

"Me, too. You and he both move well in the water. Guess you get that from your father."

"I wonder what he'd think of him, me, you, if he were still alive."

"There'd be a few surprises, I'm sure. Well, I'm off. Talk to you later."

I drove home eager to have some time with Robbie. Elena had picked him up from school and would stay with him tonight after his dinner, but I looked forward to having some time with him. He was growing fast.

Elena greeted me and left to go to one of her classes. "I'll be back in plenty of time for you to leave for dinner at the hotel," she said as she walked to her car.

Trudy jumped around my feet, and I leaned over to pet her. I noticed a few gray hairs around her muzzle, picked her up, and hugged her close. Originally Bernie's dog, she'd quickly become ours. I don't know what we'd do if she ever left us.

Robbie ran into the kitchen. "Hi, Mom! Are you ready for a swim? Elena showed me a new trick."

"I'll change my clothes as quickly as I can," I promised and left him to put on my bathing suit.

When I came out of my room, Robbie grabbed my hand and tugged me outside. There had been a time when he was leery of the pool, but now we could hardly keep him out of it. After Vaughn announced that only excellent swimmers could be on the sailboat, Robbie became determined to earn that status.

Outside, the sun was heading for the horizon at a leisurely pace. It would be hours before sundown, but I liked this time of day when everyone's pace seemed to slow. Unless you were an active six-year-old.

Robbie jumped into the pool and turned to me with a smile. "I can walk on my hands in the pool. Want to see?"

"Of course," I said, grinning. He loved to show off his latest tricks, and I was pleased to see him so happy, so comfortable with us. Ever since Mandy had asked me about Robbie being adopted, I'd thought about our taking him in—

a frightened little boy who wasn't used to routines or even a lot of love. Seeing him now, like this, my heart burst with love. At those times when one of Robert's expressions crossed Robbie's face, startling me, I tried to remember the best times my ex and I had enjoyed and vowed to always be a good mother to Robbie.

I clapped when Robbie came to the surface of the pool and then I jumped in to join him. The stress of the last few weeks lifted away from me as I moved my limbs through the water in a steady crawl. Robbie swam alongside me like an eager puppy. Trudy stood guard above us, watching anxiously. I turned over and floated on my back, staring up at the blue sky, missing Vaughn.

As if knowing my thoughts, Robbie asked, "When is Daddy coming home?"

"Soon, I hope." So much of Vaughn's timing depending on the length of shooting each episode. If everyone knew their lines it went quickly. Thankfully, Darla was a much better-prepared actress than Lily Dorio had ever been.

When both Robbie and I had had enough swimming, we got out of the pool and sat for a few minutes drying off in the warm air.

"How is school going?" I asked. "Did you bring home more papers to show me?"

His face lit up. "I got two gold stars and one silver star so far this week."

"Excellent. Why don't we go inside, and you can show me?"

Robbie raced ahead with excitement.

Smiling, I wondered how long his enthusiasm for school would last. He was a bright boy, but he'd rather be outside playing than inside doing schoolwork.

While I fixed Robbie dinner, he chatted about school and the latest space station he'd built with Brett, the boy next door, who was his best friend. They'd gone from playing space cowboys to more serious play.

Elena arrived, and after offering her dinner, I left her with Robbie and went into my bedroom to shower and get ready for dinner at the hotel with the Worthingtons.

Standing in the shower, the stream of warm water felt delicious on my skin. I closed my eyes and enjoyed the way my body loosened from the worry of spending time with the senator and his wife. I didn't know why, but I was concerned about the dinner with them. I wanted to like them, but the situation with Mandy and the baby had red flags all over it. I'd had enough problems getting pregnant and carrying Liz that I knew the longing Cassie must feel for a child of her own. And Mandy was a nice, healthy young woman who would most likely produce a healthy baby. But a nagging thought kept circling in my mind. If Mandy had had different parents, this situation might never have occurred.

I got out of the shower and wrapped a towel around me. Vaughn had said not to get involved, but the truth was both Rhonda and I already were.

I dried my hair and studied the results in the mirror. My smooth, dark locks hung to my shoulders, the tips curling under naturally. After lining my blue eyes with a dark-brown color, I swiped a subtle beige tint across my lids, bringing out the blue in them. Mascara was next. Satisfied I'd done what I could in a most natural way, I turned away.

The linen dress I chose to wear was a light-seafoam green. Any idea of ever owning a beige dress had disappeared after first meeting Rhonda. She'd looked me over and told me not to be so beige. She was right of course, but at the time, her remark had stung. And I'd never worn beige since.

Properly dressed and bejeweled, I kissed Robbie goodnight and told Elena I wouldn't be late.

Driving up to the front of the hotel, I took a moment to admire the tiny sparkling lights in the landscaping along the front, highlighting the pink hibiscus blossoms. On either side of the double wooden doors, huge pots held small palm trees whose trunks were wound with similar twinkling lights, adding a touch of magic to the welcoming front entrance.

I turned my car over to a valet and climbed the stairs, smiling at the doorman who stood ready to welcome me inside.

"Thank you," I said and stepped into the front hallway. At the far end where the bar was located, the lobby was filled with people sitting in comfortable chairs, enjoying a drink, or sitting beyond the open sliding doors in chairs on the outside lanai. In front of me, standing and looking out at the pool area, I recognized Samuel and Cassie Worthington. I noticed they stood apart and wondered, not for the first time, what kind of marriage they had.

Rhonda walked into the lobby from the back of the house wearing a tangerine-orange caftan decorated with flowers at the hem and on one shoulder. Colorful as always, she drew attention as she waved at me and then called out to the Worthingtons.

At the sound of her voice, they turned to her with smiles, and then noticing me, they walked toward me, Samuel a few steps ahead of Cassie.

I returned their smiles. "Good evening! It's a beautiful night."

"Have you had an enjoyable day?" Rhonda asked.

"Oh yes," said Cassie. "We met with Mandy for breakfast, and then I spent some time at the pool reading." She turned to her husband. "Sam finds it hard to relax so he called a friend and played some golf."

"Business, not pleasure," said Samuel crisply.

"In politics, there's never a time to relax, is there?" said Rhonda.

"I guess you could say that," said Samuel. "I'm working on a book deal."

"Oh, interesting. Will it be about politics or something else?" I asked, leading them toward the private dining room.

"Something else. We'll see," said Samuel, clearly not wanting to talk about it.

Annette was standing by the door. "Welcome," she said smiling. "I know you're about to have a delicious dinner. If there's anything at all that I and my staff can do for you, please let me know."

"Thank you," I said, and made introductions.

"You look lovely," Annette said to Cassie before taking hold of her elbow and ushering her inside.

I studied Cassie. As I'd first thought there was a resemblance to Jackie O. Faint, but there, with her graceful moves, Mona Lisa smile, and natural elegance. Her dress was a simple white one that I knew cost more than monthly salaries for many. I'd looked up some information about her online and learned she'd come from a wealthy family and was the beloved only child of a man who'd made millions in the tech industry. I couldn't help but wonder if that's what had attracted Samuel to her. They certainly didn't exhibit any kind of physical attraction.

In the corner of the dining room, a small bar had been set up. Drink orders were taken, and then, sipping cocktails, we stood talking to one another.

"What is it like being married to Vaughn Sanders?" Cassie asked me. "A bit different from being married to a senator, I should imagine."

"A little," I admitted. "Vaughn has only to concentrate on his work, while Samuel has to do that and then worry about the ramifications of his choices and how it affects everyone else and their votes."

"There's a lot of actor in him," said Cassie, wryly. "But he does want to please his constituents."

I gazed over at Rhonda talking to him. She said something, and they both burst out laughing.

"You and your business partner must be so proud of all you've done, creating a beautiful hotel like this. I admire you," said Cassie.

"Thanks. It hasn't been easy. There are some in the neighborhood who like to cause trouble, but we're able to handle them."

Cassie smiled. "I believe we might have met one of them this morning on our walk with Mandy. His name was Brock Goodwin. Does it ring a bell?"

"More like a clanging sound against my head," I said. "As president of the Neighborhood Association, he feels he has much more power than he's been given."

"Who are you talking about?" asked Rhonda joining us.

"Someone named Brock Goodwin," Cassie responded.

"The biggest effin' pain I know," said Rhonda. "Did you tell her, Annie?"

"Indeed, I did," I said, noting Rhonda's language didn't bother Cassie or Samuel at all.

"We all have our non-favorites to deal with," said Cassie. "Don't we, darling?"

He grinned. "Yes, we do."

Annette came over to us and said quietly, "If you'll take your seats, we can start dinner."

I sat next to Cassie, facing Samuel and Rhonda. "I hope you enjoy the meal. Jean-Luc does a fabulous job for us."

"Jean-Luc Rodin?" Cassie said. "Several years ago, I ate at his restaurant in Paris. How lucky you are to have him here."

"Very lucky," said Rhonda. "He wasn't quite ready to retire and has helped us tremendously from the beginning."

We sat quietly while the soup course was placed before us—a mushroom broth with a cheesy crouton floating on top.

"Yummy," Cassie declared after taking a spoonful. "So simple, so delicious."

"Nothing too rich," I agreed, knowing what was coming next.

After making sure no allergies were involved, we'd chosen red snapper with a lobster cream sauce. Because Cassie's family had a summer home in Maine, we thought having lobster in some form would be a special treat for her.

The fish was served on a bed of spinach with enough sauce that it didn't overpower the sweet snapper. A side of lemon rice rounded out the pretty presentation.

Rhonda and I kept the conversation going and listened to one story after another about life in D. C.

The salad course came and went, and then dessert was served. Jean-Luc had scooped out the insides of oranges and filled them with a light lemon-mint sorbet. A trio of cookies was placed beside the oranges, including a chocolate almond one that was my favorite. As we sat over dessert and coffee, the topic of Mandy finally came up.

"Thank you so much for taking such good care of Amanda," said Cassie. "She seems very happy here, and that's important." She smiled at me. "She loves working with your daughter, Liz. She told us she'd like to stay in the area following the birth of the baby."

"We'd love it if she did," I said. "Liz and Mandy work well together and have plans for expanding the business Liz has started."

"What about her friend Jax?" Samuel said, frowning. "I understand he's working for you."

"That's right," said Rhonda. "The timing was perfect, and he's an outstanding addition to our staff."

"Amanda still hasn't made a final commitment to us regarding her baby," said Samuel. "I'm disappointed and a bit angry, but I think we can manage to help her change her mind. We can give that baby every material thing she is unable to do. An excellent education, camps, foreign travel, and the advantages that come from my position."

"And my money," said Cassie, raising an eyebrow at him.

"And if she decides she cannot give up her baby?" I asked.

Cassie and Samuel looked at one another.

Her eyes brimming with tears, Cassie turned to me. "I pray she won't choose to do that. We've tried for several years for a baby. This seemed like a perfect solution to our desires and a way to give her a fresh start."

"I understand," I said. "Do you have other options?"

"We have a source in Washington who might be able to help us with a Russian child," said Cassie. "But it's not the same as having an American baby."

Rhonda and I exchanged silent glances. I prayed Rhonda would keep quiet. We both knew children everywhere needed homes.

"We wish you all the luck in the world with any child you're able to adopt," I said. "My son, Robbie, is adopted under unusual circumstances. It's been a joy to have him be part of our family."

"Yes, Mandy told us about him," said Samuel. "Any influence you can place on her would be appreciated."

My back stiffened. "You know I'm unable to do that. At Amelia Swanson's request, we're keeping Mandy here, seeing she has her doctor appointments and eats well. But aside from that, we must be unbiased."

"It's in your best interest that we do so," said Rhonda.

"I'm sorry. I spoke out of turn," said Samuel. "We appreciate your willingness to help both Mandy and Amelia."

"It's such a shame this happened to a nice girl like her," said Cassie. "I understand her parents have disowned her."

"Yes, that's what we've been told," I said. I wasn't about to mention Mandy's true feelings toward Jax. I had a suspicion Samuel might approach him for help, something I knew Jax wouldn't want to give.

Annette came into the room. "May I offer you anything else?"

"No, thank you," said Cassie. "Everything was delicious."

"Yes, very nice. Thank you," said Samuel. He got to his feet. "We'd better call it a night. Something has come up, and we're returning to D. C. tomorrow. We've got an early morning flight."

"I'll be sure to tell Amelia how hospitable you've been," said Cassie, standing and holding out her hand to me as I rose.

I shook it. "I wish the best for you, no matter what Mandy decides."

Cassie looked to Samuel.

"She more or less owes us to follow through," he said.

"Good night," Rhonda said, shaking hands with him and turning to Cassie with a smile. "I'm sure you'll have a family one day."

Cassie smiled. "I hope so. Thanks for a lovely stay."

Rhonda and I walked them to the stairway leading to the Presidential Suite, and then we headed to our office.

Rhonda closed the door behind us and took a seat at her desk.

I sat facing her. "Well, what do you think?"

"I pray Mandy keeps her baby. The way Cassie and Samuel talked, any child of theirs will be someone who gets all the material things but none of the love Mandy and Jax have for each other and for that baby."

"I watched them closely, waiting for a spark of affection between them, but they acted as if their marriage was a business deal, not a love match. I got the same feeling about their adopting a baby."

"Me, too. I know we're not supposed to be involved, but how can we stay quiet?" said Rhonda.

"Without saying anything, we can make sure Mandy and Jax have the opportunity to build their relationship."

"Mandy will be moving in with Jax. Maybe something will happen then," said Rhonda. "It didn't take Will and me long to discover the joy of finding each other."

"Maybe the four of us should spend more time with them. Vaughn promised an afternoon of sailing to Jax. Will could join them, talk to him about getting up the courage to propose to her, no matter what she says about being just a friend. We both know she loves him."

Rhonda rose and clapped me on the back. "Gosh, Annie. Now you're sounding like me. I like you as a matchmaker."

I laughed. "If it works, I'm going to be very happy."

"Speaking of that, I'd better head home. Tonight, I intend to enjoy my husband. Just thinking of it makes me horny."

"TMI," I said laughing. Rhonda was all about too much information.

CHAPTER EIGHTEEN

The next morning, I headed to the hotel to pick up Mandy for her doctor's appointment. I was eager to see how the Worthingtons' visit had affected her. It was such a complicated, heart-rending situation.

She was waiting for me outside the hotel entrance when I pulled up to it. I studied her and drew in a long breath. Her shoulders were slumped, and she was staring down at the ground. I beeped my horn to get her attention, and the look she gave me was startled.

"Hi, there!" I said brightly, hoping to inject a little cheer into the quiet as Mandy slid into the passenger seat.

"Hi," she said without animation.

I reached over to clasp her hand and noticed her nails were ragged with chewing. "What's this?" I asked, lifting her hand.

Mandy made a face. "I chew my nails when I get nervous."

"Oh, sweetie. Let's talk. What happened?" I asked as I drove away from the entrance and parked the car in a parking spot farther away.

I faced her. "Now, tell me what's going on."

She let out a sigh. "I realize I have to give up my baby."

"Oh?" I held my breath.

She swallowed hard and nodded. "Yes, Senator Worthington told me all the things they could do for her—like a top education, summer camps, and other things. And then his wife, Cassie, showed me pictures of some cute little dresses she's already bought." Tears filled her eyes. "She can live like a princess with them."

"Material things don't necessarily make a happy life," I said, trying to be neutral but unable to be quiet.

"I love my baby. I really do ..." Mandy caressed her abdomen.

"Time may help you sort things out," I said.

She looked at me, her cheeks wet with tears. "That's just it. I'm running out of time."

I squeezed her hand. "One thing at a time. We'll get you to Dr. Benson's, and then while you're with Liz at the store, we'll move your things into Jax's apartment. Being with him might make things easier for you."

Mandy sniffed and nodded. "He always makes me feel better."

I studied her. "That says a lot about him. Don't be afraid of that."

"I know," she said quietly.

Later, after dropping off Mandy at the store and checking in with Liz, I headed back to the hotel deep in thought. I don't know what, if anything, Dr. Benson said to Mandy, but she seemed a different person, more confident.

When I entered the office, I saw a note from Rhonda on my desk. I picked it up.

Katherine isn't doing well and asked to see me. I'll talk to you later.

I headed down to Mandy's room. Living with Jax might help her decide about the baby. With him, she might not feel so burdened by the Worthingtons' generosity.

The room was tidy when I entered it. She'd already packed most of her belongings. I called housekeeping, and together a staff member and I loaded Mandy's belongings, including drinks and other items from the small refrigerator, onto a cart and headed to Jax's apartment.

There, we hung up Mandy's few items of clothing, placed her suitcase on a rack in the bedroom that contained two queen beds, and put her food items into the refrigerator or a kitchen cupboard. Seeing how little food they had, I decided to go to the grocery store and surprise them with some basics.

I'd just returned to the office when Rhonda entered, plopped down in her desk chair, put her head in her hands, and sobbed.

I went over to her and rubbed her back. "What is it?" I asked softly.

"Katherine wanted to see me. She's not doing so well with this frickin' disease. Gawd! She looks terrible." Rhonda sat up and dabbed at her eyes with the tissues I handed her. "Anyway, she wanted me to make sure her grandchildren wouldn't forget her. She gave me some jewelry to hold onto for Sally. She thought it would mean more if it came to her through me."

Fresh tears stopped Rhonda from speaking.

"Such a sweet gesture," I said, remembering how mean Katherine had been in the past.

"We sat and talked until Katherine grew too tired. She told me all kinds of things about her life that she wanted her grandchildren to know about her. I made notes as she spoke and promised to type them up to put in a book for them. She knows Angela is too busy to do this, and I'm happy to help."

Rhonda stood and looked out the window. When she turned back to me, her expression was full of sorrow. "You never know what someone's life is really like. Katherine had an unhappy childhood with a pushy single mother who eventually married for money and insisted Katherine act as if she hadn't grown up poor. It twisted her, in a way, made her act superior when she didn't feel that way at all."

"That's sad," I said. "And it caused so much hurt in your family. What about Arthur? He apologized to me. Have he and Katherine settled things between them?"

"I think so. He's being very attentive." Rhonda sighed. "It's too bad it's taken her illness to change things around. Arthur is even thinking of keeping a small office here in Will's building as a permanent thing, though he'd spend most of his time in New York."

"A permanent office? That's interesting."

"Yeah, he and Will have a truce goin' on. Will is such a phenomenal guy," said Rhonda, taking a seat at her desk. "I'm very proud of him for all he's doing for Arthur."

I faced her. "I was with Mandy this morning."

"Oh? How is she?" Rhonda said. "I don't have a good feeling about that situation."

"The poor girl is distraught. The Worthingtons have made it clear they could give her daughter a better life than she ever could. It's eating away at Mandy because she loves her baby."

"That's so unfair," said Rhonda, pressing her lips together.

"I tried to stay out of it," I said, "but I did say that material things didn't always bring happiness."

"You're so nice, Annie. I would've said a whole lot more than that."

"While she's working with Liz at the store, I arranged to have all her things moved from her room to Jax's apartment. She admitted he makes her feel safe. And if she realizes what a sweet life they could have together, she might be able to choose to keep the baby."

"I hope so," grumbled Rhonda. "They're both coming to dinner at my house tomorrow. I made sure to set it up. You're invited too, if you'd like."

"Thanks, but I think I'll opt-out so that you have a better connection without my interfering."

"Okay. Hopefully, I can have a private talk with Mandy, and Will can speak man-to-man with Jax." She stood. "It's been a grueling day. I'm going to go home. I have a sudden need to be with my kids."

"I understand. I'll stick around here and make sure everything is set for the Restaurant Association reception tonight. I promised Bernie I'd make an appearance."

"Great. I don't think I could face it tonight," said Rhonda. She gave me a quick hug. "See you tomorrow."

I watched her leave, respecting her wish to have time with her family. Saying farewell to someone like Katherine and doing those favors for her was taking a toll on Rhonda. But then Rhonda's soft heart was easily bruised.

That night, as I was getting ready for bed, Vaughn called.

A wave of happiness washed through me. "How are you?" I said, wiggling my toes with contentment at hearing his voice.

"Fine, fine. A change in plans. Tina called me. I'm flying to California for a couple of days to read for the part in the movie. I've agreed to stay with Tina and Nicholas and will fly back to New York before making my way home."

"How exciting! I know how much you want that role." No way would I show my disappointment at not seeing him soon.

"What's going on down there?" Vaughn asked, and I gave

him an update on all the news. "Will you do me a favor and call Katherine tomorrow? It would mean a lot to her. She's fading fast."

"I'd be happy to do that for her. I'll make a note and take care of it before I leave for the airport. And tell Robbie next time I'm home we'll go for a sail, and for him to keep up the swimming. Speaking of that, do me a favor, Ann, and make sure all items on the boat are tucked away and secure. The chances of Hurricane Allison brushing the east coast of Florida are growing. Even if it swings away, we'll likely have tropical wind and rain in Sabal."

"Oh, right. Bernie is keeping an eye on the hotel. I'll check the deck furniture here."

"Thanks. I'd better go. I love you. I'll call you tomorrow morning after I talk to Katherine."

"Okay, love you, too." I clicked off the call and sighed. Talking with Vaughn on a regular schedule kept me centered. He was a kind listener and understood me well enough to know what to say to make me feel better. Especially when it concerned someone like Mandy.

The next day was bright and sunny. Worries about any storms seemed like overkill, but I dutifully moved the pool furniture closer to the house inside the screened lanai.

At the hotel, when I found Bernie, he was discussing the weather with the head of housekeeping, warning her that her team might be called to action in the next day or two to help with furniture on the guest balconies.

"Anything else on the agenda today that I should know about?" I asked.

He smiled. "Pretty quiet. The weekend wedding is under control. But nothing out of the ordinary."

"Good. Let's keep it that way."

I went outside to find Manny and Jax to make sure they were aware of the weather and to check with them about anything they might need. I found them working together, trimming some of the larger shrubberies.

"*Buenos dias!*" I called to them, and they both turned around and smiled at me. It was a relief to see Manny pleased with Jax's help. He was getting too old to do as much work as he'd been doing by himself.

I walked over to them, and we talked about any branches that might fall or damage that could occur.

"Don't worry, Ann," said Manny. "We'll take care of everything. It's just a tropical storm."

"I guess y'all are used to it," said Jax. "But we've got things under control, right?" He looked to Manny.

Manny nodded. "*Si. Todo bueno.*"

"*Todo bueno,*" Jax dutifully repeated. Learning Spanish was part of his agreement with Manny.

"Jax? May I talk to you for a minute?"

He nodded and stepped away from Manny. "Is this about Mandy?"

"Yes. I'm worried about her. She's so conflicted right now that it's not healthy for the baby."

"We talked about it, but she's not willing to make a decision. It's so much more than deciding the baby's future. She knows how much I love her and want us to be together. I'd like to, but I haven't asked her to marry me. Not yet. Not until I'm sure of her answer."

"I'm glad she has you to help her. For what it's worth, I think you'd make a great couple."

"Thanks. That means a lot." He shook his head. "She has this idea that she'd be hurting me if we ever married. It's those parents of hers. They've made her believe she's an awful person. And not just because of the baby, but also because she chose to go to Washington D.C. for her internship. Instead of being the honor that she thought it was, everything blew up in her face." His nostrils flared with anger. "Her parents told her she was evil."

"God! That must be so devastating. We all have to keep telling her otherwise."

"One of the reasons she's afraid to keep the baby is that she's worried her parents are right, and her baby will never be happy because of her."

My stomach churned. "Maybe it's time for another session with Dr. Holmes. I'll give Mandy a call and ask her if she needs a ride."

"That would be great," said Jax. "Once she stops thinking about her parents, she's okay. She tried to call them yesterday. That's why she was so upset last night."

"I'd better not detain you any longer," I said, aware of Manny standing by. "I think instead of calling Mandy, I'll stop by at the apartment."

"Okay. Thanks," said Jax giving me a salute as he trotted across the grass toward Manny.

Upset by all I'd heard, I crossed the lawn to the building, climbed the stairs to the second floor of the building, and knocked on the door.

"Who is it?" Mandy called from inside.

"It's Ann. Can I talk to you for a minute?"

The door opened and Mandy motioned me inside. "Hi. C'mon in."

"Thanks. I wanted to check in with you. I know you've had a couple of tough days and wondered if I might help."

The worry lines on her brow softened. "I just got off the phone with Dr. Holmes. I'm due for my regular visit and wanted to make sure she'd scheduled me."

"Oh, I'll be happy to drive you there."

"That would be nice," Mandy said. "I appreciate it. You, Rhonda, and Liz have all been very kind to me. It makes me feel special."

"You are special, and we want you to be happy," I said.

Mandy's face crumpled. She pulled a tissue from her pants pocket and dabbed at her eyes. "I'm so mixed up. Everyone except my parents seems to like me. Jax even says he loves me. Why can't I believe it?"

I placed a gentle hand on her shoulder and studied her. "Maybe it's time to let the bad stuff go. Even if it doesn't seem normal to you."

"I'm pretty sure Dr. Holmes will say pretty much the same thing. I keep thinking of being a parent and my own parents thinking I shouldn't even consider it because of who I am, that someone else should raise my baby."

"I'm sure Dr. Holmes would have a better answer than mine. Have you ever thought that they are the ones who have issues, that they are the bad parents? Honestly, I've never heard of such cruelty."

Mandy's jaw dropped. "You think they're cruel?"

"Yes. Without a doubt. Don't you?"

"They tried to be good parents. I'm the problem, despite everything they did. At least that's what they tell me," said Mandy. "That's why I don't think I'd be a good mother to my baby. I love her so much I'd never want to hurt her."

The words I wanted to say got stuck in my throat. I knew if I spoke, I might say something I shouldn't. I drew a breath. "What time is your appointment?"

"Eleven o'clock. Then I'm going to help Liz. She got a lot of new orders in." Mandy's lips curved. "If I stay in the area, I want to continue working for her. She wants me to."

"That would be fantastic. Lots of things to look forward

to," I said hoping for a more cheerful note. "I'll meet you in front of the hotel at quarter to eleven. See you then."

We exchanged quick hugs.

"Thank you so much," said Mandy giving me a shaky smile.

"You're welcome." I was so distressed over her situation I couldn't wait to get out of there and privately let off steam.

I was at work in the office when Vaughn called. "Just wanted to let you know I talked to Katherine." His voice caught. "She said goodbye to me and thanked me for saying her name on the show, and the note I sent. It sounds like it's not going to be much longer. A Hospice nurse was there when I called."

"Oh, dear! I'd better call Angela and find out what's going on," I said. "I'm glad you had the chance to speak to her."

"Me, too," Vaughn said. "I'll call you later. I'll let you know how things go."

"Good luck. I know how important this is to you. I know you'll do a great job. You told me you really connected with the character."

"Thanks," said Vaughn, and I could hear his nervousness.

After the call ended, I immediately phoned Angela.

"Hi, Ann," she said, and I could tell she'd been crying.

"What's going on? Vaughn told me a nurse from Hospice was there."

"Katherine has taken a turn for the worse. We just want to make sure she's comfortable. We've been talking quite a bit, and she seems at peace with her situation. She and Arthur have resolved things between them. He's having a hard time thinking of letting her go. It's such a shame."

"How's Reggie?" I asked. Even with all the difficulties of

defying his parents by marrying Angela and moving to Florida, he clearly loved them.

"Reggie is having a hard time. I suggested he speak with Barbara Holmes, and he's agreed to go. He has some issues with his father that need to be addressed. Honestly, Ann, this has been such a difficult time."

"Call me anytime, and we can talk about it. And if you need to get out of the house, I can pick you up and take you to lunch."

"Thanks. That sounds fabulous. Maybe in the next day or two," Angela said, her voice wobbling.

"Talk to you later, sweetie. I love you." I ended the call, saddened all over again.

I decided to take a walk on the beach to settle my emotions. I wrote a note for Rhonda, who'd left to pick up Willow from pre-school for a dentist appointment and headed outside.

The hurricane that everyone had been talking about was expected to graze the east coast of Florida in a matter of hours. The sky was bright blue, but to the east, a band of gray clouds was heading our way. The wind had picked up, and the agitated waves rolling into shore were crowned with a ruffled appearance. I thought of my promises to Vaughn and decided to go home after dropping off Mandy to Dr. Holmes so I could check the boat and the lanai for objects that needed to be stashed away.

As I walked, the wind tousled my hair, lifting it from my shoulders. The breeze felt pleasant against my skin, and I told myself to let my worries go, that time would take care of them with or without me.

The waves smacked against the sand like an angry slap instead of its usual kiss. Shorebirds raced along the lacy edge of the water dodging clumps of seaweed deposited there earlier, seeming frantic to get food before the storm.

My skirt whipped against my legs, but I stood my ground in the shallow water, looking out at the continual movement, finding solace there. Life would go on, I told myself, as it was meant to be.

I heard someone behind me and turned to see Brock.

"I thought I saw you heading down here," said Brock. "I was at the hotel having a late breakfast, checking the competition. Looks like we're about to get the back end of Hurricane Allison. Hope The Beach House Hotel doesn't get much damage being so close to the water."

The insincerity in his voice made me fist my hands. *Could he be more annoying?* I took a moment and then asked, "What's going on with The Sand Castle? Anything new?"

"Business is booming in spite of Terri Thomas's article on Tina Marks. How much did you pay either one of them for doing it?"

"Really?" I said, shaking my head. "You're going there?"

"You have to admit it was a slap to The Sand Castle," said Brock, letting his gaze rest on my skirt billowing in the wind.

I gathered it as best I could. "I'd better go in and see that our guests are comfortable. See you later." I turned and walked away from him.

He ran up to me. "We're going to turn around the property. Just wait and see."

I faced him. "Turn it around? I thought you were doing a booming business."

"Any business can improve." His face grew red, and he shuffled the toes of his foot in the sand, and I realized he'd misspoken.

"Goodbye, Brock." I moved away from him at a fast clip, grateful he decided not to follow me.

As I entered the hotel, Rhonda met me. "Was that Brock

you were talking to?"

"Yes. He made a slip of the tongue when he told me they were going to turn around The Sand Castle. He'd already said their business was booming."

Rhonda clucked her tongue. "That frickin' liar. With him, believe the worst, which means that little sandbox hotel isn't such a great playground after all."

"How'd Willow do with the dentist?" I asked, changing the subject. Rhonda's cheeks were already flushed with anger over Brock.

Rhonda chuckled. "She was brave until she was alone in the car with me. Willow doesn't like anyone to think she's a baby. One of the kids at school called her a baby once and she's never forgotten it."

"She's such a darling," I gushed. From the moment I first saw her, I'd always loved Willow. She was such an irresistible blend of gentle, calm Will and boisterous Rhonda.

"Let's check in with Bernie about the preparations for the storm," said Rhonda.

"Okay, then I have to drive Mandy to see Dr. Holmes. These past two days have been very difficult for her."

"That poor kid," said Rhonda. "What a tough decision, made even tougher because Samuel and Cassie are definitely not in love."

"I don't know how much she sees of that," I said. "She's concerned because they've told her about all the things that she's unable to do for the baby herself."

"I don't like it," grumbled Rhonda as we made our way through the hotel.

We knocked and opened the door to Bernie's office. He looked up at us and smiled. "Come in. I suppose you're here about the storm. I just checked the weather, and Allison is doing more than grazing the coastline, which means the rain and wind will be heavier here. I've put housekeeping and Manny and Jax on alert. We'll begin storing furniture soon."

"Great," I said. "I'll be taking some time myself to take care of things at my house."

Rhonda frowned. "I'd better talk to Lorraine Grace about the plans for the upcoming wedding."

"We'll have to make some changes if the vegetation suffers and the rain lingers," said Bernie.

Rhonda nodded and waved as she left us.

I went to my car and pulled it in front of the building holding Jax's apartment.

Mandy walked out of it to greet me. "Thanks for driving me."

"No problem," I said smiling. "It's going to get quite windy, so I'm going home after I drop you off. But I'll still pick you up after your appointment and take you to Liz's store."

"Thanks," said Mandy, her voice quiet.

I sighed and kept my worries to myself. Barbara Holmes would, no doubt, help Mandy sort things out.

CHAPTER NINETEEN

I dropped Mandy off at Dr. Holmes' office and drove home. Earlier, I'd pulled some of the furniture closer to the house, but with the change in the weather, I thought I'd better store most of it in the garage. I didn't want those items blowing around and destroying the screen barrier around the pool area.

With Robbie at school, Trudy was ecstatic to see me. I picked her up, laughing as her pink tongue washed my cheeks with loving excitement. When I walked out to the back of the house, *Zephyr* was straining against the lines tying her to the dock. I went down to check on her and make sure the rubber bumpers were tied tightly. She was a lovely boat, perfect for an afternoon or better yet, an evening sail, my favorite time to be on the water. I'd hate for anything to happen to her.

I opened the hatch and carefully lowered the two cushions that had been placed on the benches on either side of the cockpit. After locking everything up, I left her and went to collect the pool furniture. The plastic and metal casual chairs I tossed into the swimming pool. They'd be safe there. The better furniture I carried out of the lanai and stored in the garage.

By the time I was done and ready to head back to pick up Mandy, I was sweaty. But with no time to spare, I got into the car and drove to Dr. Holmes' office.

Mandy was waiting outside. When she saw me, she grinned and waved.

"Hi, Ann!" she warbled as she got into the passenger seat.

I hadn't driven far when Mandy's cellphone rang. She looked at it, clicked it off, and tossed it into her purse with a sound of disgust. "They've got to stop calling me."

"Who?" I asked.

"The Worthingtons. They call all the time. Cassie keeps showing me pictures of the baby's room and the new clothes she's bought her. It makes me furious."

"Rightly so," I murmured.

"Can you please take me back to Jax's apartment? I'll call Liz and tell her I'll be in touch later. I need some time for myself."

"No problem," I said, turning the car around.

It was silent in the car as I drove to the hotel.

"It's all going to work out," I said, as I dropped Mandy off at the apartment building.

Mandy scowled but nodded, and I wished I could be sure I was right.

I parked the car in back of the hotel and slipped through the employees' entrance, relieved to have something to do to take my mind off of Mandy's troubles.

Rhonda looked up from the spreadsheet in front of her. "I need you to look at these numbers. This month has been slower than I'd thought."

"And now a stormy weekend. Late September and October are iffy times."

Rhonda and I checked our numbers, compared them to the previous year, and wondered what the two of us as ambassadors to the hotel could do to make things better. The New Mothers Program had received a slight bump from the Tina Marx interview but wasn't doing as well as we'd thought. Maybe more national advertising was needed.

We grabbed a sandwich from the kitchen and worked all

afternoon on various advertising options and budgets.

I was startled by a call on my cell and looked to see that it was Liz.

"Hi, Honey! How are you?"

"Fine. Just wondering if you'd seen Mandy this afternoon. She phoned to say she'd let me know when she wanted me to pick her up to help me with the jewelry. But I haven't heard from her; I tried reaching her, but no answer. I'm worried."

"Hmmm, let me check. I'll go to Jax's apartment and I'll get back to you."

"What's up?" asked Rhonda.

I told her, and we both got to our feet.

"Let's go," said Rhonda. She glanced out the window. "I didn't realize it was raining so hard. Better grab an umbrella."

"Not in this wind," I said. "We'll have to run for it."

We went out the front entrance of the hotel and dashed across the front lawn to the building. By the time we got there both of us were out of breath and soaked.

"Mandy better have a good explanation as to what's going on," said Rhonda, wiping the rain off her face.

We climbed the stairs, passed Manny and Consuela's apartment, and continued to Jax's place.

I knocked on the door and waited for an answer.

When I knocked again, I noticed the door was cracked open.

My heart pounding, we walked inside. The apartment was tidy. The kitchen counters were clean, but the table that held Mandy's jewelry project was covered with groups of beads. I walked into the bedroom and saw dresser drawers open and the closet empty of Mandy's clothing.

Rhonda and I faced one another with shocked expressions.

I noticed a piece of paper on top of the bureau held down by Mandy's cell phone and snatched it up.

Dear Jax – I need some time alone to think. No matter what I do, I'll be hurting someone. I know you understand. Mandy

"What the fuck?" roared Rhonda. "She doesn't know this area. Look at the weather! Is she crazy?"

"Crazy enough to do something stupid like this," I said, furious she'd put us through this and even angrier to know why she'd done it. "She was being harassed by the Worthingtons, which is so unfair of them. No wonder she took off. But she should've known not to leave in weather like this."

"Let's find Jax and get details on the truck," said Rhonda. "We've got to think. If we were in her shoes, where would we go?"

We looked at each other and then cried together, "Miami."

"Hurry; let's get Jax. If we're right, she's going to try to hide out somewhere in Miami."

We raced to the front door and shrieked in surprise when Jax burst through the entrance toward us, dripping wet.

"What are you doing here?" he asked, as surprised as we were.

"It's Mandy. She's taken off and your truck is gone." I thrust the note in my hand at him. "We're guessing she may be heading to Miami. Does that make sense to you?"

"We talked about going there on my day off. We even talked about how to get there." He ran a hand through his wet hair, looking grim. "We were going to take Alligator Alley and see if we could discover any gators."

"I'll get my car and bring it out front and pick up the two of you." I grabbed a jacket on a hook by the door, tossed it over my head, and ran down the stairs and into the rain, running as fast as I could.

I was breathless and trying not to cry as I rushed into the office, grabbed both my purse and Rhonda's, and raced out to my car.

Thinking of every minute flashing by, I started the engine and pulled the car around to where Jax and Rhonda were standing under shelter.

Jax opened the back door for Rhonda and then climbed into the passenger seat beside me.

"I'll be able to spot the truck more quickly here."

"Okay. We don't know when she took off," I said. "That will make all the difference in finding her and maybe catching up to her."

Jax turned to me with a sad smile. "I have a feeling she isn't going to get very far. The needle showing the amount of gas in the car is broken and I haven't filled the truck with gas in a long time. We weren't going anywhere, and I like to walk to town instead of driving. For the exercise."

I glanced at Rhonda in the backseat. "Keep an open eye for a red truck. Looks like fate may have dealt us a nice hand."

Rhonda nodded glumly as she took a tissue from her purse and began dabbing at the moisture running down her face from the rain.

I drove through town keeping to U.S. 41 thinking that if Mandy were trying to escape, she'd take the less-traveled route to avoid being seen, the way to Miami she knew about.

The rain hit the car like angry slaps from above. The sound of it rattled my nerves. I glanced at Jax. Though he didn't say anything, he leaned forward as if he was willing the car to go faster.

"I wish Mandy hadn't left her phone behind," said Rhonda.

Dessert at The Beach House Hotel

"She probably didn't want another call from the Worthingtons," I said. "Apparently, they've made a habit of calling her often. Mandy was fine after seeing Dr. Holmes earlier today and then she got a call from them. She didn't answer it, but she immediately wanted to go home. Mandy told me she'd call Liz and work on jewelry projects at the apartment. I understood how upset she was, but I didn't think she'd do anything like this."

"Don't blame yourself," said Rhonda. "I wish I'd known about the phone calls. I would've said something to the Worthingtons. They're putting too much pressure on her."

I drove as fast as I dared on the wet road. Normally you could see miles ahead of you because the landscape was so flat. But the heavy, torrential rain made it impossible to see even a few feet ahead. I turned on the radio to a smooth jazz station hoping to ease the tension inside the car.

"What's the situation between Mandy and you, Jax?" asked Rhonda.

He turned to her, shaking his head. "I wish I knew. She knows I love her. She says she loves me too, but she keeps saying it isn't a good idea for us to be together. I'm hoping as the time gets closer to her having the baby, she realizes we could be great parents to her."

"I don't know what it's going to take for Mandy to realize it," said Rhonda. "It's obvious when I see the two of you that you love one another. You're a sensible, hard-working guy who not only would help take care of the baby but would be there for her too."

He turned back to staring out at the road.

We'd traveled mostly in silence for almost an hour when Jax called out, "Stop! I think I see the truck up ahead."

I slowed the car, and as I did, I noticed the red truck pulled to the side of the road. I drew up behind it and watched as Jax sprang out of the car and ran over to it.

Rhonda started to get out of the car to follow him.

"Wait," I said. "Better give them some time alone."

"Right. But I can't wait to put my arms around her and tell her everything's going to be okay. I hate to think what position the Worthingtons have put her in."

"I'm sure they think they're building a relationship, but they don't realize how trapped Mandy feels."

"Or maybe they think they can bulldoze her into believing that's what she wants," said Rhonda.

We stopped talking as Jax returned to the car with Mandy.

Rhonda got out of the car and hugged her. "You had us worried sick."

"I'm so sorry to make you come after me," Mandy said. "Especially in this weather. I just had to get away. I can't even think anymore without waves of guilt washing over me."

"You oughta be sorry, but the most important thing is that you're okay. Don't you dare pull another stunt like this. We're here for you. Got that? We're here for you." Rhonda gave Mandy another tight hug. You two sit in the back together, and we can talk."

"Hi, sweetie," I said as Mandy settled in the backseat. Her clothes were dry, but her cheeks were wet with tears.

I handed her the box of tissues I kept in my car.

She took one, blew her nose, and let out a long sigh as she gazed at Jax.

"Thank you both for coming to get me. I've got a lot to do, a lot to think about." She smiled at Jax. "Especially with you." She snuggled up against his broad chest.

Rhonda and I exchanged glances. Maybe this was going to work out better than we'd thought.

By the time we found a gas station, traveled back to the truck, and filled it with enough gas to get it home, the four of us were exhausted.

Jax drove Mandy in his truck, while I followed with Rhonda in my car.

"What do you think, Annie?" Rhonda asked, sipping on the bottle of water she'd bought at the gas station.

"The situation got out of control." I shook my head and wondered what it would take to help Mandy make up her mind. "I think she's beginning to realize that this idea of her ruining someone else's life is something no one else but her parents believe. The Worthingtons talk about what they could give the baby materially, but Mandy's never mentioned them saying anything about love for the baby."

"She's got to give Jax a fair chance," said Rhonda. "He's amazing with her."

"I just hope he doesn't get hurt." Having grown close to Vaughn's son, Ty, I better understood how sensitive young men could be.

CHAPTER TWENTY

After dropping Rhonda off at the hotel to get her car, I headed home. I'd have just enough time to have a hot soak in the tub before Robbie came home from his after-school sports program.

At my house, I greeted Trudy and decided to call Liz while I got ready for my bath. I filled her in on what had happened and said, "I know you'll support Mandy in making any decision she chooses. I know how you feel about her giving away her baby when you've waited a long time to get pregnant."

"We've talked about it some. No matter what she decides, she can work with me going forward. And if she keeps the baby, I'll pay her on a piece-by-piece basis and then we can, perhaps, form a partnership. Everything is up in the air at the moment, though."

"I understand. I wish Mandy would keep her baby, but the decision is hers to make," I said, wishing she'd never been put in such a situation.

Later, lying back in the warm bubbly water in the spa tub in my bathroom, my thoughts drifted. It was hard for me to stay neutral about Mandy's predicament when I'd tried so hard to have a large family and had been blessed with only one child. Robert had been concerned but not overly understanding with me after each disappointment. Times had changed, and men were now more involved with both pregnancy and the raising of a child. Even so, Jax was special.

Vaughn called. Surprised but pleased I answered. "Hey! How are you?"

"I got the role in the movie! I guess it was pretty much decided before I read for it. But still, I'm very excited about it."

"Of course, you are!" I said, pleased for him. "What happens next?"

"I'm staying here in California for a while to do some promo shots and to work on a shooting schedule. Though it's an excellent role, it's not the lead, which will allow me to work around my schedule for the show. If things go well and I get any other jobs in Hollywood, I'll quit the show. But no need to do that for a while."

"Who else is in the movie?"

"Aside from Tina in the lead, the woman playing my love interest is none other than Lauren Hyde."

"How fabulous!" I said, pleased. "I've always liked her in various roles."

"Me, too, though she's a bit intimidating. She knows her craft and doesn't like waiting around for others."

"Well, you wanted new challenges. Sounds like this is going to be that."

"Yeah, I think so too. So how are things there?"

I told him about the escapade with Mandy and shared some of the things I was working on at the hotel, and then we said goodbye.

I climbed out of the tub and toweled off, pleased to hear such joy in Vaughn's voice. I understood how much he wanted the change in his life. The hotel business with people coming and going meant new things happening every day. He'd been at his job with the soap opera for years, and he was beginning to lose interest.

Curious, I googled Lauren Hyde. An attractive woman in

her early fifties, she was happily married to the owner of a large insurance agency in northern California and was the mother of three sons. I smiled. There'd be no scandals with her.

I dressed and waited for the time when I could pick up Robbie from his sports program. Though he seemed young for it, Robbie was learning to play soccer.

When I got to the soccer field, he was waiting for me with a big smile. Looking at that precious face I was torn once more about the decision Mandy had to make. Adoption into a nice home could be a wonderful thing.

The next week flew by with work at the hotel, Robbie's increased activities, and helping Mandy. Liz's appointment with Dr. Benson was coming up, and I waited anxiously to know why she'd asked both Liz and Chad to attend. Liz seemed well. She was glowing after she got past a few queasy mornings.

On the morning of her appointment, I called Liz. "Just checking in. Be sure to let me know how things go with Dr. Benson."

"Sure. I've heard from a friend of mine that Dr. Benson just likes to make sure that both parents are part of the process," said Liz.

"That makes sense. I'm sorry that I took his place with her."

"Mom, I wanted you there," said Liz.

"Thanks. It was a very special day for the two of us. Gotta go. Talk to you later."

I said goodbye and told Robbie it was time to leave for school.

He came running into the kitchen, Trudy at his heels.

"Can Brett come play here after class?"

"Sure. I'll talk to his mother."

Waving his fist in the air with triumph, Robbie headed for the kitchen door.

I followed, pleased that it took so little to make him happy.

I was sitting in my office going over the figures for the latest wedding, trying to figure out ways to bring in more income without overcharging for our services. Knowing breakeven points for the events was very important to forecasting future income streams and making the events profitable.

My cell phone chimed, and I picked it up. *Liz.*

"Hi, there!" I chirped happily.

"Mom?" said Liz, tearfully.

At the sound of her voice, my heart stopped. I grabbed onto the edge of the desk. "What's wrong?"

"Nothing," said Liz. "It's good news! We're in a state of shock because it turns out we're having twins! Can you believe it? Two babies, not one!" She started to laugh hysterically. "You should've seen Chad's face when Dr. Benson told us."

"Oh, my! I'm so excited! This is such fabulous news! Are they due in late April like you thought?"

"Yes, though twins sometimes come early." Liz sighed happily. "I can't wait to tell Angela that by next spring I'll have caught up to her."

I chuckled. There'd always been a little bit of friendly competition between the two of them.

"I gotta go. We have to tell Chad's mother and a few other people."

"Thanks for calling, honey. Congratulations to the two of you. I'm so excited!"

"I knew you would be," said Liz. "Talk later."

After ending the call, I sat and held my head in my hands. Tears slipped down my cheeks. After worrying about Liz for so many months, I was so very grateful for such wonderful news.

Rhonda walked into the office, saw me, and stopped. "Annie, what's wrong?"

"It's Liz," I managed to say as the knot in my throat tightened.

"Oh my God! She didn't lose the baby, did she?"

My lips stretched in a smile I couldn't contain. "No. She's having twins!!"

Rhonda pulled me into a bosomy hug. "That's fantastic! I'm so happy for her!"

"Me, too." I grinned. "She says by April she'll have caught up to Angela."

Rhonda laughed and then grew serious. "I need something like this after coming from Angela's house. The nurses are saying it's a matter of days for Katherine. Evan's at my house for the rest of the week. Angela thought it best."

"I think so too. It's such an emotional time that it's confusing for someone his age." I studied the sad expression on Rhonda's face. "How are you holding up?"

"I'm trying to do the best I can to help, but there's little I can do for Katherine at this stage. We've had our talk and said our farewells. Arthur seems lost, but he and Reggie have been able to spend some time together, which is a healthy thing for them both."

"Let me know if I can help with anything. I've been working on a new budget for the spa. We can talk about it tomorrow."

"Okay. I'll check in with Bernie and then I'll go home. Poor Rita has her hands full with the three little ones."

Rhonda left, and I thought how ironic it was that I was celebrating new life while she was mourning another.

I took a chance on timing and called Vaughn. He didn't answer so I left a message that I was calling with good news and for him to call me back when he could.

Later, I'd just finished discussing staffing issues with Bernie and was back in my office when my cell rang. Thinking it was Vaughn, I picked it up. "Hi, darling!"

"Hi, Ann," said a voice that I recognized belonged to Tina Marks.

"Tina! How are you? I just heard from Vaughn and he's delighted he got the role in the movie."

"Did he tell you who else is in the cast?"

"Just that his love interest was Lauren Hyde, someone we both admire," I said, beginning to be concerned. "Why?"

"We all just found out that one of the minor roles is going to Lily Dorio. That's why I'm calling. She's making a fool of herself over Vaughn, but I'm keeping an eye on things. Lauren Hyde can't stand her either and has been speaking up about it. But you know how Lily is about publicity."

I let out a long sigh. Lily, like a bad apple, seemed to come in and out of our lives. She was, no doubt, responsible for the earlier gossip in the newspaper about being together with Vaughn again. She was a female version of Brock Goodwin. Enough so that I felt a little sick.

"Don't worry, Ann. I informed Nicholas about some of the social media stuff Lily was starting to put out about being in the same movie as Vaughn and he shut it down, told her that her behavior was abusive, and he'd fire her if she continued. I'm pretty sure that's put a stop to it. How's everything else?" Tina asked.

After swearing her to total secrecy, I told her about Liz's twins. "I'm still not used to the idea. It's so exciting."

"Oh, yes! She'll have her hands full, but I know how thrilled she must be after worrying about getting pregnant. Tell her I've got lots of boy things if she needs them."

"Oh, I hadn't gotten there yet. I don't care what she has as long as they're healthy. It'll be a while until we know the sexes. But thanks, sweetie, for being so kind."

"I love you, Ann. You're the mother I never had. That's why I wanted you prepared when Vaughn gave you the news about Lily. Poor Vaughn has been trying his best to be pleasant to her because it's important for him to do well with this project. But it's difficult. Nicholas is making sure there won't be much need for them to be together."

"Thanks. I'm not worried about Vaughn's behavior, but I have to admit, I don't like hers even under the best of circumstances."

"I've got your back. Love you. *Ciao.*"

I got up out of my chair, and paced the room telling myself that this kind of thing was sometimes part of the movie business. And as I'd told Tina, I trusted Vaughn not to get caught up in Lily Dorio's need for bad publicity again. Especially when he was feeling vulnerable because of his age.

That night as I was getting ready for bed, Vaughn called. "Guess you heard about Lily Dorio being chosen for a role in the movie. I bumped into Tina and she told me she called you."

"Yes. She didn't want me to worry," I said.

"Are you worried about it?" he asked with an edge in his voice.

"No, Vaughn, I'm not. I trust you, trust us," I said calmly.

"I'm glad because I have a feeling Lily's going to try to shake up things just for the attention. She's such a piece of work. But I'm going to deal with it because this may be the break that I need to get more film roles."

"I understand. So ... did Liz call you?"

"She did! How do you feel about twins, Grandma? Fantastic, huh?"

"I'm delighted for them, of course. Privately, I'll be concerned about her taking care of herself. I miscarried two babies."

"She's healthy and happy. I was very pleased she called me. Our family is growing. I like it."

"Me, too. On a very different note, Katherine's days are numbered. She and Rhonda have settled things between them. I'm planning on visiting Angela's house tomorrow. I'm so glad you managed to work her name into the show, wrote that note to Katherine, and then called her. She treasures those moments."

"The next few days in New York are going to be hectic. I'll try to make it back for the memorial."

"She's chosen to have a small, family service here in Florida. I was surprised but pleased for Angela and Reggie that she considers Sabal her home with the kids."

"Oh, then, I'll try to get to Florida. I'm taking the red-eye tonight to New York. I'm here at the airport now."

"Safe travels, darling. Let me know you've arrived safely."

"I will. Sleep well knowing how much I love you."

"Love you too," I said. He sounded both happy and tired.

CHAPTER TWENTY-ONE

T he next morning, I called Mandy. "Just checking in. I have to go out this morning and wondered if I could give you a ride to Liz's store."

"That would be great. I've done some work on special necklaces that I can't wait to show her."

"How are you feeling? It's getting close to delivery time."

"The baby hasn't dropped yet, but I feel like I've swallowed a beach ball. Jax tells me it's cute, but I don't think so. I'll never be the same again."

"You're young. You'll be surprised how your body can react. I'll pick you up at ten if that's convenient."

"Perfect. See you then," she said and ended the call.

I thought about her comment with Jax. Since she'd taken his truck and tried to run away, their relationship had changed for the better. Still, I wouldn't ask. That would be as bad as a Worthington phone call.

I called Angela next and asked if it would be okay for me to drop by to see Katherine.

"Thanks. It would be nice if you could. She and Mom have spoken and it's important. Katherine is sleeping more and more, but she'll be glad to hear your voice."

Tears sprang to my eyes. What a waste of friendship our early days of knowing one another had been. She'd been so angry at Reggie and Angela for their defiance and had decided to dislike Rhonda before they'd even met.

I picked up Mandy as planned and watched as she made her way to the car looking as if she might deliver at any moment. Liz had told me Mandy had gone to my hairdresser, Malinda, at Hair Designs. Looking at her now, her shorter, easier hairstyle suited her. Glowing with the pregnancy, she was a striking young woman. Her blue eyes looked even larger with her new hairdo, and healthy food had filled the sharp angles of her body.

"Hi," she said happily as she slid into the passenger's seat and smiled at me. She held up the small box she'd brought with her. "Here are the new designs to show Liz. I think she's going to like them."

"I'm sure she will. She thinks you're very artistic."

Mandy beamed at me. "I can't wait to set up a business with her."

My eyebrows rose. "You're staying then?"

She nodded. "No matter what happens with the baby, I want to stay here. I like it."

"I'm glad," I said, waiting for her to say more, but she simply stared out the window.

I dropped her off in front of the store.

Liz waved at me through the store window, and I blew her a kiss. This evening, she, Chad, and Chad's mother, Sadie Bowen, were coming to dinner to celebrate the news of the twins.

I pulled away from the curb and headed to Angela's full of anxiety. I'd been there when Rhonda's ex, Sal, had died and knew it wasn't an easy process. I hoped Katherine wasn't suffering but was heavily medicated. Even if we couldn't speak, she'd know I was there.

Angela greeted me at the door with a lingering hug. "Glad you came. She's semi-awake and was happy to hear you were stopping by."

She led me into one of the guest rooms, which had been turned into a hospital room for Katherine. Lying on the special bed, Katherine stirred when I walked in.

"Hello, Katherine. It's Ann Sanders," I said softly. I took hold of her hand and squeezed it.

She opened her eyes and her lips stretched eerily across her ravaged face. "Thank you for coming. I know how much Angela and Reggie love you. Take care of them, will you?"

"Yes, I'll be here for them and the children. Rhonda told me she's going to make sure the children don't forget you. She's making them a book with your stories and photos."

Katherine closed her eyes and nodded. "So sweet."

I stood a moment longer with her, even though she'd fallen asleep.

Arthur walked into the room. "Hello, Ann. Thank you for stopping by. I know it means a lot to Katherine. And to me."

"I'm here if you need me. Vaughn sends his apologies, but he's stuck in New York."

A sad smile crossed his face. "She's a big fan, as we all know."

I returned his smile though there was no joy in it. Then I leaned over and kissed Katherine.

"Thanks for coming," said Angela as I headed to the door.

"Evan is staying with Rhonda. What about Sally?"

"She's here so I can nurse her. Reggie has her out for a walk now. He's so good with her."

"Tell him I'm here for him and to please let me know if he needs me to do anything. Love you." I hugged her and left the house.

Outside the sky seemed bluer, the air cleaner, and I vowed to take more time to enjoy each day.

At the sound of my name, I looked up and waved as Reggie walked toward me, pushing a carriage.

When he reached me, I hugged him. "I'm so sorry about your mother."

His mouth turned down. "Not going to be long now."

"No, I think not. How's Sally?" I peered into the carriage. The baby was sound asleep on her back. Looking at her now, I could see a bit of Katherine in her and much to my delight a bit of Sal in her too. "She's so beautiful."

"Yeah, I know," he said proudly. "Great news about Liz and Chad. Twins? That's going to be a hard act to follow."

"What do you mean?" I asked.

Reggie shrugged. "I'm not supposed to tell anyone except my mother, but Angela is pregnant again. Not planned, that's for sure."

"Does Rhonda know?" I asked, stunned by the news.

He shook his head firmly. "No. And you can't tell her. We're going to wait until things settle down after my mom is gone. Promise?"

I nodded. "Promise." I remembered how my last promise to Rhonda had worked out. Didn't they know I had a hard time keeping secrets from Rhonda? I knew the minute Rhonda found out she'd begin to worry how Angela was going to handle three babies under five. And Liz? She'd be disappointed not to have caught up with Angela, but she'd be delighted that her twins would have a playmate their age.

I spoke to Reggie and climbed into the car my mind awhirl with everything that was going on.

At the hotel, I was glad Rhonda was at home helping Rita with the kids. I was still bubbling with the news of Angela's new baby.

Later, when my cell phone rang, I hoped it wasn't Rhonda. I checked. *Amelia Swanson.*

"Hello, Madame Vice President," I said.

"Hi, Ann. I'm calling on my private line because I'm

concerned arrangements with Mandy's baby seem to be falling apart. I got a call from Sam Worthington and he's upset. What's going on?"

"Mandy told me she didn't sign an agreement with them. Is that correct?"

"Yes, but why are you asking? They had a verbal agreement that in exchange for helping her financially, she'd let them adopt her baby."

My stomach clenched. "What do you mean help her financially? Do you mean by setting her up here for rest?"

"That and the idea that when the baby is theirs, she'll receive a lump payment as well as a payment to my charity," said Amelia. "Nothing official, mind you, but an agreement just the same."

"This makes it sound awful as if he's buying a baby and you're getting something for arranging it."

"It's not like that." Amelia sounded shocked. "I need to know what's going on. I suggested The Beach House Hotel for privacy and for the excellent care I knew she'd receive."

"A bribe, it sounds like to me," I said.

"Certainly not."

"I'm sorry, Amelia, but I think things have become more complicated than you might imagine. The Worthingtons have been hounding Mandy, telling her all the reasons why she should give up her baby while at the same time Mandy has grown to love her baby. I don't know what Mandy will choose to do. Rhonda and I aren't getting involved other than taking her places, seeing that she gets to her doctors' appointments."

"But this isn't how it was supposed to work," said Amelia. "It was all arranged."

"As a mother, I can't imagine being forced to give my baby up. Mandy was so upset after the Worthingtons came for a visit that she even tried to run away."

"Oh, dear! That isn't good. What's the real problem?"

I drew a breath and let it out slowly. I didn't care if Amelia Swanson was the vice president of the United States or not, she needed to hear the truth. "I think two things are happening. Mandy is becoming more and more attached to her baby, and she isn't sure the Worthingtons can give her baby a lot of love."

"What? For what reason?" said Amelia.

"Have you seen them together?" I asked. "There's no sign of real love between them. I think that's what she saw. She understands they can give her baby material things. And that weighs on her mind. That is all the information I can give you."

"What about this boyfriend, this Jax Thomas. Did you know he was once arrested?"

"Arrested? For what?"

"He was involved in a demonstration at his college. Several students took over the Registration Office over a matter."

I let out the breath I'd been holding. Certainly, we would've uncovered something bad in a background check. "That sounds more like rebellion on a school issue than something that will lead to a life of crime."

"Well, I suppose you're right, but Samuel Worthington has had him investigated. I understand he's now working for you."

"And doing a fine job," I said, rising to Jax's defense. "He's a hard worker and is creative as well. Manny, who's head of caretaking at the hotel, likes him."

"Okay. I just wanted to hear about the situation from you."

"Mandy has been put in a terrible position," I said. "If

she'd truly made up her mind early on it would be much easier for both her and the Worthingtons. The problem is, she says she doesn't know what she should do."

"What do you think she's going to decide?" Amelia asked.

I couldn't lie. "I think she's going to make a great mother."

"Thank you for your honesty," Amelia said. "I'll try to warn the Worthingtons that it may not go their way. Chances are another opportunity will arise. My charity is receiving calls from other young women who are troubled. We want to help them and their babies in whatever ways we can. But that isn't the real purpose of my charity."

"Does that mean you're sometimes acting as an adoption agency?"

"Heavens, no! This was an exception. There are professional adoption agencies that do that work. Mandy's situation was unique as Senator Worthington feels a bit of responsibility because members of his staff were at that party."

"No names yet as to the potential father?"

"None," said Amelia. "Doubtful anyone would come forward. It would mean the loss of their job and would mar their careers for life."

A shiver went through me. There were so many things wrong with this. My thoughts turned to Jax. He was a decent man. I hoped staying with him was proving that to Mandy.

Amelia and I talked about her sister, Lindsay, recently divorced from an abuser and now living with Jean-Luc.

"I'm sure once a year from the time of her divorce has passed, Lindsay and Jean-Luc will officially become a couple. But her need to hide from the president's family is real. Right now, living together is healing for both Lindsay and Jean-Luc. What a sweet man he is. I've never known my sister to be so optimistic, so happy."

"I don't see them often, but when I do, they glow with happiness. I'm so pleased for them. When are you coming down for a visit?"

"Not for a while. Too busy here," she said. "I'd better go. Thanks again for being so open with me. It will all work out the way it's meant to be."

"I think so, too," I said, relieved she'd allowed me to speak frankly before ending the call.

I decided to go see Rhonda at home helping with the kids.

Rhonda greeted me at the door holding Drew in her arms. They'd just had lunch by the look of the purple jelly circling Drew's mouth.

"Auntie Ann!" Drew shrieked, reaching for me.

Laughing, I said. "Hi, Drew! How's one of my favorite little boys?"

"It's been a tough morning," said Rhonda, holding Drew firmly in her arms. "Willow and Evan won't let Drew play with them and he's out of sorts. Come on in. Rita's been giving them lunch."

I followed her into the kitchen. Willow and Evan were laughing together. Hard to believe that at age four, Willow was an aunt to her four-year-old nephew. Even so, they were best friends. It was cute to see.

I gave them each a hug and then Rhonda handed Drew to me. His face was cleaned up now, so I kissed his cheek. He wrapped his arms around me, and I hugged him close. With a bossy older sister like Willow, he sometimes needed an extra bit of attention.

"What's up?" Rhonda asked as I set Drew down on his feet, and Rita took the children out of the room.

I straightened. "I just got off the phone with Amelia Swanson. Thought we'd better talk."

"Let's go to my room for privacy. How about lunch? I can whip up a salad for us."

"That sounds delicious. It's been a busy day. I stopped in to speak to Katherine this morning. She's been on my mind."

"How did it go?" Rhonda asked, pulling fresh romaine out of the refrigerator along with several other items to put into a salad.

"It was sad to say goodbye, of course, but I'm glad I had the opportunity to do so. Arthur appreciated it."

"I'm sure he did. Katherine's choice for a small, private family service is going to be so much easier than trying to do something big in New York. I think her decision is all part of the new her," said Rhonda, pouring dressing over the salads she'd quickly put together.

"Me, too. I like it."

Rhonda whipped out a tray and placed the two salad plates on it. "Why don't you carry the drinks? Iced tea, okay?"

"Perfect," I said, amazed as always by Rhonda's ease in the kitchen. She came from a family who liked to eat, and she was a great cook.

We retreated to the master bedroom upstairs and sat in the private sitting area off it. Sliding glass doors led to a balcony overlooking the large backyard and pool area. It was one of my favorite spots in Rhonda's large, two-story home.

She set down the tray on a table between two comfortable, over-stuffed chairs, and I placed the glasses of ice-tea next to it.

"Let's eat first. Then we can talk about Amelia. It's been a crazy morning, and I want to enjoy this quiet time with you. Are you still in shock over Liz's twins? I'm thrilled for you. A perfect number of grandchildren between the two of us, don't you think?"

Wishing I hadn't promised Reggie not to tell, I swallowed, nodded, and told myself not to give anything away about Angela's new baby.

We chatted about Willow's dance class, Robbie's soccer, Evan's readjustment with Katherine and Arthur in the house, and then Rhonda leaned back. "Okay. Tell me about Amelia's call. I have a feeling it didn't go well."

I set down my fork, wiped my mouth with my napkin, and turned to her. "It was disturbing, actually. For a moment I was leery of Amelia's charity work, it sounded like they were running a baby mill, but she assured me that it wasn't so. Let me start at the beginning."

Rhonda listened carefully as I repeated my conversation with Amelia, making faces at some points. When I was through, she shook her head. "I think Amelia's program is okay, but I don't like the idea of the private deal she made with the Worthingtons. I'm tellin' ya, it stinks, Annie. Samuel Worthington is like so many people in D.C. who think rules aren't for them, but for everyone else."

I let out a long sigh. "I feel the same way. The tough thing for us is that we can't make Mandy's decision for her, no matter how much we'd like to. I believe her instinct is to keep the baby, but the Worthingtons are powerful people, and she may be swayed."

"The best chance she has of keeping the baby is to stay close to Jax. He makes her feel both safe and strong," said Rhonda.

I shook my head with dismay. "Time will take care of many things, but in this instance, we're running out of it. She looks ready to deliver. She thought the baby hadn't dropped, but, to me, it looked like she has."

"How are things at the hotel? Anything I should be concerned about?"

"Nothing that I know of," I said. Lorraine Grace is so competent at her job. We got another contract for another wedding. Aside from that, Bernie has everything under control. I've been doing some budget work on raising some of our prices. Bernie told me that the Sand Castle has lowered their rates after trying to keep them at our level. The problem is they don't give the kind of service we do, and their guests expect better."

"What's new with Vaughn?" Rhonda asked. "It seems like ages since we've caught up."

I filled her in on his new contract and the problem with Lily.

"That woman is a frickin' nuisance," grumbled Rhonda. "How about Brock? Seen anything of him lately?"

"No, which makes me wonder what's going on with him," I answered. "The next few weeks are going to be very interesting."

"I'd like to do everything I could to keep him away from us and the hotel, but it's not possible. Besides, Will thinks it's better to know your enemy and what he's up to."

"Yeah, he's right." I stood. "Thanks for lunch and the chat. I've missed our time together. It's always helpful to talk things through with you."

We hugged, and I carried the glasses back to the kitchen while she followed with the tray.

"Auntie Ann!" Willow cried, running over to me. "Look at what I made." She held up a string on which pasta pieces had been strung. "It's my diamonds," she said proudly.

I laughed. Knowing Willow, the day would come when it would be true. She was a little princess who loved nice things.

"Beautiful," I said, hugging her.

Rhonda smiled at us. "She sure loves her Auntie Ann."

"And I love her." I gave Willow a kiss and left the house wondering how I could be so lucky to have Rhonda and her family in my life. It had taken quite a while to get used to the idea.

CHAPTER TWENTY-TWO

I stood in the dining room checking to make sure everything was set for dinner with Sadie, Chad, and Liz. I'd picked up food from the hotel, a fish stew that was one of Chad's favorites, and spent the time I would've taken to cook a meal myself creating a special centerpiece of Plumbago Imperial Blue blossoms, pink hibiscus, blue daze, pink penta blossoms, white gardenias, and a few white vincas purchased from my favorite florist, Tropical Fleurs.

As I placed each bloom into the white vase, I pictured my grandbabies and was already eager to hold them in my arms. It would be nice for Liz to have one each—boy and girl, but I didn't care as long as they were healthy.

Sadie arrived ahead of Liz and Chad. Though we shared a friendly relationship, we'd never be close. Sadie was head of the local theater group and loved to be the center of attention. She'd even insisted on singing at Liz and Chad's wedding, a song she'd written especially for the celebration. But she was a nice person, just a little too self-centered to become close to me.

I greeted her at the door, admired her new bright-red hairdo, and ushered her inside. "Such exciting news from the kids!" she exclaimed. "I'm over the moon! Two grandchildren at once!"

"I am too. Liz will need help, no doubt, but I'm sure we can all pitch in."

Sadie held up a hand. "I've already told the kids I'll be busy with my theater work but would be glad to help pay for a sitter from time to time."

"Of course," I said. Chad had told me that when he was a schoolboy living with his mother, he was pretty much a loner growing up except for his football and computer geek friends. A usual combination of interests that had made him many friends later in life.

Liz and Chad arrived, and I rushed over to hug them both. "Congratulations, Mom and Dad!" I couldn't help looking at Liz's stomach. There was already a roundness to it that would seem unusual for a single baby. I could only imagine what she'd look like as her pregnancy neared the end.

I smiled at Chad. "Are you ready for all this?"

He grinned. "I guess I have to be. It was a surprise, but I'm glad we can get two at once. That makes it easy to catch up to Angela and Reggie."

Chad and Liz exchanged smiling glances.

I kept quiet. Soon enough, everyone would know that the race was far from over.

"Let's sit and talk out on the lanai. What would everyone like to drink? Liz, I have some lemonade or bubbling water you might like. Sadie, I have bourbon, and, Chad, I have a beer, if you'd like one."

I took requests, pleased I'd satisfied everyone, went to the kitchen to fix them, and greeted Robbie as he came into the kitchen from playing next door with Brett. "Hi, Robbie! Lizzie and Chad are here with Chad's mother. Why don't you go out to the lanai and say hello? I'll bring you some juice."

"Okay. I want to see Lizzie's stomach."

He left the kitchen at a run and I laughed thinking of the questions I was sure Robbie would ask. We'd talked about babies and how they grew when Nell was here with Bailey. But the idea of twins was new to him.

As I walked onto the lanai, Robbie was sitting next to Liz

with his hand on her stomach.

"They're only tiny now," Liz said, "but they'll grow bigger."

"As big as an elephant?" Robbie asked.

Liz shook her head no. "Why did you say that?"

"I heard my teacher say her friend was having a baby and she was as big as an elephant."

"Oh, my word!" Liz looked aghast at me, and we laughed softly together.

"That's just an expression, Robbie," I said. "We'll see how things go with Lizzie."

I handed out the drinks and took a seat opposite Sadie seated in a chair next to Liz.

"I was just telling the kids I'm already looking through materials for plays that include young children. I can't wait to get my grandchildren involved in the theater." She glanced at her son. "Chad was never interested."

"You were having too much fun on your own," Chad said. "Besides, I'm not comfortable in front of an audience."

"Well, let me have the chance with my grandchildren," Sadie said with an edge to her voice.

"I understand you're holding auditions for your new play," said Liz smoothly, a move that came with practice, or so she'd told me.

Sadie beamed at her. "Yes. We even got Brock Goodwin to try out for the part of an old roué. I think he'll be perfect."

The sip of pinot noir I'd just taken got caught in my throat. I struggled to swallow while wanting to scream with laughter.

"Are you all right, Mom?" Liz asked as I tried my best to catch my breath.

I nodded and when I could, I said, "You're kidding! Is Brock going to take the part?"

Sadie smiled. "Yes. He's pretty excited about it. It's perfect, don't you think?"

"Totally," I said, itching to call Rhonda and give her the news. We'd needed a good laugh.

Sadie sighed. "I was hoping to get Vaughn involved with this one, but I understand he's currently working on a movie."

"Yes, he's working on both the movie and the show. We're hoping it leads to other film projects." Vaughn didn't mind working behind the scenes in support of the community theater but didn't want to get too involved, thinking it might take chances away from the locals.

"It's very exciting to have someone in the family like him. He's so gorgeous and talented," said Sadie. "How do you stand having him away and surrounded by beautiful people?"

"Vaughn and I have a solid relationship," I said, not wanting to get into my feelings of insecurity whenever I saw photographs of him with other women. The first time it had happened I'd been shattered. Now, I knew he was not being unfaithful; it was all part of the business.

"Vaughn's crazy about Mom," Liz said.

Sadie glanced at her. "Show business can be difficult. Makes it hard to settle down."

Liz and I exchanged looks. We both knew the story of Sadie leaving her husband to go to New York to try to break into theater work there. She'd left New York after only a few months and came to Sabal with Chad.

"I'll go get dinner ready to serve, and then we can eat," I said. "Chad, I brought home the fish stew you like. I'll make a salad and heat the rolls and then we can eat."

"Thanks, Ann," said Chad.

I gave him a quick kiss on the cheek and left to go to the

kitchen. I'd liked Chad from the first time we'd hired him to do some computer upgrades for us at the hotel. With his strawberry-blond hair and blue eyes, he was a strikingly handsome man who was both sweet and as bright as they come. It had taken him a while to get used to the kisses I handed out to family and special friends, but he'd quickly grown to like it.

During dinner, Liz and Chad discussed plans for the future. "We're not renewing the lease on the store. Chad is renting space in the building where Uncle Will works. And he's going to set up a home office in what was going to be the baby's room. I'll take over his old office space, and the babies will have the guest suite as their room."

I smiled. "That sounds ...."

"Awful," said Sadie. "I've been counting on your storefront for publicity for the theater. It was perfect, right on the main drag. What'll I do now?"

"I'm sure you can find someone else to accommodate you," I said.

She frowned and turned to me. "It's becoming more and more difficult. Your hotel manager turned down my request to set up a bulletin board at the hotel with all kinds of community events."

"I understand Bernhard told you that he'd be glad to have brochures behind the front desk to distribute to guests," I said.

"Well, yes, but it isn't the same as being on display," she countered.

I held in a sigh. That was the problem with Sadie. Display. She craved it.

"Mom, we can't afford to rent the store to just hang signs in the window," said Chad. "We got a good deal on the space at Will's office. Since he bought the building, a lot of us in the family are using it."

"I'll work something out," said Sadie, "but it won't be easy."

I watched Liz throughout this interchange and knew how frustrated Sadie made her from time to time. They hadn't bonded like I'd thought they would. Maybe having twins would bring them together. Chad would help, she knew, but he was busy growing his business.

"Is everyone ready for dessert? Pear tarts?"

I grinned when they all nodded. The flaky fruit desserts at The Beach House Hotel were almost as famous as our cinnamon rolls.

Later that night, after everyone had gone and I'd cleaned up the kitchen and settled Robbie for the night, I wandered outside. I lay down in a lounge chair and stared up at the sky. Stars sparkled in the darkness like candles lighting the way to heaven. My thoughts turned to Katherine, and I wondered if she'd make it through another day. Poor Arthur. The gentleman who'd seemed so quietly able to accept Katherine as she used to be, now was at loose ends, as if without her domineering presence, he couldn't function. Funny how that works, I thought, thinking of Robert and how he made sure he had his way.

I sighed and went inside. I missed Vaughn. With him beside me, life seemed complete.

The next morning, I was jarred awake by the sound of my cell ringing. I checked my caller ID. *Rhonda.* I knew what had happened before she told me in a trembling voice, "It's Katherine."

"I'm sorry. What can I do to help?" I asked, fighting the sting of tears.

"I was to meet Lorraine Grace about the wedding coming up, and I need you to take my place."

"Sure. What time?"

Rhonda gave me the details and then said, "Sorry, I've got to go."

I quickly found Angela's contact information, left her my condolences, and told her I'd take care of dinner that night.

Robbie padded into my bedroom, holding onto his favorite giraffe. Trudy followed at his heels.

"Come here," I said, patting the place beside me.

He crawled into bed and lay next to me. "Are you crying?" He touched my cheek with the tip of his finger.

"Just a little," I answered, taking hold of his hand and kissing it. "I'll be all right. What are you doing today at school?" Robbie was a kid who liked to have a schedule, and he paid attention when the teacher announced upcoming projects.

"We're going to talk about elephants," he said. "Do you know they like peanuts?"

I smiled. "Now I do. When you come home from school, you can tell me everything new you learned about elephants,"

"I know," said Robbie, giving me a smile that reminded me of Robert.

I laughed and hugged him. "Better get up and get going."

We were eating breakfast when Vaughn called.

"Morning!" I said happily. "How are you?"

"Tired. I think I finally have a schedule worked out here for the show. The producers have been kind to me. I'll make it home this weekend."

"Great. Rhonda called to say Katherine has died. We'd all

really like for you to be here for the family service for her."

"Give me the details as soon as you can, and I'll work it out. Now, how is my sweetheart and our little boy?"

"Missing you. Here he is," I said, and handed the phone to Robbie.

I smiled as Robbie told Vaughn all about the elephants they were going to study. They shared such a strong bond.

Robbie handed me the phone, and I chatted with Vaughn for a few minutes pleased for this opportunity. He always settled me.

CHAPTER TWENTY-THREE

E ven though it was a sunny day, my heart was heavy as I walked into Angela's house, carrying the chicken casserole that both Angela and Reggie loved. Funny how some people come in and go out of your life with such an impact. As difficult as it had been for me to deal with the ups and downs of having Katherine in my life, it was that much worse for Rhonda. She was an outspoken woman who didn't mind fighting for things she believed in, but her spirit was open and loving. It had bothered Rhonda no end that she hadn't seemed able to get along with Katherine.

Rhonda smiled at me as I stepped into the kitchen and placed the casserole on the counter. She was feeding Sally her mid-day meal and held the spoon in the air. "We're playing airplane," she explained. "The only way to get a little bit of food into her."

Sally cooed and waved her fists in the air from her infant's chair, knocking the spoon out of Rhonda's hand.

Laughing, Rhonda picked it up and wiped the cereal off the floor. "This little girl is proving to be a feisty one. Reminds me of Willow."

"How is my darling Willow?" I asked, picking up Sally and hugging her.

"Willow now wants to be called Princess," said Rhonda, clucking her tongue. "It suits her."

We laughed together.

I handed Sally back to Rhonda who held her in her lap.

"How are things here?" I asked, taking a seat at the

kitchen table beside her.

"Actually, okay. Reggie and his father have been spending time together working out their past differences. That's been a relief to see. Angela is exhausted, but I've promised her and Reggie a trip to the islands. I'll handle the kids ... or I should say, Rita and I will handle all the kids."

I waited for her to mention Angela having another baby and realized she hadn't been told yet.

Rhonda stared at me. "What?"

I straightened in my chair, trying to keep my face expressionless. "What do you mean?"

"Annie Rutherford Sanders, I know you, and you're hiding something."

Angela walked into the kitchen, wearing a robe. Her hair was wrapped in a towel. "What are you two talking about?"

"Annie is hiding something from me. Do you know what it is?"

Angela gave me a questioning look.

"I've said nothing to make her think that way," I said, defending myself.

Angela took a seat at the table next to me with a sigh. "Don't worry, Ann. I was going to tell her sometime today."

"Tell me what?" Rhonda said, glaring at the two of us. "You know I don't like secrets."

"Don't be angry at Ann. Reggie told her by accident." Angela took a deep breath and blurted out, "You're going to be a grandmother again,"

Rhonda stared at her with shock.

Angela burst into tears. "I don't think I can do it. Three kids four-years-old and under."

Rhonda handed Sally to me as she rose and went to Angela. Pulling her up in her arms, Rhonda hugged her. "Oh, honey. It'll all work out. I'll get some permanent help for you.

And I'll be here for you." She glanced at me. "And Annie too."

Angela took out a tissue from the pocket of her robe and dabbed at her eyes. "I'll feel better if I can just get some rest."

"When is the family service for Katherine going to be?" I asked. "Is there a way I can help with that? It's just the family and her friends from Palm Beach, right?"

Angela nodded. "Mom will set them up at the hotel. We'll meet on the beach to all say a few words and then have a nice dinner in the private dining room."

"That's what we've planned so far," said Rhonda. "We want to set a date that works for Vaughn. Katherine was very proud to be mentioned on *The Sins of the Children,* and that note he sent her. His call too."

"Just let me know what dates you're thinking of, and I'll make sure Vaughn is there," I said getting to my feet to give Angela a hug. "Dinner is set for tonight. Please give my condolences to Reggie and Arthur. I'm going to go, but I want you to know I'll help in any way I can."

"Thanks, Ann. I appreciate it," said Angela.

"You might not be ready to hear it, but congratulations on the new baby."

Angela let out a puff of air. "Thanks. I'll get used to the idea." She laughed. "Liz is worried she'll have to have another baby right away after her twins are born in order to catch up. I told her to get a puppy instead."

I laughed with Angela and Rhonda, but I was worried about Liz having more babies than she could handle. I'd seen what Angela was going through and didn't want that for Liz.

"I'll text you the possible dates after Angela and I have talked to the men," said Rhonda. "We'll go from there."

"Okay. I've got an appointment with Terri Thomas and Lorraine Grace. Terri is doing an article on fall weddings, and I want to be sure she understands her obligation to us for cooperating with her."

"Absolutely. Have you heard anything about weddings at the Sand Castle?" asked Rhonda.

I shook my head. Things had been pretty quiet from there.

As I left the house, Reggie and Arthur pulled into the driveway. I waited until they got out of the car and then went to them.

"Arthur, I'm so sorry about Katherine," I said, taking his hand and squeezing it. "She and I became friends over the past couple of months, and I'll miss her. If there's anything either Vaughn or I can do for you, please let me know."

"Thank you. Is Vaughn coming to the family service?" he asked.

"Yes. Rhonda and Angela are talking about dates now," I responded.

I went to Reggie and wrapped my arms around him. The first time I'd met him I wasn't sure he was the right person for Angela. But ever since he stood up for her at the beginning of their relationship, I'd loved him. "How are you doing, hon?"

He shrugged. "Okay, I guess. It seemed to happen so quickly. It'll take me a while to come to terms with it."

"If you ever want to talk, I'm here. By the way, Rhonda knows about the baby."

"Baby? What baby?" asked Arthur, giving Reggie a steady stare.

"We told mom but we were waiting to tell you," said Reggie.

Deciding not to get in the middle of that situation, I said, "Love to you both. Call, if I can help."

I left the two men talking in the driveway.

As I slid into my car, I turned to see how things were

going. Arthur was shaking a finger at Reggie, and I wondered what it would take to for him to understand that Reggie was a grown man now.

Parenting is hard, I told myself as I drove away. Liz was an adult, but I still worried about her. She was pretty open about letting me know when I was getting too close to an issue, but there were times when I wanted to make it easier for her by giving her advice born of experience. I suppose Arthur would learn in time that he had to let Reggie remain the man he was.

After the meeting with Lorraine and Terri, I went to Bernie's office and knocked on the door.

He looked up from his paperwork and waved me inside. "Sorry to hear that Katherine has died. I spoke to Rhonda earlier. She thanked me for the flowers we sent to the house. Let me know what else we can do. We've reserved a room for Katherine and Arthur's friends, Bettina and Chester Larkins, and also set aside the small dining room for the family for Thursday. This is contingent on Vaughn being there."

"I'll get in touch with Vaughn and get right back to you. On another note, what do you hear about The Sand Castle and weddings? So far, there's been no attempt to steal any wedding parties away. Lorraine Grace has heard nothing, and The Sand Castle wasn't invited to participate in the newspaper article. What's going on?"

"I'm not sure," said Bernie. "There's talk going around that the hotel is not doing well, that they can get guests in the door, but they don't stay long, and they don't come back."

"Interesting. Not that I'm surprised. Aubrey Lowell isn't much of a true hotel guy. Sure, he wants to get people into his hotel, but he doesn't have the patience or kindness to treat them well. We've all experienced that kind of behavior from him."

Bernie gave me a knowing look. "I guess his investors are pretty unhappy about it. I saw Brock Goodwin the other day, and he couldn't wait to avoid me."

"That alone speaks volumes about the project. I don't mind fair competition but dealing with someone who's dishonest is difficult. I haven't seen much of Brock around our hotel. I'll let you know if I do." I turned to go. "If anything comes up about any of it, please let me know."

"Will do. Let me know when you can that Vaughn's okay with the dates," Bernie said, giving me a little salute.

I left his office and went to mine to call Vaughn.

Sitting at my desk, I stared out the window, punched in his special number, and waited.

When he finally answered, he sounded out of breath. "Hi, Ann! What's up?"

"Angela, Reggie, and Arthur are hoping to have a family memorial gathering on Thursday. Are you able to make it? We won't go ahead with it without you."

"Hold on. I just came from a meeting. Let me check."

When he came back on the phone, he said. "That'll work. In exchange, I'll work late this week. I'm glad Darla is so easy to work with."

"How are things going for Darla and Meredith?" I asked. I'd been remiss about calling her.

"I guess great. They both seem happy."

"Nice," I said. "Such a change from before."

"Yes, but I'm still anxious to get to Canada and start filming. It's an important project."

"You'll do a great job with it, I know." Vaughn was a perfectionist who'd make sure of it. One reason other actors liked working with him.

"Can't wait to see you. It's been a while and so much has happened," he said.

"I'll be here waiting for you." I told him about the plans for the service.

"Thanks. I'd better go. Give Robbie a hug for me. And, Mrs. Sanders, when I get home, I'll show you just how much I missed you."

I laughed, loving his teasing. "Deal."

CHAPTER TWENTY-FOUR

I saw Vaughn swinging through the doors of the airport baggage area out to the sidewalk, and my heartbeat sped up. He always had that effect on me.

He smiled at me and trotted to the car, easily rolling his carry-on suitcase. Owning a condo in the City made it easier to travel back and forth. Something I intended to take advantage of one day.

As we drove home, Vaughn talked about his meetings with the director and told me who else was involved in the movie, sounding like an excited schoolboy.

I glanced at him and smiled.

"What?" he said.

"This is an excellent move for you. I haven't seen you this happy about work in a long time."

"I needed this change." He reached over and rubbed my shoulder. "You always make me feel so grateful I married you."

I smiled and thought of Jax and Mandy. This morning, I'd seen them from a distance as they carefully made their way to the beach. She waved happily. I wondered if Mandy was beginning to appreciate Jax's support. Life was so much easier with someone who loved you by your side.

When we arrived home, Trudy performed a happy dance for Vaughn and trailed after him as he headed into the bedroom to change clothes.

He emerged a few minutes later dressed in shorts and a T-shirt and walked down to the sailboat. After the service for

Katherine, Reggie and his father were sailing with Vaughn into the water off Sabal to spread her ashes. They'd decided to do it alone to keep a promise they'd made to Katherine. They'd bought a bottle of champagne for the occasion. Another request from her.

Vaughn returned and took a seat at the kitchen table where I'd placed plates of salad for our lunch. The informal family service on the beach was at four with a small reception in the Presidential Suite to follow. The Larkins, friends of Katherine and Arthur, would spend the night at the hotel in the Suite.

That afternoon as we assembled out by the beach in a spot often used for weddings, I found myself close to tears. I thought back to Angela and Reggie's wedding almost five years ago. Katherine had been so awful to everyone; especially Rhonda. And now, as part of the ceremony, Rhonda had been asked to speak. If only they'd started as friends instead of finally forming a friendship as Katherine was dying.

We formed a circle – Arthur, Angela, Reggie, Will, Rhonda, Vaughn, Bettina Larkin, Chester Larkin, Liz, Chad, and me. We each held a pretty seashell that had been found along the beach by Angela for the occasion.

Arthur spoke quietly. "Thank you all for being here as Katherine requested. She very much liked the idea of expanding our small family to include all of you. As she dealt with her illness, knowing the outcome, she was especially happy that she and Rhonda grew close. It was her wish that Rhonda speak at the ceremony, and then that anyone else who may wish to do so, follow."

It was quiet except for the sound of waves hitting the

shore and the mournful cries of the seagulls circling above us. I noticed the way Rhonda gripped Will's hand and knew she was trying her best to keep her emotions under control.

Finally, Rhonda stepped into the circle and spoke. "I promised to do as Katherine asked and speak to all of you as family. As you all know, Katherine and I did not start out as friends. Quite the opposite. Even a few months ago, we bickered over Sally Kate's name. It all seems so foolish now, but we were very sure we were right about so many things. Funny, how illness and knowing the way it was going to end was also the beginning of something we both wanted. A real friendship. Something I honor today."

Rhonda paused to gather her composure. "Katherine and I made a pact that I will keep. After realizing that nothing was more important to her than her family, she asked me to put together information about her to share with our grandchildren. I promised her that they would know the best about their grandmother Katherine. I have jewelry and other items that will be given to them at appropriate times. This I will do for her and them. As sad as this moment is, I'm grateful to have known Katherine not at her worst, but her best. She was a remarkable woman in unexpected, private ways. Before she died, we agreed to set up a fund to help Vice President Swanson's foundation to help women who needed it. Katherine, dear new friend, I will miss you."

Rhonda stepped back.

Each of us said a few kind words about Katherine and wished Reggie and Arthur comfort, but nothing could match Rhonda's heartfelt speech.

"And now," said Angela, "I ask each of you to return your shell to the sand or water in front of us so that memory of Katherine remains part of nature's pattern, here with us.

Tears ran down her cheeks, as she offered her hand to

Arthur. He took it.

Reggie held onto Rhonda's elbow, and they walked behind Angela and Arthur to the water's edge.

Then we all followed.

The sand, the water, and the wildlife at the beach always filled me with a sense of peace. Today was no different as I carefully laid my shell in the frothy edges of the water where it would eventually become part of the natural scene. Katherine and Rhonda had done what had once seemed impossible. That, in itself, was cause for such a touching gesture.

Later, back in the Presidential Suite, I had a chance to speak to Arthur. "After you go out on the boat with Vaughn, you're welcome to have dinner with us." Rhonda was entertaining the Larkins at her house, as she and Katherine had once discussed.

Arthur smiled and shook his head. "Thank you, anyway. I promised Angela and Reggie I'd spend the evening with them and the children. I have to return to New York. I've decided to sell our house in Newport and will be looking for housing here in the area in addition to keeping the penthouse in New York. It's time we became a real family." His eyes filled. "I had no idea Katherine felt so strongly about it. But she's right, you know. It's never too late to make things right. I want to learn to be a good father and grandfather."

"Sounds to me like it's already happening. I'm glad." I kissed his cheek.

"Angela and Reggie think the world of you and Vaughn." He gazed across the room at Will and Rhonda talking to Reggie. "Them too."

"What's that old saying—something about giving children wings to fly?"

He smiled and nodded. "Yes. I've been doing a lot of reading about those kinds of things." He stopped talking as Reggie came up to us.

"Ready, Dad?" Reggie asked quietly. "Vaughn said it might be time to set sail."

Arthur put his arm across Reggie's shoulder. "Okay, son, I'm as ready as I ever will be."

Vaughn joined us. "See you later, Ann. Time for the three of us to go."

"Good luck," I said, kissing him.

I watched as the three of them left the suite together. *See, Katherine? Your plan is working.*

"You okay, Mom?" Liz asked, wrapping an arm around me.

"Just thinking how important it is to enjoy life every day." Even at this early stage, her pregnancy was evident. We had much to celebrate.

When Vaughn returned from the sail with Reggie and Arthur, he was quiet. I understood. I was emotionally drained from the service for Katherine and all the emotions it had brought up.

We had a light supper, tucked Robbie in bed, and then sat outside on the lanai with glasses of lemon water.

"How did the sail go?" I asked, after deciding not to ask earlier.

"It was nice. Katherine's idea of having just the two of them scatter the ashes was a sweet one. I think Arthur and Reggie are beginning to resolve their differences."

"Naturally, Arthur is disappointed that Reggie won't be

joining the family firm, but I can't imagine that it would work out."

"Me, either. But Arthur told me he's going to make an effort to be part of Reggie and Angela's lives. It made me wish I could see more of Ty and June."

"Let's fly them here. I've missed them."

"Really? That would be great. I couldn't visit them when I was in California. But going forward I'll try to do that as much as I can."

I handed Vaughn my cell. "Call them. Ty should be home from work by now."

Grinning, Vaughn punched in the number for Ty.

I listened as Vaughn talked to his son. Though they were very different people, Vaughn and Ty had a strong relationship. It was heartwarming to hear their conversation.

"June's pregnant again? Great news, son!" Vaughn turned to me with a smile. "Yes, I understand. Well, maybe when she's feeling better and you think it's safe for her to travel, you'll come to Florida. Until then, I'll try to meet you in California."

Vaughn handed me the phone. "June wants to speak to you."

I eagerly took it from him. "Hi, sweetheart. I just heard Vaughn say you're pregnant again. I'm so happy for you. How are you feeling?"

"Pretty good," said June, "though after losing the last baby, we're not telling people outside the family that we're expecting. How's Liz? Last time we talked she thought she might be pregnant."

"She's pregnant and expecting twins," I said proudly. "Have you told her about you?"

"No," said June. "I didn't want any hurt feelings if it hadn't happened for her." She laughed. "I guess I shouldn't have worried. After we hang up, I'm going to call her."

We chatted for a few more minutes. I congratulated Ty, and before we said our goodbyes, I promised to accompany Vaughn to California so we could visit in person.

"Wonderful news, grandpa," I said to Vaughn. "I'm so happy for Ty and June."

"Yeah, me too. Ty sounded pretty excited about it." He grinned at me. "All this talk of babies reminds me how great it is that we don't have to worry about that. Should we ..."

Before he could continue, my cell rang. *Jax.* I took the call. "Hi, Jax. What's going on?"

"Mandy's in labor and she's asking for you," Jax said, his voice shaking. "Her pains are about five minutes apart."

"Oh, my word! You need to get her to the hospital. I'll meet you there." I turned to Vaughn. "Talking about babies, another one is about to enter the world. I have to meet Mandy and Jax at the hospital."

"The circle of life," said Vaughn, rising with me.

I grabbed my purse and with a kiss, I left Vaughn to help Mandy's baby enter the world.

Jax met me in the admitting area with a quick hug. "I'm glad you're here. She kept asking for you. They've taken Mandy up to her room. Follow me."

On the maternity ward, we were directed to Mandy's room, a suite similar to what Angela and Reggie had shared.

As soon as Mandy saw me, she started to cry. "Ann, thank you for coming. I'm so scared."

I went to her bedside where a nurse was taking her vitals. "Hi, sweetie! There's no reason to be scared. Childbirth is a natural thing." I took hold of her hand. "Jax and I are here to help you."

"You don't get it! I don't want this baby!" she said.

"Oh, honey! Let's get through this part and then we can talk." I gazed into her eyes and saw misery.

"If I have this baby, the Worthingtons will take her. I can't let that happen," she said, grimacing as pain took over.

"One step at a time," I said gently, nodding at Jax who stood on the opposite side of the bed. He'd taken hold of Mandy's other hand.

"Let's bring this baby into the world," he said. "Then we can decide what we're going to do."

Mandy nodded. "Okay. I love you, Jax."

"I know," he said softly. "Love you too."

My eyes welled with tears. They were so good together, so strong.

Dr. Benson stepped into the room. "Hello, everyone! Looks like we're having a baby."

She smiled at me. "Seems like I'm seeing a lot of you lately."

I returned her smile. "I'm always happy to be part of such an occasion."

Dr. Benson examined Mandy. "Looks like the baby is ready to come."

"Should I leave?" I asked.

"No, Ann! Stay here," cried Mandy, her voice high with pain.

"Okay, sweetie. I'm right here. Listen to Dr. Benson and do as she asks."

Twenty minutes later, Mandy, sweaty and sobbing, held her baby girl in her arms. "She's beautiful. So beautiful," she managed to get out. "Look, Jax! Isn't she perfect? 7 pounds, 2 ounces."

Tears streamed down Jax's face. I didn't know whether they were tears of triumph or sorrow.

Mandy turned to me. "Jax and I are going to keep the baby."

I glanced at Jax. "I've asked Mandy to marry me. She said yes."

While one nurse cleaned up the baby, Dr. Benson took care of Mandy's afterbirth.

Jax took me aside. "We're going to call the Worthingtons tomorrow. I have a feeling it's not going to go well. We might need to find a place to stay away from the hotel for a few days."

"If so, you may come to my house. I've tried my best to remain neutral on this issue, but I'm so pleased things have worked out between you and Mandy, and you're keeping the baby."

Jax glanced at Mandy. "We've loved each other since we were kids. My mother and father have known Mandy since she was a young girl needing a safe place away from her parents. Living down the street from them, they knew all about their cruelty."

"Jax! Ann! Come see the baby!" cried Mandy, sitting up in bed, holding the baby close to her.

I stood nearby as Mandy handed Jax the baby. "Here she is. Yours and mine."

The gentleness with which Jax held her told so much. Smiling down at the baby who was wearing a pink hat and wrapped in a green blanket, he turned to Mandy. "She's beautiful. I knew she would be because she's yours. She's ours."

"I know we're doing the right thing," said Mandy with a sound of confidence I hadn't heard before. Mother juices flowing, I thought.

"Here," said Jax. "You hold her." He handed me the baby and glanced at Mandy. "Should we tell her now?"

"Yes." Mandy beamed at me. Ann, we're calling the baby Carli Ann Belle. Carli means a woman with freedom, and Ann is for you and all you've done to help me."

"Oh, such a sweet gesture. Thank you so much." I glanced down at the pink-cheeked baby whose eyes seemed to focus momentarily on me. "Hi, Carli! Love your name!" I cooed, before handing her back to her mother's outstretched arms.

Jax sat on the edge of the bed next to them. Seeing them together like this, I was sure they'd come through the worst and were about to embark on a nice life together. Or they would after they got the conference call with the Worthingtons behind them.

CHAPTER TWENTY-FIVE

Vaughn was asleep and the house quiet when I returned home. It was too late to call Rhonda. I sent a text instead, so she'd have the news first thing in the morning.

I undressed, prepared for the night, and slid into bed, careful not to disturb Vaughn. Lying next to him, I gazed up at the ceiling fan whirling slowly above us and thought back to Liz's birth—the wonder and joy of it. I understood Mandy's desire to keep her baby. But, like Jax, I knew there'd be trouble ahead.

Morning came early with a call from Rhonda. "I heard from Jax and Mandy late last night, too late to talk to you. But I couldn't wait to talk to you this morning. Their news makes me so happy. I told them they could have their wedding at the hotel. But, Annie, I don't think it's going to go over well with the Worthingtons."

"Neither do I," I said.

Restless, I got out of bed, went to the window, and stared out at the water, hoping for my nerves to calm. The morning sun glistened on the crescents of the waves rolling atop the calmer water of the inlet, topping them with a touch of gold.

But even that beautiful sight did nothing to lower my anxiety.

"I think we ought to tell Amelia what's happened," said Rhonda. "Perhaps she can help to smooth things over with Sam and Cassie. I don't want anything to upset the happiness Jax and Mandy have found together."

"That's an excellent idea. Do you want me to make the call?"

"I think you should, considering you were there when they first announced their decision." Rhonda let out a sigh. "I knew they were a perfect match."

"What? You're not going to claim you brought them together?" I said, surprised.

Rhonda laughed. "It was too late. I realized they were together from the first moment I saw them. By the way, I love the baby's name. Carli Ann Belle. So sweet."

"I was very touched by it," I admitted. "Before we hold a wedding at the hotel for them, we probably should host their baby shower."

"They told me they intend to stay in the staff apartment if it's okay with both of us. I gave them our blessing. Hope you don't mind."

"Not at all. They have my permission to hide out at my house should it become necessary. I feel sorry for Cassie Worthington that this didn't work out for them, but I believe with all my heart that the right decision is being made."

"I promised I'd go visit Mandy in the hospital this morning. Jax is already working with Manny but will take time off to bring Mandy home to the apartment. I'm taking a bunch of food over there now and will see what they need. I thought you and I could go shopping. Why don't I pick you up in a half-hour or so after I've seen Mandy?"

"Sounds perfect. The big box stores open early. I'll get dressed and be ready. This is an even better idea than a baby shower."

I padded into the kitchen. Vaughn and Robbie were having cereal.

I gave them each a kiss, fixed myself a cup of coffee, and told them the news of the baby's arrival. "Rhonda and I are going shopping. We'll surprise them. Thankfully, we both know what they'll need with all the babies presently in our lives."

"Have fun. Be sure and get them a baby monitor like Nell and Clint own," said Vaughn.

I laughed. "Guess you've been brought up to speed on the latest, too."

Robbie gave me a serious look. "Will you buy the baby a stuffed dog like I have?"

Touched, I leaned down and kissed his cheek. "I will. A special gift from you to Baby Carli."

I left them to get ready for the day. Rhonda was an enthusiastic shopper. I'd have to take my SUV for all the packages we intended to buy.

When Rhonda arrived, she was glowing with excitement. "Mandy's baby is beautiful. Blond hair and light-brown eyes. So unusual. And Mandy's glowing. I took her some clothes that she wanted to wear home. Knowing she's going to keep her baby has created such a change in her. She's much happier, much more at ease. I just hope the Worthington's don't ruin it."

"Stop and catch your breath," I said. "I have a call in to Amelia Swanson but haven't been able to talk to her. We'll go ahead and do our shopping. Nobody is going to take that baby away from Mandy and Jax now."

"Okay. C'mon. From the looks of it, they need everything, but a crib borrowed from the hotel." She rubbed her hands together. "This is going to be fun."

I laughed, remembering how Rhonda had insisted on taking me shopping for a new bathing suit after seeing the dull black one I'd bought for the trip to Florida to meet her.

She was an enthusiastic shopper. No doubt, we were about to buy out a few stores.

I arranged the seats in the SUV to better hold a lot of packages, and we took off.

Two hours later, after loading up everything we could think of for an infant, three-month-old, and six-month-old girl, two different salesclerks worked separate cash registers to check us out.

We quickly drove to the apartment, accepted help from Troy at the spa to carry packages up to the apartment, and began work setting things up.

Jax arrived home, took one look at what we were doing, sank onto the only empty chair, and held his head in his hands, overwhelmed.

I went to him. "Hope you don't mind our doing this. We're so excited about the decisions you and Mandy have made and want to help. It's a grandmother thing."

He raised his face and though he was smiling there were tears in his eyes. "Thank you. Since we decided to get married and keep the baby, we haven't had time to even think about any of this. Mandy is going to be very happy with all you're doing. The Worthingtons made her feel as if she could never provide for her baby. Now, this is proof that we can do it with a little help from friends."

Rhonda came over to him and patted his back. "Like Annie said, it's a grandma thing. You kids are more than friends. You're like family. Ya know?"

He nodded and drew a deep breath. "I'd forgotten what it was like to be treated like this. I haven't been home in a while. Now, this is my home."

"See if you can delay picking up Mandy," I said. "I want to

launder some of these things, and we need to get other things ready for you so that after you bring the baby home, you can have some privacy."

"We'll get things put away in the baby's room," Rhonda said. "Leave it up to us."

Jax stood and gave us each a hug. "I'll call her now and work out timing with Manny."

After he left, I looked around the living room where boxes and bags still filled a large portion of the space. "We've got a lot to do. Let's start with the infant things that need to be laundered."

As we unwrapped each little shirt, each little outfit, I couldn't wait for the time when I'd be doing this for Liz. The thought of two at once was a bit of a worry, but as we'd done for Angela, and now, Mandy, we'd be there to help Liz.

We'd put the last of the cleaned, folded clothing in the bureau drawers, made sure the monitor was operative, had the diaper pail and diapers ready, along with organic lotions and other items Angela had told us Mandy would want and stood back. We'd even tucked the stuffed dog Robbie wanted me to buy into a corner of the crib next to a soft, light blanket that matched the pink in the butterfly-printed crib sheets we'd bought so they would see them.

"Looks pretty," said Rhonda. "I don't know about you, but I'm ready for a light lunch and one of Jean-Luc's sweet desserts."

"Sounds perfect."

I patted the robe we'd laid out on the bed in the baby's room for Mandy. We'd placed a note on top of it that simply read, "Welcome Home!"

"Thanks, Annie, for being my partner in this, like always."

"You're welcome," I said. "I just hope none of this has been in vain. I'm not going to be able to relax until I'm sure the Worthingtons will let the issue drop."

"We won't make them pay for any of Mandy's room charges," said Rhonda. "I'll pay for them myself." She glared at me. "Don't say no."

"Okay, I won't," I said, knowing she could well afford it. "Let me try Amelia again."

I punched in the number and this time, someone answered. "Is Vice President Swanson there? It's Ann Sanders calling from The Beach House Hotel."

"Oh, hello, Ann. It's Amelia's assistant, Beverly. The vice president is on her way to Florida to see you. She wanted me to tell you if you called again."

My heart dropped to my shoes. "Do you know what the visit is about?"

"No. Some personal business to tend to. When she checks in with me, I'll let her know you called."

"Thanks," I said, worried sick.

"What's going on?" Rhonda asked.

"Amelia Swanson is on her way to Florida to see us."

The look of dismay on Rhonda's face said it all.

We left the apartment and headed to the hotel for lunch. A sweet dessert might be just what we needed to lift our spirits.

We'd just finished lunch and were going over the list of expenses Mandy had incurred at the hotel when my cell chirped a special tone. *Amelia Swanson.*

My fingers were cold as I picked up the phone. "Good afternoon, Madame Vice President. I've put you on speakerphone with Rhonda. What can we do for you?"

"I understand you called. I just landed in Fort Myers and am driving down to Sabal. What are you calling about?"

"You don't know about the baby?" I said, astonished.

"Are you talking about the Worthingtons' baby?" she asked. "Has she come yet?"

"Yes, and it's not the Worthingtons' baby. The baby is remaining with Mandy and Jax. They are going to be married and raise her."

"Whoa! What do the Worthingtons say about that?" Amelia said.

"To my knowledge, they haven't been notified yet. Mandy wanted to wait until she and Jax were settled before calling them. We thought you might be a help if things don't go well."

"I'll do what I can, but I know how devastated the Worthingtons will be. What about her expenses?"

"Rhonda has agreed to reimburse any hotel expenses. We're going over them now."

"Ah, such a generous woman you are, Rhonda," said Amelia. "I'm both sad and happy at how things turned out. I was trying to do a favor for everyone involved. Now, the Worthingtons will have to go through an adoption agency because I don't want this to happen again. From now on, any woman my foundation helps will have to use normal channels for adopting out her baby."

"I feel the same way about being both happy and sad," I said. "But if you saw Mandy and Jax with the baby, you'd know the right decision has been made. I'll let you know how things went after they make their call to the Worthingtons."

"I don't see your name on our reservations list," said Rhonda. "Are you staying with us?"

"No, I'm not. I'm staying at Jean-Luc's house with my sister. She called to say she had something important to share with me. I have a feeling they've decided to get engaged. Even though it's early in the relationship, it's bothered Jean-Luc not to have Lindsay appear more respectable. It's sweet really."

"He's been very quiet about it, but if it's true, I think they make a marvelous couple," I said.

"A perfect solution after what that rat bastard ex-husband did to her," said Rhonda.

Amelia laughed. "Spoken like a true friend of Lindsay's."

"We hope to see you while you're in town," I said.

"I have a feeling you might. I don't think Samuel Worthington is going to let this issue drop easily."

We ended the call, and I turned to Rhonda. "What do you know? All kinds of things are happening. Some not so great."

"I knew it was a good idea of mine to have Jean-Luc and Lindsay spend time together," said Rhonda. "A match made in heaven."

I knew it wasn't entirely Rhonda's idea to put Lindsay and Jean-Luc together, but I let her think it was. With all the chaos around Mandy's baby, it was a lovely thought.

We were just about to leave the hotel together when Rhonda and I received a phone call from Samuel Worthington.

"Hello, senator," I said, "I've placed you on speaker-phone so my partner, Rhonda, is part of this conversation." No way was I going to get into a situation of "he said, she said."

"As you no doubt know, I've received a phone call from Amanda Rogers stating that she's decided to keep our baby. That is something that was never agreed upon."

My throat grew dry, but I forced the words out. "I believe she mentioned from time to time that she wasn't sure about going ahead with it."

"She told me that the two of you have set her and Jax up in an apartment and have provided all the things the baby needs. You were supposed to remain a neutral party in all this. You advertise being discreet with guests, but it appears you're not. Jax mentioned several people who know about the baby being theirs. What happened to your integrity in this situation?"

My voice grew icy. "We have remained discreet about any information between you and Mandy. What she or Jax talks about is out of our hands. We've supported her; we've done as we've been asked in caring for her needs as our guest. As much as I think she's doing the right thing, neither I nor my business partner knew anything about her decision until after the birth of the baby, which is when she and Jax announced their intentions."

"What am I going to tell Cassie?" he asked with genuine hurt, and I felt for him.

"I'm so sorry. I know how disappointed you are and how difficult it will be to tell your wife, but neither my partner nor I made that decision for Mandy. It's her decision and Jax's alone."

"I'm flying down there tonight. She's going to have to face me and give me reasons why the baby is better off with her than with us. She knows what we can do for that child."

"I'm not going to tell you all the things she can do for the baby herself. It's not my place. But I will warn you not to put undue pressure on her. She and Jax are together on this."

"One thing more," Rhonda said. "Any expenses paid to the hotel will be reimbursed by us. That's one thing we can do to help."

"Yeah? Well, Mandy is missing out on a lot of money. Enough to give her a financially sound start in a better life."

"I think there's nothing else we can say or do," I said. "I'm truly sorry for your disappointment. Please give our condolences to Cassie. Good evening."

"I'll see you tonight. I'll be staying at the hotel. I

understand the apartment Mandy is living in is right there on the property."

"Safe flight," I managed to say while my stomach whirled in sickening circles. He sounded so threatening.

I ended the call and turned to Rhonda. "I think Mandy, Jax, and the baby better not be at the hotel when Samuel Worthington arrives."

"I agree. Didn't you offer to have them come to your house if there was trouble?"

"Yes," I said. "It might be better if when the time comes for a meeting, the baby isn't there. That would only make it worse for the senator. She's a beautiful baby."

"I think you're right," said Rhonda. "What a sticky situation for everyone involved."

CHAPTER TWENTY-SIX

I called Vaughn and told him about my conversation with Samuel Worthington. He agreed it sounded ominous and also thought it was a wise idea for Mandy, Jax, and the baby not to be accessible.

"Though I think they'd be better off here at our house, Ann," he said, "It concerns me that you and Rhonda got caught up in another situation like this."

"I understand. Believe me, I don't plan to get involved in another project of Amelia Swanson's. I'll help her in other ways. I agree we can't have someone staying here at the hotel who might cause trouble for our guests."

"You and Rhonda are caring women," said Vaughn. "But I don't want anything to happen to you or the hotel. It's pretty rotten of the senator to suggest that you and The Beach House Hotel don't live up to your reputation. I can't imagine what he'll say to Mandy."

"And that's why Rhonda and I want her out of the apartment. It will force him to set up a time and place for them to meet. Rhonda, Jax, and I will be at any meeting between them and Mandy."

Vaughn sighed. "Hopefully, that will be the end of it."

"I know. Thanks for being concerned, but we'll handle it." I didn't dare mention how worried I was that the situation would backfire and hurt the hotel.

"What about dinner? Are they eating with us?" Vaughn asked. He was great at grilling food outdoors.

"I'll see what they want to do. The senator won't be here

until late. Mandy and Jax might want their first meal together with the baby to be at home. After talking to them, I'll come right home and make sure they have everything they need. Good thing we've got all the necessary baby equipment up after Nell's visit."

"Nell called a short while ago," Vaughn said. "She says Bailey is smiling all the time now."

"So sweet!" I could hear the happiness in his voice and knew how proud he was.

"I'll see you soon," I said.

Rhonda gave me a thoughtful look. "We can't let our reputation or that of the hotel be ruined by the likes of Senator Samuel Worthington. He's an entitled prick!"

"Let's take care of this problem and rethink how best to help other young women without the pressure of having them stay here."

"Sounds like a plan," said Rhonda. "Though with all the new babies in the family—here or soon to be born, I don't regret helping Mandy with hers."

"Me, too," I said. "Let's go talk to them now."

We walked over to their building and climbed the stairs to their apartment.

Rhonda knocked gently on the door.

Jax opened it with a worried look.

"Hi, Jax!" I said. "May we talk to you and Mandy about a problem?"

"Problem? Do you mean Senator Worthington?" A pinched expression transformed his handsome face. "He's tried to call three times, but I won't let Mandy pick up the call. She answered once and broke down in tears."

"Can we talk to her?" Rhonda asked, giving him a look of concern.

"Sure. Come on in. She's lying down on the couch."

We walked into the apartment. Soft music was playing from a cell phone perched on the coffee table in front of the couch. Mandy was stretched out across the cushions holding the baby in her arms.

She looked up at us. "Hi, glad you're here. I think I'm in big trouble."

"What do you mean?" I asked, frowning at the fresh tears that filled her eyes.

"If you're talkin' about Senator Samuel Worthington, leave 'im to me. I'll tell that bastard where he ..." Rhonda began, stopping when laughter burst out of Mandy.

"I'm so glad you're on my side," Mandy said between breaths. "Sorry, my hormones are going crazy. But really, I appreciate the two of you so much."

"We've been talking and think it's a good idea for you, Jax, and the baby to stay at my house until you can get things resolved with the senator," I said.

"Yeah, he's flying in tonight," said Rhonda.

"He is?" Mandy clapped a hand to her chest. "But I don't want him here."

"Neither do I. If he harasses Mandy, I'm not going to hold back," said Jax grimly. "Mandy, the baby, and I are making a home together." He glanced at Mandy. "I love them and will take care of them."

"And I love him," said Mandy gazing at Jax.

"I'm glad to see you standing firm on this, but I think we all need to be together when you meet with the senator," I said, gazing at Carli. "I also think it's wise and kindest if he doesn't meet the baby. She's so beautiful that seeing her would make it that much harder."

"Annie's right. It's going to be difficult enough as it is," said Rhonda.

"When would I have to meet with him?" asked Mandy in a

tiny, frightened voice.

"I think it best if you meet mid-morning. That will give you a chance to get things settled with the baby and you ready. My babysitter, Elena, will take care of the baby for you. She's highly trained."

"You and Rhonda and Jax would be there with me?" Mandy said.

We looked at one another and nodded.

"Okay," said Mandy, pressing the baby up against her.

"I have everything you need for the baby except newborn diapers and what clothing you want to dress her in."

Mandy's smile was forced. "I'll use the diaper bag you gave me." Her shoulders straightened. "No one is going to take away my baby. He has no claim to her."

"Right. Legally, he doesn't. Thank heavens you didn't sign any papers with him," I said.

"Smart move," said Rhonda.

I turned to Jax. "What time do you plan to come to my house with Mandy and the baby? We have a private guestroom for the two of you with a nursery."

"How about after dinner?" He glanced at Mandy for approval.

"Let's say eight o'clock," she said. "Are you sure you want us, Ann? The baby and I will be up in the night making noise."

"No worries. We'll deal with it. If you come by eight, Robbie and Trudy can say hello before settling down. It's a school night."

"Okay. Eight o'clock," said Jax. "We'll text the senator and tell him we'll meet with him tomorrow morning around ten. Does that sound all right?"

"Yes," said Rhonda. "That way, you're not ignoring him, but you're setting the boundaries, not him."

"With you unavailable here at the apartment, he won't be able to see you until you're ready," I added.

Jax let out a long breath. "Okay. That's how we'll play it. Thank you both."

The baby started to cry.

"I think she's hungry again. I'm trying to breast-feed her so I'd better go see if she'll latch on."

Holding the baby, Amanda got to her feet. Standing there in a robe we'd bought her, she was nineteen-years-old, so vulnerable that I was glad we'd stepped in to help.

At home, I sat with Vaughn enjoying a glass of wine as I told him all that had happened.

"I hear stories about young women in trouble and I'm glad both Nell and Liz have never faced that situation," said Vaughn. "I think Amelia Swanson deserves a lot of credit for setting up her foundation. But, in truth, I've never liked the deal with Senator Worthington."

"She told me she has no intention of ever doing anything like it again," I said. "It's too bad that this happened to Mandy. But Amelia was only trying to help."

"I get it," said Vaughn. "Another baby in the house, eh?"

"For one night only," I said. "A way to get used to the idea of another visit from Bailey and future visits from Ty and June and their baby, and Liz's babies from time to time."

He grinned at me. "I have to say you make a damn sexy grandma."

I laughed. "If anybody had told me how happy I'd be to hear that, I'd say they were kidding. But, truthfully, I love the sound of it. By the time our grandkids are ready for independence, Robbie will be grown and perhaps we'll start all over again."

"Whoa! That' would make me a decrepit grandfather."

"Not if you stay in shape," I said.

"Hmm. I know of one way to get my exercise," he said, wiggling his eyebrows.

I laughed, wondering if most grandparents still acted this way or if it was because in many ways Vaughn and I were still like newlyweds.

I took a last look at the guest room and the alcove where the crib was set up. I'd loved the idea of a separate wing holding three ensuite bedrooms when we'd first looked at the house. Robbie used the one closest to the rest of the house, leaving the other two open to guests. It had worked well on several occasions. This, I hoped, would be one of them.

With Nell's arrival with the baby, one of the guest suites had been transformed into a very practical layout for both parents and baby. In typical fashion, I'd bought and set up everything I thought she'd need and added even more following their visit. Mandy would be as comfortable here as I could make it. Still, it seemed a shame that she'd had to move even if it was for only one night. At the sound of the doorbell, I left the room and went to the front of the house.

Jax stood in the doorway with Vaughn holding onto the baby's infant car seat in one hand and a small suitcase in the other. Mandy followed him into the house carrying the diaper bag Rhonda and I had given her.

"Welcome!" I said, signaling Trudy to stop barking.

Robbie joined us.

"You remember our son, Robbie," I said, ruffling his dark hair.

"Hi, Robbie!" Jax said, smiling. "Want to show me to our room?"

Robbie grinned and motioned him forward.

I quickly hugged Mandy and said, "Come with me. We'll get you comfortable and then if you like, we can relax on the lanai unless you'd rather just go to bed."

"I'm pretty exhausted, but I can relax for a while," she said, following me into her room.

Her eyes widened when she saw the crib, and the special little dresser filled with clothing and holding a collection of lotions and health care supplies on top in a colorful arrangement. Several different styles of pacifiers were there, wrapped in plastic.

Jax sat on the edge of the bed holding Carli. Robbie was at his side, staring down at the baby.

"She sure is little. I thought Bailey was small, but this one's even smaller," said Robbie.

"Bailey is my granddaughter," I explained. "Why don't we let you get settled and if you wish, come join us on the lanai for a while. Robbie has a little time before he goes to bed."

"Aw, Mom," Robbie said. "Not so early!"

"On the weekends you don't," I replied, ruffling his hair. In reality, he was a child who loved sleep. Without it, he was a grouch.

"The baby's very cute," said Vaughn to me as we walked away. "I think it's a smart move that the senator won't be able to see her. That would only make matters worse."

"My thoughts, as well."

After a few minutes, both Mandy and Jax joined us. Mandy held up the baby monitor. "Thanks. I love the one you gave me. Now I can see and hear the baby if she begins to cry."

"And Trudy can hear her, too," said Robbie. "She likes guarding babies."

Mandy laughed. "She wouldn't leave when I asked her if

she wanted to come."

"We'll force her out of the room when you're ready to go to bed," I said, grinning at the thought of that little dachshund guarding the baby. But I knew if anyone tried to harm Carli, they'd have to fight Trudy off. She might be small, but she had the heart of a lion.

Jax, sitting next to Mandy, clasped Mandy's hand and lifted it to his knee. I noticed the diamond ring on her finger and said, "You're officially engaged?"

Mandy beamed at me. Holding up her left hand she wiggled her fingers, so the diamond sparkled in the light from the fan above. "Isn't it beautiful?" She smiled at Jax. "I was so surprised. I'd told him I didn't need a ring as long as I had his promise."

The most tender look filled Jax's face as he studied Mandy before turning to me. "We have another favor to ask. Is it possible for us to be married at the hotel? I don't mean anything fancy. I know of a space in the side garden where we could recite our vows."

"That would be lovely. We'll help in any way we can. If the small dining room isn't booked, we can set up a little celebration there." I knew Rhonda would want to be involved. She'd thought Mandy and Jax were soul mates before anyone else. It would be worth her bragging to work with her on a special celebration for them.

"That would be great but uh ..." he coughed with embarrassment.

"No worries about expenses. You're on our staff. We take care of things like this for free if we're not booked and rooms are available."

"Really?" He turned to Mandy and smiled.

"That would be lovely," she said. "It would be just us and those we want, if they will come—you and Vaughn, Rhonda and Will, and Manny and Consuela, Liz and Chad. Right, Jax?"

"I might even have a surprise guest for you," I said, thinking of Amelia Swanson.

"My parents are coming for a visit, but we want to be married before they get here so there's no question about the future. No doubt Mandy's parents will hear some talk. We live in a small town."

"Well, then," I said cheerfully, "let me talk to Rhonda and Bernie and we'll come up with a plan."

Mandy couldn't help yawning, and I realized how tired she and Jax must be. "Robbie, time for bed. Mandy? Jax? Do you need anything else?"

They stood. "We have everything we're going to need," said Mandy. "You've even put bottled water and flowers in the room. I feel as if I'm at The Beach House Hotel."

I laughed. "Once in the hotel business; always in the business."

The three of them left the room with a promise to Robbie from Vaughn and me that we'd be in to tuck him in for the night.

Alone on the lanai, I faced Vaughn. "Weddings and babies. Why does it seem as if that's been our lives lately?"

"Because it has," he said. "But after Katherine's unexpected death, I'm ready to enjoy it. More babies to come."

"I look at Liz and think of two babies at once and wonder how she'll manage. She looks huge already, and she's not that far along. And with Ty and June far away I don't want to disregard them. I'm wishing for a boy to carry on the name."

"Or a sweet girl like Bailey," he said.

I smiled at the best grandpa I knew.

CHAPTER TWENTY-SEVEN

The next morning, I waited anxiously to hear that the meeting between Jax and Mandy and the senator was finalized. After more thought, we all agreed it should take place in a neutral location like the library at the hotel. There was no need for the senator to see and judge the kids' living quarters. We all knew they were fine accommodations, if not fancy.

When Mandy and Jax walked into the kitchen dressed just before ten, I put aside my coffee cup. Elena was sitting in a chair at the kitchen table holding the baby.

"Ready?" I asked.

"As ready as we'll ever be," said Jax, his voice tight with nerves.

"I didn't mention that you and Rhonda would be there," said Mandy. "But I'm glad you will be. He sometimes scares me."

Jax put his arm around her. "You have me to protect you."

"I know. But it's Ann and Rhonda's hotel he keeps threatening," said Mandy.

"What do you mean?" I asked as my stomach turned a somersault.

"He said you were the main reason for my changing my mind," Mandy said. "I told him that wasn't true, but he's very upset."

"Well, then, I'm glad we'll be present," I said. "You go on ahead to the hotel. I'll meet you there. We want to give an appearance of your being independent."

"My truck is in pretty bad shape, but I've worked on it since Mandy tried to run away," said Jax.

I smiled. "No worries. A truck or car doesn't make a good parent or a bad one."

He nodded his acknowledgment but didn't speak. Turning to Mandy who was kissing the baby, he took her elbow and gingerly walked her to the truck as I watched.

I raced to my car, got in, and took off after them.

At the hotel, I parked in the back as usual. Rhonda's Cadillac was already there.

Inside the office, I told Rhonda about the phone call Mandy had had with Samuel Worthington.

"If that bastard tries to pull any punches, I'm gonna blast him wide open," said Rhonda. "He's as bad as Brock with all his threats."

"Wait and see what happens. We need to join the kids before he pulls any stunts."

We walked to the library. I heard the sound of voices before I opened the door and we walked in.

Surprised, I stared at the man sitting with the senator on one side of the table. Facing them, Jax and Mandy glanced at us and I noticed the relief that crossed their faces.

"Hello, senator," I said and studied the man next to him. He jumped to his feet along with Samuel and held out his hand. "Geoffrey Cohen, representing Mr. Worthington."

"Is there a reason Mr. Worthington can't represent himself?" Rhonda asked, glaring at the senator.

"My understanding was there were no documents signed," I said, shaking Geoffrey's hand reluctantly.

"True, but there are other issues to be resolved," he said, shaking Rhonda's hand.

Samuel spoke. "This is Ann Sanders and her business partner, Rhonda Grayson, owners of The Beach House Hotel."

"Ah, yes, I assumed as much," said Geoffrey.

Rhonda and I took seats on either side of Mandy and Jax.

My heart pounded as I faced Samuel. *What did he have in mind?*

Samuel wasted no time in letting us know. "As far as I'm concerned, Amanda, you had an agreement with Cassie and me to provide you with care in return for the baby you didn't want."

"I never said I didn't want her. I said I didn't know if I did. Then you started in on me about all the material things you could give her." She swallowed hard and blinked back tears. "But I've never seen you look at Cassie the way Jax looks at me."

"My marriage is as solid as they come," said Samuel, his cheeks flushing with anger. "I won't be judged by a child. A child whose word cannot be trusted. You accepted our gifts of medical care and a restful stay here at the hotel where you'd be treated well and have privacy." He looked directly at me, then Rhonda. "And that's where our trouble began. You two women had no right to get involved in my business."

"One step at a time," counseled Geoffrey. "Let's talk about you, Amanda. You agreed to give your baby to Samuel and Cassie Worthington. Is that correct?"

Mandy squirmed in her chair. "Yes and no. When we first talked, I thought I might be able to do it. But when I realized my parents would never let me bring her home, I got to thinking about raising her on my own. But each time I tried to talk to Senator Worthington and Cassie about it, they kept telling me the baby would be better off with them. Though I knew Jax loved me, I told myself I shouldn't let him know I loved him too, that he'd be trapped into an awful marriage like my parents have."

Jax spoke up. "I've loved Mandy since high school. Her parents didn't approve of anyone outside the church her father runs, so we had to keep it pretty quiet. And her parents ... well, they're different." He glanced at Mandy. "Not very nice."

"They never want to see me again," said Mandy. "Jax's parents understand the issues within our family and support me."

"Do they know the baby isn't Jax's?" said Samuel.

Mandy sniffled and nodded. "They know she's mine and that Jax loves her."

Samuel sighed and looked away.

"May I ask what you do for a living, Jax?" asked Geoffrey.

"I work here at the hotel as a landscaper and man of all trades," said Jax proudly. "It's a great job with competitive pay and provides us with a place to live."

"Sounds like a lot to give a landscaper," Samuel said, studying Rhonda and me.

"I don't know what you're thinking, but I can assure you that the job requirements include being on the property should anything go wrong with the buildings," I said. "Peace of mind is worth a lot, and Jax has already proven to be very reliable."

"You're out of line. Don't question us about how we run the hotel," said Rhonda, her lips thinned with anger.

"Now, now," said Geoffrey. "We're just trying to find out to what extent you've influenced Amanda into changing her mind."

Ah! That's it! "I think you should concentrate on the matter of Mandy choosing to keep her baby herself." I turned to her. "Mandy, would you explain when you told us about your decision to keep the baby and to marry Jax?"

Mandy drew a long breath. "I told Ann when she came to the hospital after I went into labor. Jax had asked me to marry him, and I said yes. We'd decided to raise the baby together. I've loved him for a long time even though I thought he could do better than me."

"I see," said Geoffrey. "There's the matter of repaying the Worthingtons for the hotel bill and other items."

I straightened in my chair. "Without a written document, I don't think she'd be required to do that. So, if you were planning to use this ploy to have Mandy change her mind, you can stop now. All hotel expenses that have been paid for by the senator for Mandy's stay will be reimbursed. It's a non-issue."

Geoffrey's eyebrows rose. "Really? I was unaware of that." He turned to Samuel. "You didn't mention that. I think under the circumstances, we have no standing. Our business here is completed. I'm sorry."

"Senator Worthington, I'm sorry to disappoint you and your wife," said Mandy softly as tears rolled down her cheeks. "But I tried to tell you that I wasn't sure it was something I wanted to do. That's why I never signed the papers. I'm sorry, but she's my baby and I deserve to try to give her a good life and a lot of love with Jax and me."

Samuel held his head in his hands briefly. When he lifted his head and settled his gaze on Mandy, his eyes drilled into her like silent bullets. "I'm just so damn disappointed in you! You have no idea the damage you've done to Cassie and me! You should be ashamed of yourself! Now, before I throttle you like I want, I'd better get out of here." He rushed from the room.

Geoffrey stood. "There's nothing more to be said. I'm sorry it's ended like this. For what it's worth, I wish you two luck with each other and the baby."

Jax bobbed his head. "Thank you, sir. We already have a lot of that." He took Mandy's elbow, and they left the room together, their backs straight.

Geoffrey turned to us. "I'll make a list of expenses and submit them to you."

"No need," said Rhonda. "It's already been done. If you can wait around for a few minutes, I'll have a check drawn up for you, along with a copy of the expenses."

"Wow! I'm impressed," said Geoffrey. "Such a sad situation for the senator, but a reason to be very cautious in circumstances like this. I want you to know that in D. C., the reputation of the hotel remains high. I told Sam it would be difficult to prove that Amanda was swayed by you two to keep the baby. But, as usual, he wanted to press forward. He's pretty used to getting his way. This has been a severe blow to him and his lovely wife, Cassie."

"I'm sorry this has happened to them, but I think Mandy's concern about love is genuine. More than anything, those two will give that baby love. Especially because Mandy grew up with so little of it."

"She's a strong person," said Rhonda. "Just watching the joy on her face when she looks at the baby is enough to make me cry."

I simply nodded my agreement. I didn't want to let on that Rhonda was one of the biggest softies I knew.

We shook hands with Geoffrey again.

"How long are you staying?" I asked.

"We're booked on a late afternoon flight." He held up a finger of warning. "But I intend to eat lunch here. If the rest of the food is as delicious as those cinnamon rolls, I have no intention of missing out."

Rhonda and I laughed with him. It wasn't the first time

we'd heard such a thing.

Back at my house, Rhonda and I sat with Mandy. Jax had gone off to work, and Mandy was taking it easy on one of the couches on the lanai. The sun spread a glow around us. I reveled in the warmth of the sun. Fall temperatures went from hot to not so hot, and I loved it all.

"By suppertime, it'll be okay to go back to your apartment," I told Mandy, telling her about the conversation with Geoffrey.

"I was so scared to meet with Senator Worthington," Mandy said, "but I know I'm doing the right thing. And I'm right about him and Cassie. There's no real love there. And I wouldn't want that for my baby."

"You and Jax are perfect for one another," said Rhonda. "I knew it. I have a special knack for putting people together."

I rolled my eyes and burst out laughing. We were going to have fun with this wedding.

"Well, I'm glad you were right about us, Rhonda," said Mandy. "Jax and I are happy together. I don't know why I listened to my parents telling me I wasn't right for him. Jax's parents don't respect mine at all. And they don't know all the things I know about them. It's too bad, but I don't want Carli near them. They're such cold and unforgiving people."

As much as I hated to hear of family predicaments like this, I knew from others that sometimes distance from family was best.

CHAPTER TWENTY-EIGHT

With Jax's parents due to arrive, Rhonda and I went to work on the wedding we had just two days to make happen. It had taken some convincing, but Mandy and Jax finally agreed to wait until his parents could be part of the ceremony. I was glad. I knew Mandy and Jax would need their support in the future and there was nothing like weddings and babies to bring people together.

Unbeknownst to Mandy and Jax, I made a call to Amelia Swanson to tell her what had transpired and to suggest she attend the wedding as a means of closure for all concerned.

"I like that idea," said Amelia. "I'd be happy to attend. By the way, Lindsay told me she and Jean-Luc are going to announce their engagement at Christmas."

"Wonderful news!" So much had happened in the past year it was difficult to keep up with all the changes.

I went to find Rhonda, who was meeting with Lorraine Grace in the small dining room. The library was booked the night of Mandy's wedding, but we'd decided to use the small dining room instead. That room had been used for many happy occasions. This would be one of them.

Rhonda was ecstatic to hear that Amelia Swanson would make the effort to come to the wedding. "It makes everything seem right, ya know?"

"I think so too. Now, let's see about a menu. Something simple and wholesome is what Mandy requested," I said.

"Jax told me he wanted steak on the menu," Rhonda said.

"We could offer a choice of steak or fish of some kind," I

said. "We'll see what Jean-Luc has to say about it."

"The color theme will be pink and white," said Lorraine. "Rhonda and I have discussed it and wanted to honor both the wedding and the baby."

"I love the idea. What does Mandy think of it?"

"She told us to do whatever we thought best," said Rhonda. "Jax has told her not to worry, but I think she's become nervous about seeing his parents again and having their approval."

"I'm curious about his parents," I said. "I know Jax loves them, and he's told me they accepted Mandy back when they were in high school."

"I've learned they own a successful car dealership in town. That's why they wanted to pay for the wedding," Rhonda said. "There's more to Jax Thomas than we've been led to believe. Mandy told me he was the star quarterback for the football team, and though he was offered scholarships at a lot of schools, he went to UVA to stay close to her. Heaven knows what Mandy's mother said to her to make her believe she'd harm Jax if they stayed together."

"I'm glad her parents won't be present to ruin this occasion," I said. I could imagine Rhonda's reaction to them and theirs to her. I would've tried to be polite, but I'm not sure I could carry it off after learning about their abuse of Mandy.

"Mandy told me she sent a picture of the baby to her parents, but they told her to stop, that neither she nor the baby had a place in their family. Pretty heavy stuff for a new mother." Rhonda shook her head. "We'll make this wedding the best ever."

"As long as we make sure Mandy is happy with all the details," I reminded her.

"Of course. With Amelia coming, we're up to fifteen

people, including Liz, Chad, Angela, and Reggie. That's a nice size."

"It's so sweet that Jax has asked Manny to officiate. When Consuela told me, I almost cried," I said. "But then she had tears in her eyes too. They both adore Jax."

Annie threw an arm around my shoulder. "You know, Annie, sometimes this hotel business is better than you could ever dream."

"Some days are a nightmare, but sweet gestures like this and seeing how happy our guests and staff are makes it all worthwhile."

We grinned at one another. There'd been both ups and downs.

Rhonda and I were in our office when we received a call from the front desk that Mr. and Mrs. Ned Thomas had called from the airport as requested and would be arriving soon.

"Thanks. We'll be out shortly to greet them," I said.

Twenty minutes later, Rhonda and I watched as a heavy-set balding man got out of their rental car—a silver convertible— and stretched. A short, plump woman with blond hair pulled back into a bun at the neckline emerged from the passenger seat and gave us a little wave as we headed down the front steps of the hotel to greet Sharlene and Ned Thomas.

Sharlene's pretty face split into a broad smile and her blue eyes sparkled as she rushed to meet us. "You must be the owners of the hotel. I've heard so much about you."

"Welcome to The Beach House Hotel," I said, accepting her warm embrace. "I'm Ann Sanders and this is my business partner, Rhonda Grayson."

As Rhonda and Sharlene embraced I approached Ned. "Welcome to The Beach House Hotel! We're so glad you're here."

"Thanks! Shar and I are happy to make the trip for the kids." Not much taller than Sharlene, laugh lines at the corners of his dark eyes gave a pleasant look to his classical features. His dark hair was sprinkled with gray and balding at the crown of his head. There was something so natural, so friendly as we shook hands that I instantly liked him. *No wonder he was so successful selling cars.*

"I'm trying to decide who Jax looks like," said Rhonda after greeting both his parents. "A little bit of both of you, I guess."

Sharlene laughed softly. "So funny you mention it. We adopted Jax when he was just two months old. He's a handsome, sweet boy, and we're proud to call him ours."

Rhonda and I exchanged looks of surprise. Neither Jax nor Mandy had ever mentioned it.

Sharlene patted my arm. "We don't usually talk about it. It seems so irrelevant. His parents died in an auto accident, and Heaven blessed us with the baby we always wanted."

"He speaks so well of you both," I said, blinking back tears. Mandy was one lucky young mother to be part of this family.

We led Sharlene and Ned inside as their suitcases were brought into the hotel.

"We have a nice first-floor room for you not too far from the swimming pool and the beach," I said.

"Well, I don't know about being in a bathing suit, but I'll love walking on the beach," said Sharlene, laughing softly.

Ned put his arm around Sharlene. "Now, honey, I've told you that you're just fine the way you are. Curves make a man happy. You know that's true. We've been together for almost thirty great years."

Rhonda grinned. "You know, Ned, I like you."

"All the ladies do," said Sharlene. "He fixes them up with real nice cars, and then I see that they're trained in taking care of it. Changing tires and all."

"That's remarkable," I said, charmed by the two of them.

"Hopefully, I can convince Jax to give up that old truck of his. Time for something suitable for a family," said Ned.

Jax came into the hotel wearing his work clothes and a straw hat, which he quickly took off. "Hey, Mama! Dad! Glad you're here." They hugged each other warmly.

"As soon as your room is settled, I'll walk you over to the apartment," Jax continued.

He joined us as we showed his parents to their room.

"Gorgeous! Simply Gorgeous. Reminds me of the French coast minus all the hills and such," said Sharlene.

Ned laughed. "That was a great trip, huh, Shar?"

Smiling, Jax shook his head. "My parents love to travel whenever they can get away."

Sharlene smiled. "We're giving you and Mandy a honeymoon whenever you're ready. Along with a proper family vehicle. Now, let's go see her and that adorable baby."

Jax led them away, and Rhonda and I went to our office.

"Mandy is a very lucky woman," Rhonda said. "Jax's parents are terrific. So warm and accepting." She dabbed at her eyes with a tissue. "This wedding is going to be one of the best ever."

Trying to control my own emotions, I nodded. No wonder Jax was such a steady, sweet guy devoted to Mandy. His parents were perfect examples.

The morning of the wedding, the skies were gray and

hinting of rain. I wasn't worried. Rain on your wedding day was considered good luck. Besides, the weather prediction was for clearing skies, perfect for a late afternoon ceremony.

I'd heard from Amelia. She was in Florida and excited about being part of the wedding celebration. It seemed only right to have her in the group.

Vaughn padded into the kitchen wearing shorts and a T-shirt. "A great day to work on the boat," he said. "I'm going to take care of some things below deck."

"How about some coffee?" I asked, already heading for the machine.

Vaughn kissed me and accepted the cup I handed him. "What time is the wedding?"

"Four-thirty. It should be a pleasant afternoon and a perfect time for it. It's going to be a happy affair. I think you'll like Jax's parents."

"I'm glad things are settled after all the business with the senator. Where's Robbie?"

"Next door. He's been invited to spend the day aboard their boat. They're going to motor up to Sarasota for lunch."

"It'll be good for Robbie to experience the difference between a sailboat and a powerboat."

"After breakfast, I'm going to the hotel to check on things for the wedding. Willow has her ballet lessons this morning, and both kids have birthday parties this afternoon, so I told Rhonda I'd take care of it."

"You two work together so well. With all these babies and children to help with, it's important."

"Liz and Chad's twins will be a lot to handle. Thankfully, Robbie is becoming so easy. Elena will help Liz at her house instead of my paying her to be here."

Vaughn set down his coffee cup and pulled me into his arms. "You're the best grandma ever."

"Various pieces of equipment make things easier for mothers today, but it's still exhausting, constant work to raise a child."

"I know. Ellie was great at it and so are you. My kids are lucky you'll step in to help them. Nell has spoken to me about it several times."

"I'll try to get up to D.C. to see her as often as I can. But it won't be for a while. I'm beginning to think the doctor miscalculated Liz's delivery date. She's looking so big."

"As big as an elephant, to quote Robbie?" said Vaughn.

I pushed him playfully. "Those words better never reach Liz. She's already so emotional, they would crush her."

Vaughn held up a hand. "I swear I'll never mention it."

Amused, I said, "Okay, let's talk breakfast."

At the hotel that afternoon, I checked the small dining room. Instead of setting up a long table, three round tables had been set up for five people each. It would be an easy way for the group to mingle. Pink-linen cloths topped the tables, and a small white vase filled with pink roses and lilies sat in the middle of each one. The effect was lovely—both bride-like and baby-sweet.

I left the dining room and went to the kitchen to check with Jean-Luc. Together Rhonda and I had selected the main course of steak or grilled salmon with all the usual veggies and potato accompaniments. To begin we'd have a selection of hot hors d'oeuvres. The meal would start with cream of roasted tomato soup and a Caesar salad. For dessert, Mandy had requested a chocolate cake with white icing. Jean-Luc had dressed up that idea by making small individual cakes with a smooth pink buttercream icing topped with pale pink rose petals made from the same buttery icing, served with a small white truffle.

I went outside to check the area Jax had chosen for the ceremony. Behind a strip of protected seagrass, an open area remained a part of the beach isolated from traffic. It was perfect for a late afternoon wedding. One could hear the waves, seem part of the beach scene, and still have a sense of privacy.

As I turned to walk away, I saw Manny heading toward me.

"Hi, Manny!" I went to him and gave him a quick hug. "Are you ready for the ceremony? It's so sweet that Jax asked you to oversee it. I didn't realize you were a notary and could marry someone. The hotel may want to use you from time to time."

Manny smiled and bobbed his head. "I've married a few other couples before. Mostly relatives and in Spanish. But Jax has been learning the language and said he wanted me to do it."

"But you'll speak in English?"

"Oh, yes." His lips curved. "Jax is a fine young man. I'm happy he's with me."

"Me, too," I said, ruing the day when Manny wouldn't be able to handle the work. It was one reason we'd been so eager to hire Jax.

I left him and returned home to get ready for the wedding.

As promised, the sun came out as Vaughn and I walked to the spot on the beach where Jax and Mandy would be married. Sharlene and Ned were already there.

Wearing a pale pink sleeveless dress and wiggling her toes in the sand, Sharlene looked adorable. Beside her, as requested, Ned wore tan slacks, a white dress shirt, and a pink tie. They'd agreed to stand up for the couple and had dressed accordingly.

The others soon joined us.

Looking very official, Manny wore a dark suit and carried a black, leather book. He walked behind the wooden podium that had been secured in the sand and set the book down beside the white basket full of assorted pink and white flowers.

I was anxious to see Mandy. Elena had agreed to babysit Carli for the afternoon, and I knew Sharlene had taken Mandy shopping for a dress and to get her hair done.

The sound of the waves kissing the shore and the cries of seagulls and terns above provided the music by which Jax and Mandy walked toward us together. My breath released in a rush of admiration. Mandy's dress was a simple, sleeveless ankle-length, white-eyelet gown with a lace border at the hemline and a ribbon of it at the jewel neckline. She wore a corsage of pink roses. Her recently highlighted hair fell to her shoulders and swayed gently in the onshore breeze. Mandy was, I thought, one of the sweetest brides I'd ever seen. Beside her, wearing tan slacks, a white shirt, and a pink tie like his father, Jax stood straight and tall, his elbow extended so Mandy could loop her arm through his. His dark curly hair gleamed in the sun but couldn't match the delight on his handsome face.

Rhonda was already dabbing at her eyes, while I struggled to hold my emotions in. When Liz had arrived with Chad, she'd looked away from my questioning glance at the redness I noticed around her eyes.

Manny spoke slowly and carefully as he led them both through the ceremony. After vows and rings had been exchanged, Manny said, "May you both be very happy for the rest of your lives. *Que sean muy felices todas sus vidas.*"

Sharlene clapped. "Yay! They did it! Congratulations, Mandy and Jax!"

We all applauded as Mandy and Jax kissed and then embraced his parents.

It was one of the sweetest weddings ever.

I'd noticed the look of surprise on Mandy's face when she noticed Amelia. Now, she and Amelia were hugging. A happy ending to what could've been the saddest of events.

I turned to speak to Liz, but she was already hurrying away.

Rhonda approached. "I want to remember this exactly as it was for Willow's wedding. So simple, as sweet as one of Jean-Luc's desserts."

"Truer words were never spoken," said Amelia, joining us. "I'm very glad this situation has worked out the way it has. I talked to Cassie Worthington, and she's accepted that it's best to go through a regular adoption agency."

As we headed into the hotel for the celebration, Angela walked beside me. "I'm so glad I got to know Mandy through Liz. I hope her little girl and mine will be friends one day."

"How are you feeling?" I asked her.

"Surprisingly well," she said. "It could be I'm already so exhausted that it doesn't feel much different from not being pregnant."

"You're young and healthy. That's a blessing."

Angela nodded. "What's up with Liz? She seemed upset."

"I don't know. I noticed it too and can't wait to talk to her." I slowed our steps when Sharlene came close. "What a beautiful wedding," I said to her. "Mandy looked gorgeous in her dress. And her hair styled this way is very becoming."

Sharlene beamed at me. "We had fun doing it. That's what's important to me. Poor child has such awful parents. From the time Jax brought her home in high school, I told him it was important to keep that girl safe. Looks like he took it to heart. She's as safe and as happy as I've ever seen her."

"She tried to reach out to them after little Carli was born, but they want no part of her or her baby. I'm so very glad you're supportive, Sharlene."

Sharlene's smile was a little sad. "I don't understand people like that. We've had words with her parents. They don't believe in music or dancing or having fun of any kind. They actually told me their daughter was the devil. Can you imagine that?"

"Yes," I said, feeling sick to my stomach. "They're very abusive people."

I stopped walking, turned to the water, and whispered a quiet, "Thank you" to the sky above for helping to save Mandy from their treatment of her. The fact that she turned out to be such a kind and caring person was a testament to her strength.

Inside the hotel, we walked to the small dining room. I waited by the door so I could see Mandy's reaction when she saw what had been done. Jax and Mandy walked with Manny and Consuela through the open doorway.

I heard Mandy's gasp of delight.

"Happy Wedding," I said, hugging her.

"It's beautiful!" Mandy cried. "Thank you! Sharlene told me you and Rhonda are doing this for us as your wedding gift."

Rhonda came over to us. "Do you like it?"

Mandy shook her head. "No, I *love* it!"

"*Sí*, so beautiful!" said Consuela. "But you two always make things nice."

I looked around the room for Liz, but she and Chad weren't there. A waiter approached with hot hors d'oeuvres and another took my drink order.

I was about to go find Liz when she and Chad walked into the room holding hands and smiling.

My "mother nerves" quieted. "Where did you go?" I asked her.

Liz rolled her eyes. "In my state? Guess!"

I hugged her. "You look beautiful! Pregnancy becomes you."

"We'll see as time goes along," she said, glancing at Chad, who was talking with Jax.

Later, as I was talking with Ned and Vaughn, I noticed Chad talking to Mandy and was pleased to see that they were becoming friends. Liz had told me earlier that week that she and Mandy were going to run the jewelry business together.

"Ladies and Gentlemen, will you please be seated for dinner," Annette announced. "Your meal is about to begin."

We all found our seats and watched as several waitresses and waiters carried trays holding bowls of soup into the room and placed one before each of us.

"*Bon Appetit!*" said Annette, overseeing the service staff leaving the room.

While some of us were finishing our soup, Jax stood. "Thank you, everyone, for being part of our celebration. My parents, Sharlene and Ned, have met all of you and are pleased we'll be with such nice people. Mandy and I want lots of family and friends for Carli. We've found them here this evening." He raised his glass. "Here's to all of you."

Ned got to his feet. "And I toast you and Mandy. May you have many happy years together." He smiled at Sharlene. "As happy as Shar and I have had. Mandy, we've thought of you as family for a long time and now we can finally say you truly are."

Mandy smiled and wiped tears from her eyes.

Jax stood up again. "We have another occasion to celebrate." He waved Chad to his feet.

Chad stood and gazed around the room. "Liz and I received permission from Mandy and Jax to use this time with our families together to make an announcement." His voice shook. "Liz, want to tell them?"

Liz got to her feet and went to Chad's side. "We just learned today that we're going to have triplets, not twins!"

I felt my heart stop and then sprint forward with excitement. "Triplets? Oh, my!"

"I know," said Liz, and burst into tears. "We're still in shock."

Chad patted her back. "Pretty scary, but we're going to be all right."

Here's to more babies!" said Rhonda. "We'll love them all!"

I jumped up out of my seat and ran to Liz, sweeping her into a hug while we both laughed and cried at the same time.

Everyone clapped, and several people in the group rose to give Liz and Chad hugs or hearty pats on the back.

Still dealing with the idea of triplets, I gazed around the room. The past year had been full of baby news for all of us. Manny and Consuela had welcomed a fifth grandchild three months ago. Angela and Reggie were expecting their third, June and Ty were expecting, Nell was enjoying Bailey. Sharlene and Ned were delighted with Carli and Jax and Mandy. And Amelia would, no doubt, help other young mothers.

As Rhonda had recently said, life was as sweet as one of

Jean-Luc's desserts.

She and I exchanged glances. Life would continue at a hectic pace at the hotel and at home with all the sweetness we had to share. But we'd do it happily. Together.

CHAPTER TWENTY-NINE

Following the announcement at Mandy and Jax's wedding, Vaughn and I talked about how best to help Liz and Chad. Twins would be difficult, triplets even more so. I could divert Elena to Liz part-time and hire Elena's sister as a full-time nanny. More pressing than that was housing for all of them. Liz and Chad owned a two-bedroom plus den house that would never be big enough.

We met with Liz and Chad to discuss the idea of their moving before it would be too great an effort for Liz.

"I don't know if we can afford that," said Liz, glancing at Chad.

"Hold on. We'll be able to sell our house for a profit after all the work we did on it. And by giving up the expense of renting the storefront, we might be able to make something work."

"We'd like to offer you financial assistance," said Vaughn. "Find a house you think will be suitable, and we'll talk."

"Thanks," Liz said, her voice wobbling. "This is all so overwhelming."

"One thing at a time," I told her gently. "Do you want to look for a house in Angela's neighborhood?"

"You think we could?" A smile spread across Liz's face. "That would make it easier to get together and help one another."

"Call a real estate agent now, and let her know we can't wait too long," I said. "Whatever you end up buying, you'll want to take time to make it your own."

"Okay. I'll make the call and let you know what we've found." She sniffled. "Thanks. I was having nightmares about how we'd all fit into our house, especially when Chad and I were trying to have home offices."

"Don't worry. It's all going to work out. I can't wait to meet these babies of yours. I prayed you'd get pregnant. Maybe I prayed too hard," I said, attempting humor.

"It's a miracle," said Liz, looking a lot less worried. She caressed her stomach, and a smile broke across her face. "Now I'll be even with Angela."

I laughed. "Rhonda's already mentioned it. She's so excited about triplets, you know. She can't wait to see them!"

"Dr. Benson says they'll come early, around 32 weeks. She told me to take care of myself. I've set up an appointment with Troy at the spa to see what I can do about safe exercises."

"That's great. It's worked out well that Troy isn't opening another spa right now."

"I know. Elena and I talked about it, and she's happy they decided to wait."

"All right, you two," said Vaughn. "Get to work and let us know what you find."

After Liz and Chad left, I turned to Vaughn. "Thank you for being so generous. I couldn't imagine the family functioning well in their little house."

"I liked how Chad immediately thought of what they could contribute rather than just letting us pay without adding any sources of their own."

"We're very fortunate that we can help," I said. "Not many families could."

"Good thing I'm still the mayor of that terrible town," Vaughn joked.

"Good thing you're such a nice man and a great father," I

retorted, going to him and wrapping my arms around him. "And I must say, a very sexy grandpa."

He laughed. "All these babies are making me very glad we're past that stage. It means we can practice all we want."

I smiled up at him. *Practice makes perfect,* I thought, quoting a familiar phrase.

Throughout the fall and into the winter months, I waited impatiently to see the three little ones expanding Liz's stomach. Thankfully, Robbie didn't mention elephants as he studied Liz's round tummy. But his wide eyes spoke words of their own.

Though I remained focused on the triplets, life continued.

Nell, Clint, and Baby Bailey came for Thanksgiving, which turned out to be a lovely affair, reminding me of all I had to be grateful for even when the press of business kept me focused on the hotel.

Then, Tina Marks called to say that though she wouldn't see us at Christmas, she was making plans to come to Sabal in the spring after the babies were born. I was both disappointed she wouldn't be with us for the holidays, but I was excited about the opportunity to share the magic of the triplets with her.

Amelia returned to the hotel for a stay at Christmas, celebrating the recent engagement of Jean-Luc and Lindsay. It was nice to see her, but I was glad she didn't ask Rhonda and me for another favor.

Darla and Meredith bought a house in a town up the coast and joined us for Christmas dinner looking as happy as ever. I loved the feeling that our Christmas family was growing. Though Sharlene and Ned couldn't join us for the holiday, they often came to visit so they could be part of Carli's life with Jax and Mandy.

Right after the holidays, Liz and Chad moved into the same neighborhood as Angela and Reggie and were now living in a four-bedroom house. It was an ideal neighborhood for young families. Katherine had once thought it wasn't good enough for Reggie, but as it turned out, it was perfect. Both Angela and Liz made friends quickly, and Liz soon felt at home there.

The house they chose needed work inside, but Chad was handy and did a lot of the improvements himself in the evenings, including painting all the bedrooms. One ensuite bedroom was reserved for the nanny with another bedroom and bath for the babies nearby. The master was in a separate wing with a small office nearby, which would initially be the nursery and later Liz's workspace. The two-car garage had a loft above it, which would be Chad's home office. A swimming pool would be added to the backyard later. Until then, Liz and Chad could use one of the two neighborhood pools. Best of all, because of the cosmetic work required, they got it for a reduced price.

At the hotel, Rhonda and I worked on developing additions to the New Mothers Program, bringing in physical therapists, Barbara Holmes, and other experts to give us advice on how best to improve the program. We'd seen the women in our family prepare for or go through birth and wanted to be a help to them and other women in the same situation. Renovations of rooms would take place after the high season had come and gone.

One wintry day, as I walked along the beach huddled in a thick sweater, I thought of all the changes in my life. I'd been so blessed to meet Rhonda and, later, Vaughn. The life I had now was something I could never have imagined.

The waves met the shore in a shiver of cold air and rolled

back as if trying to snuggle together for warmth. I liked rare winter days like this. It reminded me of winters in New England when I'd longed for warmer weather. Here, I knew the cold would soon be chased away by the warmth of the sun and the gentle breezes that would follow.

I looked up to see Brock Goodwin headed toward me.

Frowning, I realized I hadn't seen him in the usual round of holiday parties. Too distracted to inquire, I'd let it go. Now, my curiosity forced me to stay where I was.

"Good morning, Ann!" said Brock, his voice holding no warmth.

"Hello, Brock! I haven't seen you for some time. How are you?"

"You mean you haven't heard?" He let out a snort. "I thought everyone knew."

"What are you talking about?" I asked, stepping back from the anger that rolled from him in waves.

"You and all the others won! The Sand Castle is closing down. Are you and Rhonda happy now?"

"Wait a minute, Brock. Neither Rhonda nor I would wish this for you and Aubrey and the others. All we'd ever hoped for was to work together. What happened?"

"It's all Aubrey's fault. He promised me I'd make a bundle of money on his crazy idea. People who can pay money don't want to play in a sandbox. They want excellent service and great food."

Like The Beach House Hotel? But I couldn't say the words aloud.

"Well? Are you going to say I told you so?" Brock said, his nostrils flared.

"No, I'm not. I truly am sorry that it happened. We need all kinds of hotels in the area. It's beautiful here, and guests love to come. There should be room for all of us. What else happened?" I knew there had to be more.

"Besides staffing problems, poor finances, and Aubrey taking care of himself and friends before guests?"

"Ah, I get it. Aubrey is the same as when we fired him. What are you going to do now?"

Brock shook his head. "I honestly don't know."

Studying him, I felt a wave of regret sweep through me. We could've been friends, could've helped one another, but he'd let his ego get in the way, trying to tear apart the hard work Rhonda and I had put into the hotel from the beginning.

"Good luck, Brock. I mean it."

He studied me and then slowly nodded. "I think you do. 'Bye."

I waited until he'd gone a distance before heading back to the hotel for a hot cup of coffee and something sweet. Rhonda, I knew, would be delighted with the news.

As Liz's 32nd week drew near, I remained on high alert for a call. Dr. Benson had put together a special team to help with the birth of the babies. We knew now that she was having one boy and two girls. Their names had yet to be decided.

As luck would have it, I was in a meeting with Rhonda and our hotel accountant when I got the call from Liz that she was heading to the hospital.

I jumped up from my chair. "This is it! Liz is on her way to the hospital!"

Rhonda stood and hugged me tightly. "Call me if you need me. I'm waiting to hear from Angela. She's been having some discomfort. But she thinks it's just Braxton-Hick contractions and isn't her time yet."

The accountant, a nice but dull man, gazed at us with discomfort. "Maybe we'd better finish this meeting another time."

"Absolutely. I'm leaving now." I grabbed my phone. "Oh, my God! I have to get hold of Vaughn. He's got to get here!"

"Go!" said Rhonda. "I'll call him now. You can talk to him from the hospital."

"Okay, my hands are shaking so badly I'm not sure I could even punch in the number."

I ran from our office to my car behind the hotel, drawing my breath in and out in nervous gasps. My pulse was racing as I slid behind the wheel. *Slow down!* I warned myself, as I pulled out of the hotel lot and drove the short distance to the hospital.

When I arrived and asked for Liz's room number in maternity, the volunteer behind the receptionist desk smiled. "We're all so excited for the birth of these triplets. It's the first case since 2009. Good luck!"

"Thanks," I said. "We're going to need it." I'd researched information from parents of triplets online and knew how much Liz would depend on Elena, the nanny, me, neighbors, anyone to help feed and care for the babies. Even Chad's mother had finally agreed to help. Liz's initial tears had been ones of fear. I understood better just how overwhelming the situation could be when faced with the practicality of taking care of three little ones at the same time.

Upstairs in the maternity ward, I entered Liz's room with a sense of familiarity. Angela had given birth here a little more than a year ago and was about to deliver again.

Dr. Benson looked up at me and smiled. "You're becoming a familiar figure around here."

I laughed. "It does seem like I've been at the hospital a lot." I focused on Liz. "How're you doing, honey?" A nurse was monitoring Liz's vital signs, another the heartbeats of the babies.

"I'm uncomfortable," said Liz, "and can't wait to see these babies outside of me."

Dr. Benson stood by. "We're going to take you into the delivery room for your Caesarean very soon, Liz. Everything looks just fine. The corticosteroids you've been given will help with the babies' lungs, and their heartbeats are strong."

Chad took hold of her hand. "You can do this, baby."

"Says the guy watching," she griped.

Chad held onto Liz's hand as she was wheeled into a delivery room. Two nurses, an OB specialist for multiple births, and an experienced pediatrician accustomed to births like this were there to assist Dr. Benson.

"Okay, Chad. Kiss her goodbye. You and Ann can stay in the waiting room. We'll call you as soon as you can see the babies and Liz," said Dr. Benson.

Chad bent over and kissed Liz. "Love you, babe! I'll be right here."

Sitting in the waiting room, I remembered I hadn't called Vaughn. I punched in his number. He answered right away.

"Hi, Ann! Rhonda called. I'm packing now and will be on a flight this afternoon. How's Liz?"

"They're doing the Caesarean section now. I'm waiting with Chad." I glanced at him. He looked sick with worry. "Thanks for coming home right away. I'd better go."

"Good luck with everything. Let me know when they're here, and Liz is all right."

"All right, will do," I answered, feeling an urge to cry.

I hung up and turned to Chad. "What a tremendous day, huh?"

"A momentous occasion," he said, giving me a wobbly smile.

I felt suspended in the air not feeling or hearing anything but the words I whispered in my head for Liz and the babies to be safe.

Sometime later, Dr. Benson appeared. "We have three healthy babies, two girls, and a boy, and Mom is doing great."

I couldn't stop tears from escaping my eyes. Chad was equally emotional.

"When can I see Liz and the babies?" Chad said.

"Soon. The babies are being checked and cleaned up a bit. After showing them to you, we'll be taking them to the neonatal unit. Liz will be placed in the recovery room for a couple of hours to make sure things are going as they should before we release her to her room."

"We'll wait right here," I said, needing to remain close to my daughter.

It seemed to take forever before three incubators were wheeled toward us on their way to the neonatal unit.

Chad and I peered at each one. I stared at their perfectly shaped heads and their sweet faces and filled with love. One of them, a girl, opened her eyes and blinked at the light.

"They're perfect babies," said one of the nurses to Chad. "Congratulations, Dad!"

"When can I see my wife?" he asked, not bothering to wipe at the tears on his cheeks.

"Come with me," she said to Chad. "They're getting ready to take her to recovery."

I stayed with the babies while Chad left.

The nurse and Chad returned several minutes later. Chad's eyes were red, but he managed a smile. "She's fine."

"C'mon, I'll buy you a cup of coffee, and then we'll see if

you can visit her in the recovery room."

"Those babies. All three of them are mine. Hard to believe." Chad said, sniffling.

I nodded, too emotional to do more.

Later, Chad and I stood outside the neonatal unit. A nurse brought each of the babies over to the window to give us a better look. All three had light brown, almost blond hair which seemed natural considering that both Liz and Chad were blondes.

"What are you going to name them? Still sticking to Emma, Olivia, and Noah?"

"We have to." He chuckled. "My mother's written some lullabies with their names in them. Wow! I still can't believe it. Three at once."

"It's fantastic! If you don't need me for anything, I'm going to go home and fix dinner for Robbie before coming back to see Liz. Want to join us for a hot meal?"

"That sounds great." He gave me a sweet smile. "Thanks, Ann, for all you do for us."

"I love you both and now your babies," I said.

"See you later, grandma."

I grinned. "That's a grandma with a capital G."

A few weeks later, Rhonda and I sat in our office with coffee and the sweet rolls that had helped to make breakfast at The Beach House Hotel so special.

I looked at the circles under her eyes and laughed softly.

"What's so funny?" she asked.

"Us. Wiped out grandmothers. Who knew we'd have so many babies to help take care of besides our own?"

Rhonda reached over and squeezed my hand, an affectionate smile spreading across her face. "It'll always be you and me together with our families. Remember, The Beach House Hotel is our baby too. That's what brought us together."

"Who would've thought all this began with our daughters meeting?"

"Life sure can be sweet," said Rhonda.

I grinned, remembering one of Rhonda's latest sayings. "As sweet as one of Jean-Luc's desserts?"

She laughed. "You know I've always loved Dessert at The Beach House Hotel."

I hugged her, knowing more challenges awaited us. "Me too."

# # #

Thank you for reading *Dessert at The Beach House Hotel*. If you enjoyed this book, please help other readers discover it by leaving a review on your favorite site. It's such a nice thing to do.

And for your further enjoyment, here is an excerpt from my book, *A Road Trip to Remember*, a Seashell Cottage Book. Here's the link:

https://www.amazon.com/gp/product/B08XJZB
8S4/ref=dbs_a_def_rwt_hsch_vapi_tkin_p3_i2

CHAPTER ONE

AGGIE

Gran! You can't be serious! I can't do that!"

"Yes, my darling, you can, and you will. I need your help." Agatha "Aggie" Robard put as much pleading into her voice as possible without breaking down and crying. She had a plan for a road trip, and by damn, she was going to do it! At seventy-two and just through recovering from pneumonia, she couldn't make the drive alone, and there was no way she was going to let down the man she'd promised to visit. He was, in some respects, the one who got away. Not that Arnold, God rest his soul, would mind. He'd always known she'd loved Donovan Bailey too.

"Just think about it," Aggie urged. "A road trip to remember."

It would be good for her granddaughter, Blythe, to get out of town, get over her boyfriend, and find a decent young man who'd adore her for being the loveable young woman she was. Two women on an adventure. That's what they'd be. Aggie grinned with anticipation. What could be better on this

March morning when the rest of their family was about to leave for a fourteen-day vacation in Hawaii?

Aggie listened to Blythe go on about the need to stay in Ithaca to wrap up her college courses at Cornell before graduation. Aggie knew her beloved granddaughter had used that excuse to escape going home for Spring Break, gotten into an argument with her stepmother, Constance, about it, and was left out of the trip to Hawaii in the process.

"A Spring Break trip to Florida in early April will do you good," Aggie said, dangling this last piece of information in front of Blythe like a piece of her favorite toffee candy.

Blythe let out a breathy, "Oh? *That's* where you want me to take you?"

"Yes. I've rented a place on the Gulf Coast of Florida, the Seashell Cottage, for a week, starting at the end of March. That will give us time to get there, enjoy a week in the sun, and get back home again before anyone suspects a thing."

Suddenly, Blythe began to laugh. Her musical trills filled Aggie's ears and brought a smile to her face. "Gran! You're outrageous!" She paused. "Do you think we can pull off something like this? Constance will be furious if she ever finds out."

The smile disappeared from Aggie's face as if it had been ripped off with tape, leaving stinging skin behind. Constance Robard, her only child's second wife and Blythe's stepmother, was a pain in the behind, always trying to tell her what she could or could not do. Aggie fought to find the right words.

"Constance doesn't need to know every little thing I'm doing. Just because she manipulated me into selling my house and moving into the New Life Assisted Living Community, it doesn't mean I can't have a life of my own. There's a dance or two in this old lady yet." No one was going to take away the power to live her life her way. Not even if it meant ruffling a few feathers.

"Gran, you're not that old," Blythe protested.

Aggie made her final plea. "So, will you do it?"

"You bet!" said Blythe, a new eagerness in her voice. "Florida sounds fantastic right now. I swear I haven't seen the sun in Ithaca for a week or more. I'll bring some work with me and do it there."

"Good," said Aggie. "Pick me up Tuesday morning at eight o'clock, and I'll take care of the rest. And pack suntan lotion. We'll take the convertible."

"I love you, Gran. Don't worry. I'll come home over the weekend and see you Tuesday morning. This road trip is going to be fun!"

"Don't I know it," Aggie said, feeling as if she was about to be handed a get-out-of-jail-free card.

Still smiling, Aggie clicked off the call. Blythe was a serious young woman in the final semester of her senior year at Cornell. She'd spent years doing what others had dictated and was just beginning to understand that life should be fun too. Aggie hoped if she left Blythe with anything to remember her by, it would be this.

Aggie's one suitcase sat beside the front entrance of the main building of the assisted-living complex she now called home. It wasn't a bad place to be. It had every convenience possible, good food, and lovely surroundings both in and outside the buildings. Best of all, she'd made some good friends here. Two of them, Edith Greenbaum and Rose Ragazzi, had suggested the Seashell Cottage as a place for her getaway. They'd once made that suggestion to Noelle North, the former head of the health program at New Life, and she'd ended up married to some hotel mogul. You never know what could happen. Aggie had sworn these friends to secrecy but felt it was only right for someone to know her true location should anything untoward happen. She owed that to her son, Brad, and daughter-in-law, Constance.

"So, you're going on vacation with your family," commented one of the staff. "How nice for you."

Aggie glanced at Edith and Rose, who'd come to say goodbye, and nodded. She didn't like lying in any form and was relieved she actually was going on a family vacation, even if the only other family member was Blythe.

Her eye caught sight of something. She looked through the glass-paneled front door to see her white Mercedes convertible pull up to the front of the building with Blythe at the wheel. This car represented so much to Aggie. Her purchase of it had sent Constance into a rage, claiming Aggie was losing her mind to buy something like this at her age. It was the beginning of Constance's campaign to get her to move out of her big, old house in Dedham outside of Boston and into New Life.

Aggie had finally given in to Brad's pleas to put his mind at ease about her safety and had made the move. But she'd refused to get rid of the car. She kept the shiny new beauty in a storage facility nearby and gave Blythe the extra key fob to it. After she died, Blythe would have her car for her own use. For now, Aggie needed to know she had "wheels."

"Here's your ride," said Edith, hugging her. "Safe trip! And good luck with Donovan!"

Rose grinned at her and wrapped her arms around Aggie. "We'll be with you in spirit. Remember every little detail so you can tell us all about it."

Aggie held in a laugh. There was nothing Rose liked better than a good, romantic story.

Blythe hurried over to them and grabbed hold of Aggie's suitcase. "Hi, everyone." Green-eyed, black-haired Blythe reminded Aggie of a beautiful young woman who was just coming into her own. Long-legged, thin, and with a wild taste in clothes that drove her stepmother crazy, Blythe was the perfect person to take this trip with her. By the time they got back, Aggie hoped Blythe would have a better appreciation of herself.

After chatting politely, Blythe took hold of Aggie's arm. "C'mon, Gran. Time to hit the road."

Aggie marched to the car alongside Blythe, feeling like she was sprouting wings with each step, loving this new sense of freedom. After she buckled herself into the passenger seat, she turned to the small crowd gathered at the doorway and waved.

"Okay, pedal to the metal, girl," Aggie said, sitting back in her seat, eager to begin the journey ahead.

# # #

We're happy to announce you can order this book now! Here's the link where you can find *A Road Trip to Remember:*

https://www.amazon.com/dp/B09RRR38FR

Happy Reading to All!

# # #

About the Author

Judith Keim, a *USA Today* Best-Selling Author, is a hybrid author who both has a publisher and self-publishes, Ms. Keim writes heart-warming novels about women who face unexpected challenges, meet them with strength, and find love and happiness along the way. Her best-selling books are based, in part, on many of the places she's lived or visited, and on the interesting people she's met, creating believable characters and realistic settings her many loyal readers love. Ms. Keim loves to hear from her readers and appreciates their enthusiasm for her stories.

Ms. Keim enjoyed her childhood and young-adult years in Elmira, New York, and now makes her home in Boise, Idaho, with her husband and their two dachshunds, Winston and Wally, and other members of her family.

While growing up, she was drawn to the idea of writing stories from a young age. Books were always present, being read, ready to go back to the library, or about to be discovered. All in her family shared information from the books in general conversation, giving them a wealth of knowledge and vivid imaginations.

"I hope you've enjoyed this book. If you have, please help other readers discover it by leaving a review on Amazon, Bookbub, Goodreads or the site of your choice. And please check out my other books and series:

Hartwell Women Series
The Beach House Hotel Series
Fat Fridays Group
Salty Key Inn Series
Chandler Hill Inn Series
Seashell Cottage Books
Desert Sage Inn Series
Soul Sisters at Cedar Mountain Lodge
The Sanderling Cove Inn Series

ALL THE BOOKS ARE NOW AVAILABLE IN AUDIO on Audible, Audiobooks.com, iTunes, Kobo, Google Play, Findaway, and others! So fun to have these characters come alive!"

Ms. Keim can be reached at **www.judithkeim.com**

And to like her author page on Facebook and keep up with the news, go to: **http://bit.ly/2pZWDgA**

To receive notices about new books, follow her on Book Bub:
https://www.bookbub.com/authors/judith-keim

And here's a link to where you can sign up for her periodic newsletter! **http://bit.ly/2OQsb7s**

She is also on Twitter @judithkeim, LinkedIn, and Goodreads. Come say hello!

Acknowledgments

In addition to my regular team:
Editors – Lynn Mapp, Peter Keim,
Cover Artist – Lou Harper
Audio Narrator – Angela Dawe

I wish to thank my Wednesday Morning Coffee Group – Authors Cate Lawley, Lynn Mapp, Peggy Staggs, Jeanne Triska, and Megan Bryce – for their continued support and friendship while carrying on the business of writing.

And as always, I thank my readers for their enthusiasm and support. They are the ones who keep me writing new stories that I hope delight them.

Made in the USA
Las Vegas, NV
30 May 2022

49556427R00177